JEREMY STANFORD
RAPTURE

Tale Publishing

First Published 2018
Copyright © 2018 Jeremy Stanford
All rights reserved.
ISBN-13: 978-0994439994
ISBN-10: 0994439994

National Library of Australia Cataloguing-in-Publication
entry:
Creator: Stanford, Jeremy, author.
Title: Rapture / Jeremy Stanford.
ISBN: 9780994439994 (paperback)

Tale Publishing
Melbourne Victoria

Cover design by John Canty incorporating Shutterstock
image #440638300

Other Titles by Jeremy Stanford

Memoir

Year of the Queen: The Making of the Hit Show
Priscilla Queen of the Desert the Musical

Feature Film

The Sunset Six (Director / Co-Writer)

For Annie

1

Nicole had anticipated a quiet, stay-at-home Saturday night—a night spent shuffling around in ugg boots and fluffing cushions in the nursery. Instead, she'd found herself creased over in the doorway of her husband's study, clutching at the woodwork for balance.

Like a sinner in the congregation, labour had leapt to its feet and proclaimed itself.

Up until now, Nicole had taken an intrepid approach to her pregnancy, painting it as an adventure that agreed with her—a leap of faith she shared with only the most fortunate of women. She'd caused even her most eager champions to flinch when she'd settled on a home birth. But this sudden stab had her suspecting she may well have been a little cavalier about it all as she came face to face with the brutal end of the whole pregnancy adventure.

She cried out for her husband's attention, but Tim—lit by his iMac Pro—was buried beneath space-age headphones, tearing out another riff into the melting pot of a new tune, and didn't hear a thing. As a new jolt of pain hit, she unsuccessfully reached for him, but his silent concert went on.

'Tim!' she repeated.

In a single motion, Tim spun around and tore off his headphones.

'Shit—' was the best he could manage, and she watched the random essentials of their birth plan explode out of the filing cabinet in his head and flitter slightly beyond his fingertips.

Moments later the bath was filling, and Nicole found herself being undressed. Tim moved fast, but he was so tender she felt like a piece of easily bruised fruit.

'Bath,' he said. 'Bath.' And he repeated it as if it was the only word he'd ever learned.

Before she knew it he was lowering her into the water following the steps laid down by men of centuries past.

'Holy fuck,' he squeaked, 'you're going to have a baby.'

It was sweet, but Nicole needed no reminding.

'Maybe you should go and get Gail,' she said.

Tim's eyes went dead. 'And leave you here like this? She can get a fucking cab.'

Nicole knew that was never going to happen. Gail, their highly-sought-after midwife, seemed to have been coughed up by another century. She made a point of only ever travelling on foot. The one exception to this rule was when she was conducting a birth, so you could pick her up, but she refused to get into a cab.

'You'd better go,' Nicole said.

Tim laid Nicole's phone on the floor beside her and hurried out.

As the front door slammed behind him, Nicole braced herself for the solitude that would accompany her next contraction. No hand to squeeze, no gentle words at her back. She breathed down into the warmth of the bath. But as the next contraction rolled ominously towards her there came a surprise. Rather than feeling the agonising jab, something resembling a wave of bliss washed over her. It was as overwhelming as any contraction but from the opposite end of the scale. Nicole had no choice but to surrender to it. It seemed to fill her from the toes up, and she no longer understood anything anymore. Without even knowing it, she fell into unconsciousness, floating limp and alone in the bath.

***

Tim pulled out of the driveway. Darkness had already set in. The spicy smoulder of a barbecue hung in the air all along the cul-de-sac, and Tim opened his window to get the full whack of it. That the neighbours should be entertaining while he and Nicole were hunkering down to bring a child into the world made him feel deeply disconnected. The tectonic plates of their lives were shifting, and at the end of whatever was in store for Nicole tonight they'd end up with a baby. How could the world still turn while *that* was going on?

When he hit the main road, Tim called Gail to say he was on his way, and by the time he arrived at her house minutes later she was already waiting for him in the street. He hardly recognised her at first glance. Since their last meeting she'd shaved off all her hair. As she approached the car, Tim couldn't help noting that this made her chin the more hirsute end of her head.

Gail was difficult to get a handle on. She vaguely frightened Tim. She presented as a kindly and dusty little-old-lady, but lurking in her dark, South American eyes was the kind of steel you wanted to avoid provoking.

He leant across the passenger seat and opened the door for her. Gail cowered, like she was standing at the jaws of a giant beast. Tim was afraid she might not get in at all.

'Gail?' he said, but she didn't move. 'Gail,' he pressed. This broke her from her funk, and she climbed in bringing a cloud of essential oils with her.

As he took off, Tim noticed her squirming, trying to get comfortable in her seat. The whole experience of being in the car seemed to be making her extremely anxious. It now occurred to him why she'd laid down her ridiculous rule in the first place, and it made him soften towards her.

'The contractions came on really suddenly,' he said, attempting to distract her with facts.

'How far apart?'

'About a minute.'

Gail turned on him. 'And you left her there?'

Tim wasn't sure if he'd heard right. 'I had to come and get *you*.'

'Well, I hope we don't arrive to find a surprise.'

Tim's new-found empathy crumpled, and if she weren't a senior citizen he may well have told her to go fuck herself.

When they reached the cul-de-sac, thick smoke now filled the air, and it curled around the car, brassy and acrid. Clearly something had gone awry with the neighbour's barbeque.

On any other night, Tim would have rushed to investigate, but Nicole needed him now, so he ignored the potential calamity and continued into the driveway.

Tim and Gail headed for the house, but as they approached the front door something stopped them dead in their tracks. A beautiful, ringing soprano emanated from inside. It was the kind of singing that filled concert halls and rained wonder down on its listeners.

Tim focused. Had Nicole been self-sufficient enough to abandon the bath and crank up the stereo? The answer was almost certainly no.

He opened the door a crack. The singing seemed to spill towards him from deep in the house. He looked to Gail, who had her eyes closed, drinking in the music. She turned to him and gave him an enigmatic smile.

'She's singing,' she whispered.

'I know. Nicole doesn't sing.'

Tim raced to the bathroom where he found his wife folded inside in a moment of reverie. Her eyes were open and distant, staring above her at something glorious and unseen.

Without thinking he reached out to her. It was the same instinct that occurs when you come across a sleepwalker: shouldn't you wake them?

Gail caught his arm. 'Leave her.'

But Tim wanted the singing to stop; his wife seemed too far away from him. What if it turned ugly? What if she hit a fork in the road and chose the dangerous path.

Just as he was about to defy Gail and give Nicole a shake, she jerked her knees up to her chest and stopped singing. There was a moment of silence. Then she cried out as a contraction hit.

Tim slid to the floor next to her and took her hand—which became a vice—and she panted through the pain until it subsided. She turned to him, as if woken from a dream, and searched his face.

'Didn't you just leave?' she stammered.

Tim didn't know what to tell her. He turned to Gail for guidance, but she was fixed on the challenge soaking in the bath before her. She crouched and edged Tim out of the way.

'Hello, sweetheart,' she crooned, 'why don't we see how you're progressing.'

Gail brought Nicole's feet up to her bottom for a look.

'Oh, my. You're already about eight centimeters dilated. Let's get you into the nursery.'

This was the agreed signal that the game was really on. Tim went to help Nicole out of the bath, but as he reached for her, sirens wailed outside.

Gail read the look on Tim's face. 'I'll be fine here,' she said.

Incrementally, he could feel Gail taking charge, and it was now an easy thing to leave Nicole in Gail's peculiar yet capable hands.

He stumbled out of the house and onto the street. Orange flames were erupting out of the house two doors down. The heat of it toasted his face, and the smoke turned the air into a meal. Police shepherded onlookers behind a perimeter tape as a fire crew unrolled hoses.

Tim watched vacantly, breathing through a handful of his T-shirt. What could he do? This was not his crisis to fix. He took one last look at the fire, mushrooming into the night sky, and headed back inside.

***

Gail shouldered Nicole along the hallway to the nursery. As Tim rushed to help, Nicole was thankful to give him all her weight.

'What's going on out there?' she said.

'Jake and Trudy's house is on fire.'

'Jesus.'

6

'I know, right? You just keep your mind on the job.'

They continued into the nursery where he laid her across a bed of cushions. She found herself draped with towels as though she was in a beauty salon.

This was the moment the night seemed to close in around them. They could have been the last people on earth. Nicole lost all track of time as the contractions endlessly rolled over her.

Gail's internal clock proved impeccable. She could predict Nicole's next contraction with spooky precision and always made sure she was in a comfortable repose when it hit.

Just when it seemed like the torture would never end, Gail placed her hands on Nicole's belly and said, 'In a moment you'll have another contraction, my darling. When that's over, I want you to push with all your might, do you understand?'

Nicole nodded.

'Are you comfortable?' she pressed.

Again, Nicole nodded, and right on cue the predicted contraction crashed through her.

Tim held her. 'You're going great, honey,' he croaked. 'You're nearly there.'

As the contraction subsided, Nicole snatched a few breaths and obeyed her body's instinct to push. Her head felt thick with blood, and the task of squeezing out a baby seemed completely improbable. When she couldn't push any more, she collapsed back into the cushions and gasped for breath. Sweat ran off her in streams.

Gail was praising her and dabbing her face with a cloth. The cool of it felt good on her skin. She wanted only to lie there and rest for a while, but without even knowing it she was automatically preparing for it to start all over again. Instinctively, she'd hooked into a cycle that wouldn't let up until the baby came.

Outside, another siren wailed. Her labour had closed in around her so tightly that the sound of it didn't seem bizarre anymore. It was simply one more crazy texture neatly filling the silence between contractions.

Another shot of pain exploded through her. She doubled over, crying out and bracing against it.

'Honey, there's an ambulance outside if it's too intense,' Tim said.

'She's doing fine,' Gail said, keeping them on message. 'It'll be any minute now.'

The contraction subsided, and Gail reached under Nicole's back to support her.

'Big push now, darling.'

Nicole gave it everything, heaving what little energy she had left into the squeeze.

Gail glanced up to Nicole, eyes flashing with excitement.

'That's it, my darling, you're nearly there,' she said.

Nicole felt like a wild animal was slowly eating her; she was barely keeping delirium at bay. The break between contractions had deserted her, so there was no time to regroup anymore. Too soon the next one smashed into her, and for the first time she felt like she couldn't handle it.

But as this doubt took hold, the feeling of bliss that had overtaken her in the bath returned. It started at her feet and ran up her body in waves, vanquishing the pain. Her head swam. In the far-off distance she could hear singing again—and urgent voices beyond that. Time seemed irrelevant as she turned and tumbled in the air, ecstasy stroking its delicious fingers along her skin. Was it moments or hours she remained like that: vibrating with bliss, her eyes seeing nothing but light and vapour?

Feet first, she raced towards earth again, landing hard.

The singing stopped. The voices stopped. As the world came flooding back to her, she became aware that the outward swell of the baby inside her was gone.

She looked up to her husband—who was holding their child—but one glance at his contorted face told her something was terribly wrong. He wore a mask of shock that chilled her to the bone.

'What's wrong?' she heard herself saying. 'What's wrong with my baby?'

Tim's eyes were filling with tears, but he wasn't saying anything. She wanted to demand he speak, but she couldn't find any voice of her own.

Gently, he lifted the baby to show it to her, and as she took it from him she finally saw what had so rocked Tim to his core.

Their baby had a halo.

2

The SUV made a slow pass along the deserted main street of a country town. Simon, tattooed and Christ-like (if Christ had spent time in the big house), sat in the passenger seat, paying keen attention to the little supermarket that ended the shopping strip. The cover of darkness made it defenseless—ripe for his purposes. He gestured to Charlie to take them into the car park at the rear and then waved for the vehicle trailing them to follow.

They came to a stop, and the engine died. Charlie was the first out. A harder looking man than Simon, he never wasted time getting on the move. Duck was in the back seat and followed quickly. He was younger and wore the men's toughness like training wheels. Simon waited for the other car to pull to a stop and watched as Aamir and Rob jumped out carrying their rifles.

'Leave 'em in the car, boys,' Simon said with a relaxed smile, and they obeyed, tossing their weapons onto the back seat. 'A quick prayer.' The men locked arms around him. 'Oh, Lord, bless this raid,' he intoned. 'Keep us and watch over us that we may tend to our flock, and we will praise and serve you with the muscular faith that you have so wisely planted inside us.'

The men broke. Each knew their role. Simon dragged a giant set of bolt cutters from the back seat and set out for the rear door of the supermarket. While the others collected their sacks, he clipped off the padlock, and they slipped quietly inside.

With a wave from Simon, the men fanned out. He supervised while they gathered the goods the community would need for the next month or so: cooking oil, rice, canned goods, soap.

Even as he noticed the blinking light of a security camera find them in the dark, Simon was calm. God had set them on this path. He would manage their safety. And besides, from his armed robbery days, Simon could approximate how long they had before the feed from this camera brought any action down on them. He barked a word of encouragement and made a mental note of the time.

**

Out on the main street, not far from the little supermarket, a patrol car pulled to a stop as a call came in from the station. Moments later, the engine roared, and the car pulled a U-turn. It slowed by the front of the store, and the cop in the passenger seat raked his powerful torch into the darkened building.

No sign of life.

The cops dashed to the front entrance drawing their guns. One reached for the door handle to test it. All was secure, so they crept around to the rear of the supermarket.

There they found the back door wide open. The sight of it caused them to flatten themselves against the building. They inched towards the door.

One gave a signal, and they burst inside.

Silence.

The two cops stood alert, torches slicing the darkness. The store was deserted; the thieves were gone.

On the road heading out of town, Simon was leading the men in an open-throated sing-a-long, as they made the long trip home to the compound. Their voices were tuneless, but their devotion was beyond reproach.

Jesus is on the mainline, tell Him what you want. Jesus is on the mainline, tell Him what you want. Call Him up, and tell Him what you want.'

***

Tim glanced from the baby to Gail, who'd slid to her knees and prostrated herself on the floor, mumbling words only the gods could interpret. Should he follow suit? Is this what one did when faced with apparent divinity? Five minutes ago he was in no doubt the concept of God was a load of bullshit. Now he had no choice but to accept the idea that he was actually under the same roof with Him.

He looked back to the baby once more and was confronted with a vision straight out of an oil painting: Madonna and Child. If it wasn't so iconic, it would have been wacky. He stared mutely, thinking the old masters hadn't quite captured the electric density of the halo. It hung in the air a centimeter above the baby's head, and it blazed bright enough to light the entire room. The glow had a palpable, internal voom.

The baby wasn't even crying. He just lay peacefully in

Nicole's arms, blinking. If not for Gail's muttered word salad, the room would have been completely soundless.

Nicole seemed to be in shock. And why not? If she felt remotely the way Tim did, the child in her arms would feel like an object that had been planted as a joke. One that precluded any possible parental bonding. Was it even their baby? And if not then where the hell was he?

While Tim was still processing the impossible, a knock came at the front door. It broke the silence in a truly surreal way. All heads craned towards the sound. Who the fuck could that *possibly* be?

'Should I get it?' Tim said.

'I don't know,' Nicole muttered.

He sat for a moment not knowing what to do. Maybe the knocker would bring with them some bead of sanity—either that or an explanation.

Tim felt like he was the obvious person to find out who was out there, so he got to his feet. He gave Nicole an unconvincing smile and sensibly pulled the nursery door closed behind him as he left.

Human shapes were dimpled through the glass of the front door. He knew he had to reorganise himself before he could deal with them, so he closed his eyes and breathed through the strangeness of it all. When he was sufficiently reassembled he opened the door and found three figures outside, silhouetted against the darkened sky beyond: a policeman, a fireman and a paramedic. He stepped onto the porch.

'Good evening, sir,' the fireman puffed. 'We've just attended a substantial fire at number seven, and we're here to reassure you that everything is now under control.'

The three of them seemed charged by their recent heroics. Their uniforms were dusted with soot.

'We're aware your wife is pregnant,' the paramedic said.

'Was,' Tim said automatically. 'She's just delivered the baby.' His face reddened with the magnitude of his secret. He might as well be standing on a thirty-foot pile of cocaine.

The paramedic stepped forward.

'Perhaps I should take a look at her.'

Tim blocked his way, and with way too much conviction assured him that everything was fine and that their homebirth had gone perfectly to plan. He even threw in a joke about the fire emergency failing to upstage their fun and games.

Tim read suspicion in their demeanor. He could see none of them were convinced that this was where they should leave the conversation. After a long pause, the policeman tested Tim one last time.

'Well, if everything's under control—'

'Absolutely,' Tim said, 'we'll be absolutely fine.' And he gave them a dead-eyed smile.

Reluctantly, the men backed away and headed into the night. Tim went to go inside, but something caught his eye. As the men marched away, the tops of their helmets were picking up a light from above.

Tim followed them off the porch and looked skywards. Beyond the wisps of smoke still hanging in the air was the brightest star he'd ever seen. It had four long beams that made the shape of a tapered cross, and one of them pointed straight down towards the roof of his house.

Tim's blood ran cold. What now? Were a hundred thousand frenzied worshippers about to mass at their door? Doing his best to bat away this alarming thought, he slipped back inside. Nicole was positioning the baby onto her breast, and her damp hair was tumbling all around him. It was a scene of excruciating beauty. He approached and drew them into him. Suddenly they were a family. Love swept around them. It may have been emanating from the baby, or it could have been the beauty of the knot he found himself in, but he held onto them, riding it out. Minutes passed. Finally, Nicole broke away.

'Who was it? At the door?'

Tim wanted to forget everything that had happened outside.

'Faark,' he said. 'This is all just completely bat shit.'

Nicole gave him a look. Tim had no choice but to elaborate.

'Three wise men,' he mumbled.

Nicole didn't understand, so he went on. 'Nic, it was a policeman, a fireman, and a paramedic. There's a star above the house. The brightest star you've ever seen.'

Nicole's face twisted, and Tim knew she'd finally got it. She glanced down at the baby and stroked his face.

'I thought when I first saw him I was hallucinating, because I can't remember delivering him. I blacked out, and I could hear this voice, singing.'

'That was you, hon. You were singing.'

'And then I thought—when I saw him—he's an angel. We've brought an angel into the world. I figured, maybe it's just *us* who can see it. Everything will be okay because we're the only ones who'll know.'

'It's the Rapture,' Gail said, as if ordaining it to be true. 'The Messiah is born.'

Tim and Nicole glanced at her, feasting on her certainty.

'What the hell should we do?' Nicole said.

Gail held them in a steady gaze. 'Don't shy away from him,' she said. 'He's yours, and he needs you.'

Tears wet Nicole's face. Gail was right. He was their

baby, and that eclipsed everything else. She turned to Tim and touched his face.

'Can you get my mum and my dad?' she said. 'I really need to see them.'

***

As Tim stepped out of the house, he searched skyward for the star, but it had vanished. The emergency vehicles and onlookers were gone, and the street rested with an eerie stillness. The only reminder of the evening's drama was the stink of charcoal and steam, which drifted along the cul-de-sac.

This neighbourhood still felt foreign to him. It was so out of character that he and Nicole should have moved to this part of Malvern in the first place. Before they'd met, Tim had been your rusted on Fitzroy-boy, floating from shared household to bachelor flat, and Nicole had settled like leaves amongst the art deco strip along Alexandra Avenue by the Yarra. But as a couple they'd decided to plant themselves in the hushed backstreets of old Malvern, where shop fronts like uneven rows of teeth concealed the cul-de-sacs and plane trees beyond, where all sound and character were sucked out of the world, and where the owner/occupiers were reduced to tending their gardens for their daily hit of excitement.

Here their focus faced inwards. They'd colonised their rented Cal bung like a couple of sightless chicks in a nest. Malvern was a physical manifestation of the new life their relationship had rung in for them, and they were happy to borrow the surrounding calm while they added a baby to their count. But what would it do to this quiet, inner-suburban oasis if the news broke that the outsiders had brought the Messiah into their midst? Would they come marching with torches held high, or form a stampede to honour him?

Tim shook his thoughts loose and got into the car. At this point his insistence that he drive Nicole's parents around rather than ask they hire a car seemed over-generous. So far his night seemed to be defined by him driving away to collect people at significant moments.

The apartment Nicole's parents were staying in was all sandstone facades and water features—the kind you only stay in when you're interstate on business. Tim crunched his way along the manicured gravel path and paused at the door before knocking. Inside he could hear his in-laws fussing with the unmistakable vigor of a couple poised to meet their first grandchild. How could they predict the bombshell that awaited them?

Nicole's father, Garry, was the one to swing the door open. Typically, any hint of fluster was airbrushed away as he wrapped Tim in his generous embrace.

Garry was one of Perth's leading Ear, Nose and Throat specialists and inspired an almost mystical following amongst his patients. It was only recently that he'd cut his practicing days to three a week to care for his wife, Clare, who was now edging him out of the doorway with her wheelchair.

'L-L-Look at you Y-Y-Y big hairy father,' she said, beaming. She tried her best to slap him with an unsteady hand. 'What D-D-Did we get… a B-B-Boy or a girl?'

'Boy,' Tim said, dodging the slap.

Garry took control of the wheelchair. 'Everything went to plan?'

Tim nodded. 'Yeah … yeah it was good.'

The couple shared a look that Tim did his best to disregard, then Garry dug deeper.

'And the baby?' he said, testing him. 'He's doing all right is he?'

'He's … yeah … he's doing great.'

The grandparent's excitement was fast deflating. As always, Clare reached for humour when things got tense.

'Is he B-B-B-eautiful like his G-G-Grandmother?'

When the truth is so impossibly big anything else feels like small talk, and so as they made their way through the sculptured gardens towards the car Tim struggled to give them more than a monosyllabic account of the night's events. What on earth could he tell them? The only practical way to explain was for them to see for themselves.

***

When they reached the cul-de-sac, the grandparent's chirpy celebration had sunk to polite solemnity. Tim led them to the front door and paused, keys in hand.

'I have to tell you something.' Clare and Garry braced themselves. 'I know you're thinking the worst, but ... it's just ...' Tim's words flapped helplessly before him like beached fish, '...you just need to be prepared that's all.

Tim pushed through the front door and led them down the hall to the lounge.

The house was dimly lit, and there was a distinct post-natal hush. When they reached the lounge they were greeted by the warm glow of candles and a moody silence. Clare waited for Tim to gesture them forward, and as they entered the room she could just make out Nicole sitting on the couch, with Gail lounging at her feet.

From where Clare was it looked like Nicole was cradling some kind of bedside lamp, which was illuminating her face. Nicole looked up and gave them a smile, and that's when Clare first understood what it was she was looking at. The swaddling blankets fell away so she could now make out it was actually the baby, and floating in the air above his head was a halo.

Clare could feel Garry rooted to the spot beside her. There's little else one can do when a lifetime of belief is turned on its head. As a couple, Clare and Garry were richly marinated in religious skepticism. God was a dinner party discussion held at arm's length from faith. Even when Clare's multiple sclerosis began to bite hard, turning to God was never an option for them. But now the two of them were gawking at the miracle their own daughter had delivered. How could it be true?

Gail looked up and seemed to measure them.

'As you can see, the baby has a halo.'

That was all that Clare needed. She rounded on Garry.

'Take M-M-Me to her! Please! T-T-T-Take me to her!'

Garry rolled her forward. The moment she was within reach, Clare launched herself at Nicole.

'Oh my D-D-D-Darling,' she stammered, 'are you all right?'

Nicole was beaming; she held her mother tight to her. 'Isn't he beautiful?'

Clare steadied her torso against the armrest of the couch and chewed at the air wildly. Then she reached out to touch the baby. By chance, her first point of contact was with the baby's tiny fingers. One seemed to curl around hers, and suddenly their hands were bound together. She glanced up to Nicole and giggled.

'Oh, look, he's—'

A tiny shiver shot through her. It threaded its way through her finger all the way down into the deepest part of her intestines and knotted itself there, fizzing and tingling. It made her gulp for breath. Then the sensation was gone.

Clare gave another shiver, shrugged it off, and leaned into Nicole.

'My, you're a clever girl,' she said. 'Always the over-achiever.' Then she turned to her husband and gave him a wicked grin.

'Kid's got a halo. Betcha didn't see that coming,' she said.

***

The SUV bounced along a broken dirt road deep into the bush; the headlights raked the towering trees all around them. Simon, resting a lazy foot out the window, glanced into the back seat where Duck was playing funny-buggers with a rifle—taking imaginary pot shots at make-believe wildlife.

'Put the fucking gun away,' Simon barked, and Duck snapped to attention, dutifully laying it in his lap.

Up ahead the gates of the compound loomed. Even from a distance they seemed to reach into the night sky. Beyond them all the brothers and sisters would be sleeping. Tomorrow they'd wake to find a bounty only a successful raid could bring, and it made Simon smile to think of the gratitude they'd shower on him come morning.

'I'll get the gates,' Duck said, and he was out of the car before it had even pulled to a stop. Simon sighed with frustration as he noted the kid had set off carrying the gun.

After he'd dragged open the gates and the SUVs began to rumble inside, Duck raced back to the car and jumped onto the bonnet for a cheap ride back through the compound. Simon turned to Charlie and gave him permission to drive on.

Along the path through the community, all the huts

were still. No lights burnt. No sound. It warmed Simon to know that inside those huts were the hearts that beat for him; this was the world he'd given breath to.

As the cars neared the end of the track, Charlie turned to Simon and gave him a dead-eyed smile. He accelerated slightly then planted his foot on the brake. The car came to an abrupt stop, and Duck slid from the bonnet and vanished from sight.

Charlie and Simon threw back their heads, but their laughter was short-lived when there was a crack from the gun. A howl followed.

Simon leapt from the car to find Duck lying in the dirt, a hand clamped to his bleeding shoulder. He was whimpering, and his eyes were wide with shock.

Simon sucked air through his gritted teeth. 'You are a fucking idiot, Duck!' he bawled, and he grabbed the boy by his shirt, dragged him up, and slammed him into the side of the car. Duck screamed with pain. Simon gave him one for being so noisy, then another one for being so stupid. 'Put him back in the car and take him to Garnerville,' he snapped at Charlie. 'With any luck he'll cark it on the way.'

Charlie grimaced at the idea. 'Nothing's open this time of night, boss.'

'Work it out,' Simon snapped, and sank a boot into the door of the car for good measure. 'Fuck!'

***

Tim eased himself in through the door, careful not to disturb the picture of beauty before him. Nicole was stretched out on the bed with the baby, both of them breathing deep and long.

Nicole's eyes rolled open.

'Did you get them home all right?'

Tim grinned. 'Your mother kept crying. Gail said she'd come back early to check on you. And you just know she will.'

Tim eased himself onto the bed. The baby lay between them, his little eyelids closed against the exhausting world. Tim toyed with the thin beam of light floating above the baby's head, testing for any sensation it might radiate, but he felt nothing: no electric tingle, no transformation, no enlightenment, only a beam of light floating there—waiting to blow up their lives.

He shook his head in wonder. 'What the actual fuck,' he muttered. 'I keep expecting to open my eyes and this is all some bizarre dream.' Nicole offered a tired smile. 'I mean ... why the hell *us*, you know? A couple of clueless atheists.'

'Maybe we're special,' Nicole said. 'Maybe we're incredibly righteous and we just don't know it.'

'Maybe you are. This has got nothing to do with me.'

Nicole whacked him. 'That's not even funny.'

But Tim wasn't really joking. He was certain if God had chosen them it was all about Nicole not him.

'So what now?' he said. 'What do we do?'

'I don't know. I mean ... who would? We could name him.'

'Jesus is already taken,' Tim said with a grin.

'We were going to call him Billy if he was a boy.'

'Shouldn't he have a name with some enormous significance? Like Abraham, or Noah?'

'I like Billy.'

Tim wriggled in closer and rested a hand tenderly on the baby.

'Billy,' he repeated, testing how it sounded in his mouth. 'Nic, you know there's a giant shit storm coming. We're going to have to love him a lot.'

'I can do that. Can you?'

'I bloody hope so.'

Nicole rolled onto her back. Tim ran his fingers through the halo again.

'I bloody hope so,' he repeated, and his eyes finally closed.

3

Simon woke, as always, just as the sun's first rays touched the rough-sawn bark of the hut's roof. The damp air was already warming, and the pounding surf was a distant roar behind the foothills, which ran all the way down to the coast.

The return from last night's raid had been late, but Simon was eager to lead the morning jog around the perimeter fence, so the moment he woke he gently peeled Joanne's arm from around his waist and got up to dress.

He caught her opening a slit of an eye as he slid into his boxer shorts. Kara stirred as well, then Shayne, then Mayling. He dripped a honey smile on them and ceased the charade of dressing so quietly.

'Come on, my hearts, who's for a run?' he said. The hut filled with sleepy groans. 'Come on. God has given us another perfect day.'

The last to stir was Adele. The other girls giggled as

she groaned with the injustice of the hour. She was always the last to wake, always missed curfew with her mysterious, late night bush walks. Simon struggled to find patience with her, but something about the spill of her blonde hair across the pillow, her spoilt aloofness, the mystery of her, reached into his body and tugged at him. He wanted to go to her right now and rouse a sleepy caress from those pouty lips and hold her like she was his own.

'Will "Miss" be joining us this morning?'

'No!' Adele bleated, rolling onto her stomach and pulling the sheet up over her head.

'Some of us have been up half the night and we're still running.' Simon winked, and the other girls chuckled obediently.

'It's fucking dawn.'

'Suit yourself,' he said, 'but come breakfast time we'll be feasting with lungfuls of the Lord.'

The girls were dressing. Simon cast an eye over them as they tugged on shorts and slipped T-shirts over their nakedness. Adele would come around to him eventually—would sleep with him the way they did— once she'd let go of Anthony.

'Simon,' Joanne said, drawing his attention away from Adele, 'I heard a shot last night.'

Simon cringed. He didn't like things that weren't within his control.

'Duck had an accident,' he said sharply. 'Charlie's taken him to Garnerville. He'll live.'

'Praise the Lord,' Joanne said.

'Praise his might,' Simon added, and he clapped his hands. 'Now. Who's running?'

The girls squealed and made for the door. Unable to resist, he crept over to Adele and pressed a kiss into her neck. After waiting a moment too long for a response, he retreated out the door of the hut.

Simon led the girls along the track towards the perimeter fence, where a group of joggers had already assembled. With the success of last night's raid still fuelling his mood, he plunged into their midst, and they gladly drew him into their embrace.

'My hearts,' he cried. 'Try to picture a more perfect day.'

The brothers and sisters all hooted. Their reverie was interrupted by the sound of an engine. Everyone turned to find Charlie's SUV approaching the gates further along the fence. Simon broke from them to greet him, but his ebullient mood disintegrated the moment he saw there was no passenger in the car.

'Where's Duck?' he said tightly.

'He's fine,' Charlie replied. 'Doc said he couldn't be moved.'

'Fuck, Charlie! You know Duck doesn't have the sense to answer a fucking question. Go back and get him.'

Charlie hesitated.

'Now!' Simon roared, 'before he says something stupid!'

Charlie picked a newspaper off the passenger seat and handed it to Simon.

'You brought me a newspaper.'

'Look at it,' Charlie said.

Simon unrolled it. Almost the entire front page was devoted to a picture of a giant star accompanied by a headline that read: Holy Miracle?

Simon practically inhaled it. When he'd finished reading he turned to the gathering and held up the picture.

'This is our sign, my hearts! God has spoken, and we

shall hear. Because if you're not listening to God then who are you listening to?'

The brothers and sisters cheered.

Simon handed the newspaper back to Charlie.

'Come, my hearts,' he bellowed, 'we run!'

Simon pushed through the crowd. He'd almost disappeared down the dirt track before anyone had the sense to follow.

'We run!' he cried again without turning back, and they all sprang into motion, a fluid mob, pressing together along the skinny bush track.

***

It was dawn when Tim and Nicole were woken by Billy's canine snuffling. It took them a moment to refresh: baby, halo, potential ruin. Sleep had changed nothing.

Tim batted away the dawn. This was not his time of day. His limited experience of it was a vague awareness of Nicole kissing his cheek as she tiptoed out for work. He opened an eye to see Nicole juggle Billy onto her breast like Gail had shown her. Billy tugged hard at her colostrum.

'Did you get any sleep?' he asked, battling phlegm.

She chuckled. 'I didn't move. What's the time?'

He reached for his phone. '5.20 am,' he said and groaned.

'Toughen up.'

With phone in hand, Tim automatically flicked through to Facebook. He scrolled through the first world soap opera until something stopped him dead.

'Oh, shit.' He tapped the screen and held it out to her. 'This is the star from last night.'

The clip was grainy and bleeding, but the idea that it was "out there" was alarming.

Once it had played out he flicked through to YouTube to search for more in-depth footage. The splash page was littered with it. He opened the top ranked clip. Mercifully, it ignored their house in favour of the star. Maybe they were safe after all.

He leapt out of bed and made for the window, parting the curtains.

'What are you doing?' Nicole asked.

'Checking for pilgrims,' he said. 'If there are that many videos out there, maybe the house has been recognised. Maybe there's a bloody congregation on the front lawn.'

'Well?' Nicole said, her patience deserting her.

Tim dropped the curtains and bounced back onto the bed. 'Nope.' He grinned. Nicole gave him a look.

'You're very casual about it,' she said.

'Well, there's no one out there, so we must be safe.'

Tim returned to YouTube, randomly checking videos. 'This is cool you know,' he said absently. 'We're famous. Anonymously. There's only five of us on the planet that know the truth about this, and you and I are two of them.'

Nicole seized the phone from him. Perhaps the newspaper could give them a better insight into the scale of the threat. She opened *The Age*. The splash page headline read: "Holy Miracle?"

Tim skimmed the article. It listed the popular theories of what had caused the star to appear: secret aircraft tests, alien visitations, and, of course, claims it was a sign of the second coming of Christ. He snatched the phone back and read out loud from the article. "'According to Professor Found from Deakin University's School of Astrophysics, it was more than likely an occurrence similar to the Aurora Borealis. A particularly dense solar wind passed through the magnetosphere causing a phenomenon appearing to the eye like a star.'"

It sounded so rational even Tim and Nicole were tempted to buy it. Was this what it felt like to dodge a bullet?

They lay back into their pillows.

'Someone's going to find out,' Nicole said. 'What the hell happens then?'

***

Gail was no stranger to the church in Curzon Street. Most Sundays she was cocooned on the back pew, while the priest, Father Jim, unleashed one of his passionate and controversial sermons.

She came for his subversive wit and his bluntness, which regularly bruised the establishment. She liked his brand of Christianity, which skipped the fire and brimstone in favour of kindness and tolerance, and she thought his larrikin charm might well have been sexy in his day.

Gail wasn't the slightest bit denominational. She was as happy in an ashram as she was in a mosque; she just had to feel it. So when the congregation opened their hearts in hymn it was like the drapes had been unfurled, and sunshine had poured in all around her.

Gail had no stomach for communion though, so she'd always disappear the moment the sermon had finished. As a result, she wasn't a familiar face within the flock, and, having marked Father Jim as the man she needed to speak to, she knew all that needed to change.

She parked herself in the very front pew. With her blue velvet cloak and shaved head she imagined she'd catch the Father's eye the moment he took the pulpit.

Today he singled out tolerance and inclusion, making the case for gay marriage. Gail couldn't help but smile as a ripple of outrage swept through the church.

'I won't do a gay marriages,' he was saying, 'because I *can't* do gay marriages. I support them; I advocate for the rights of those who want to marry, but until my Church changes its mind I am bound. How is this right?'

It was these kind of sermons that famously put him at odds with his bosses. An hour long documentary about his rebelliousness had recently aired, and this had only fueled his popularity.

When the sermon was over, she hung on the outskirts of the milling crowd and bided her time until the final parishioner had left.

'Nothing like an unexplained celestial event to fill your congregation on a Sunday,' he quipped. 'It even dug you out of the back row.'

Gail could tell he was revelling in her surprise. There had to have been a hundred people packed into that church, how could he possibly have noticed that?

'Last week you were wearing a floral dress,' he said. 'This week it's blue. And you've shaved your head.' Gail must have been gaping. He winked. 'It's my curse. Nothing gets past me. Ask me about any of my flock, and I could tell you exactly what they were wearing down to the buttons.'

Gail smiled.

'Do you need a word?' he said.

This was the opportunity she'd been waiting for. She led him down the long row of pews and sat.

'Are you happy here,' he asked, 'or should we go into the confessional?'

'No, it's nothing like that, Father.'

'Then I'm all ears.'

Gail took some time to begin. She introduced herself as a midwife and a lover of God. She'd chosen to come to him specifically because he had an open heart and an open mind. 'I sense that you will trust me and listen to what I say without judgment. Can you do that?'

Father Jim betrayed his curiosity by leaning forward a little too heavily. 'Of course. I'll certainly try.'

Gail straightened her cloak. 'You must have seen the videos that are circulating online, the ones of the giant star?'

'I'm more than handy with a mouse you know. About twenty parishioners have already emailed them to me.'

'And what do you make of it?'

'It's phenomenal.'

'But is it God's work?'

'Isn't everything?'

Gail cocked her head. Touché.

'I know some people who need your help. I delivered their baby last night.' She shuffled closer to him along the pew. 'The reason I say this, Father, is that … I believe the child is blessed.'

'Every child is blessed,' he said, suggesting that so far nothing he'd heard had warranted such a hushed tone.

'This is the part where I need you to listen without judgment, Father.' She held his eye. 'The baby has a halo.'

Gail saw him flinch. She guessed she was losing him, so she continued on. 'The star that you saw in those videos appeared directly above the house where he was born. It was to herald his arrival.'

The priest's eyes narrowed. Gail couldn't tell if she'd lost him or if he was lost in thought.

'This is a very unusual story.'

'I promise I'm not trying to fool you. And I'm not insane. I hoped you'd come with me and visit him so you can see for yourself. If you believe what you say from the pulpit, you'll come and see him.'

Father Jim stood and paced between the pews. 'I

believe that *you* believe this. But these people … they haven't tricked you, have they?'

'Father, I know this is beyond belief, but it's also beyond doubt. You'll be making a terrible mistake if you pass up the opportunity to see him for yourself.'

Father Jim returned to the pew and took her hands.

'Okay,' he said, 'I'll come. But I have to warn you. There are protocols. If this child is what you say he is I'll need to talk to my people.'

'If he is what I say he is you *must* talk to your people.' She allowed herself a secret celebration that in some small way she'd just done God's work. He had to have a plan for the child, and she knew in her heart that she had to be part of it somehow.

'I'm going there now,' she said, 'but I think arriving with you unannounced would be a mistake. Let me talk to them first, and perhaps we could visit together … tomorrow.'

The Father nodded.

'Good. I'll see you then.'

***

Father Jim dithered as he dressed down from the service. He couldn't settle or turn his mind to any other tasks of the day. There was something powerful in Gail's story, something threaded between her words that compelled a feeling of exhilaration in him.

He flipped open his laptop and clicked through to his emails. The first message he'd received that contained a video of the star popped up. Many of his congregation had already ordained it to be the coming of the Lord, and if he was honest, even in his cautious priest's mind, he'd been excited by the idea.

He watched it over three times asking himself, if it

wasn't God's work then what was it? It simply couldn't be explained without at least bringing the possibility of God's hand into it. Then add to that, news of a blessed child. If Gail's story were true it would be a revelation so huge the consequences would be unimaginable.

So what to do about it? Could he even wait twenty-four hours?

Father Jim paced his little vestry for an hour, intermittently watching the video. At the end of the hour, after beseeching God's guidance, he surrendered to the need for help and dialled the Bishop of his diocese.

'Your Excellency?' he said, 'it's Father Jim here. I have something rather important I need to discuss with you.'

***

Garry was accustomed to waking before Clare. His first instinct was to reach out for her, as if his initial morning touch would set her for the day ahead. But when his hand searched for her under the covers, he found no warmth there and no imprint in the mattress.

In an instant, he spun, only to find that he was alone in the bed. How had he missed her leaving his side?

Panic quickly set in. Maybe she'd fallen out. Perhaps she'd dragged herself to the toilet in the night and hadn't been able to return. A myriad of these catastrophes raced through his head, but before he could even throw back the covers and investigate, the door to the bathroom swung open, and Clare appeared. She stood before him—smiling, upright, healed—just as she did in his dreams, but her smile was more intense now, and tears soaked her cheeks.

Garry sat up and looked her over as if she were a

stranger. Somehow, someone had rewound the years and placed the former version of his wife in the space before him.

Clare giggled. Garry could hear the relief in her laugh that, finally, her struggle was over.

Filled with an emotion too intense and too unfamiliar to identify, Garry put his head in his hands and sobbed.

4

Simon dashed between the reaching bracken along the uneven track. He felt unleashed, like he could burst out of his skin and dart spirit-like into the air. He tore off his shirt so the brothers and sisters—scrambling to keep up with him—could fully see him. The muscles of his naked shoulders would parade to them his tattoo of Christ and His blazing halo and would stir the ink into life. They would *see* him. His most recent tattoos—all celebrations of the Lord that obscured the skulls and bare breasted women inked from his bygone prison days—would tell a tale of a man changed forever by the voice of God.

Those bygone days seemed like ancient history now. Incarcerated for armed robbery, Warwick Carson, as his name appeared on the prison roll call, was fresh meat to begin with. For his whole first year inside, he spent more time in medical from beatings than he did in his own cell.

Despair cruelled him into a ball, and it was then that God began to speak to him. It was whispered messages of comfort at first, but soon God's voice became a boom inside his head. It prophesied that he would become a leader of men, and that he would bring a new faith into the world.

On his release, he wandered from town to town, spending nights squatting in the half-finished skeletons of new estates, disappearing by morning before the workers arrived. He took in the gospel from the back row of country churches.

Warwick took a job as a fencer in Mildura, busting a gut on his weekdays and devoting his weekends to the church. His zeal earned him a semi-regular stint on the pulpit where his blistering sermons warned that God was not in a building or in a book, but inside any man who found the correct internal frequency. When the outraged pastor finally bundled him out with a slap to the back of the head, Warwick called on anyone with dreams of 'finding the way' to join him in the local cow paddock.

His flock collected thick and fast. Every Sunday morning and Wednesday evening he'd sharpen his tongue with stories of the times when God had His lips to his ear.

Word spread like fruit fly; his congregation became aggressive with their devotion. The turning point happened when one Sunday a sad looking stranger arrived. He was in his fifties, and he wore the residue of several mid-life crises: the street-wear, the bling, the annoyingly reversed baseball cap. He sat hunched on the damp hay behind the congregation with his head hung in shame.

Warwick noticed him, and after the sermon he took the man's large, meaty hands in his.

'What's your name, brother?' he said, gently.

Simon could see the man barely had the strength to look at him.

'Anthony.'

'What's your story, Anthony?'

That was all it took to make Anthony's large shoulders heave.

'Walk with me,' Warwick said, and he invited Anthony to unpack all of his misery before him.

A financial consultant with no wife or family, and whose parents were long dead, Anthony had woken one day to the thought that the world he inhabited was filled with greedy bastards who he shared nothing in common with besides the pursuit of money. He longed to start again, but his compass was spinning uncontrollably.

The way forward was obvious: Anthony was to move into Simon's derelict farmhouse.

Living off the fruits of Anthony's corrupted past allowed Warwick the time to go deeper into his readings of the Bible.

Hunched over the good book like a dim-sighted monk, Warwick began to notice the almost hidden presence of an apostle named Simon in the Gospel of St Luke. Not Simon Peter, but Simon Kananaios. This shadowy figure fascinated him. He was barely mentioned in the Bible, but when Warwick dug around he found Simon had joined the Zealots and their rebellion against the Romans, and there were varied tales of him meeting all kinds of violent deaths.

One night, as he strained into the text, the words on the page seemed to evaporate into the air around him, and for the first time since prison Warwick heard the familiar boom of God's voice. He said it was time to set the foundations for a new faith that followed the muscular path of the Zealots.

Warwick finally understood, and from that moment on he would only answer to the name Simon.

He instructed Anthony to liquidate his assets and tip everything into a single bank account, and the two of them hit the road in search of a property big enough to host the stream of followers God had ordained would follow them.

Instinct drove them north through the hinterlands of Northern New South Wales, through Kyogle, Murwillumbah, and up into Queensland, where months of snaking around back roads bore little fruit. Their quest often brought them agonisingly close, but the vision emblazoned in Simon's mind would not be compromised.

After nine months of hunting, God finally parted the vines and revealed their home. It had been under their noses all along. In the shadows of Mount Warning, Simon, for no particular reason, took a turn off the highway and bumped for miles along a dirt track that seemed to offer no potential at all. Anthony swayed silently in the passenger seat, sending him curious sideways glances. But at the end of the track Simon pulled the car to a stop on the soil of their future life. He knew it the moment he stepped out of the car and breathed the sweet, humid air.

This was country you could roam with your shirt off. The mystical bush hid mango trees, which dumped their yield with generous abandon. Rich pastures waved tall in the breeze, ripe-sewn for goats and sheep. The nearby woods were stacked with timber for building huts. It was coastal for fishing, and the planting soil was good enough to eat.

Simon and Anthony uprooted the willing—fifteen disciples ready to turn their hands into leather. Anthony's remaining spoils bought the land, the water

38

tanks, the sewerage system, and a 15-foot perimeter fence topped with razor wire, which encircled the entire property. The leftover cash bought vehicles, a small fishing dingy and weapons. In the end, Simon had replaced Anthony's miserable cash with the promise of a future.

In less time than they spent searching for the property, the brothers and sisters shaped it into a civilization. Twenty wooden huts were assembled from timber milled by hand. The prototypes swayed clumsily, but they quickly learnt to turn them out larger and stronger, and they soon became structures to stand back and admire.

A large prayer hall was built—not much more than a sprawling bark roof straddling six massive sawn tree trunks. The walls were crafted from tie-dyed fabric, which beat like slack drum skins in the open air, and the earthen floor was draped with cushions and hand woven rugs. Simon used a chainsaw to carve an altar from a single piece of felled lumber.

Anthony's contribution was to establish an ornamental pond. It was to be a place of reflection, a place to commune with the majesty that vibrated out of the bush. He turned the first sod of the hole, which filled with water when the rains came. Statues modelled from clay were dressed into the surrounding garden beds, and lumber was dragged alongside to sit on. Two men hiked for three days along creek-beds to return with water lily plants, which quickly made the pond their own, and gave the frogs a stage to sing from in the evenings.

The dining shelter was built to be the heart of the community. Pagodas twisted with vines sheltered long benches, and the huge kitchen coppers bubbled with soups and curries all day long. Market gardens were planted out and tended to with religious verve. Rows of potatoes, broccoli and silver beet were punctuated at the ends with flowering shrubs, like a French vineyard.

But even with all this natural bounty self-sufficiency was unrealistic, and Simon knew it. If he was completely honest, he was glad. It gave him the license to follow the tradition of the Zealots and go out into the corrupt world and take whatever-the-fuck they needed. Just like the old days, he relished the thrill of a break and enter, and it soon became the norm for the community.

With the compound now set, the family grew quickly. The cluster of huts reproduced like cells in a Petri dish, and within a year the brothers and sisters totalled fifty.

The compound called to all those searching for a safe place, and Simon watched over them with a quiet, benevolent sheen.

He hosted daily congregations in the prayer hall, where he beseeched his followers to listen for the internal frequency of God, claiming that proximity to him was all they needed to hear it. They drank him in. Simon gathered a clutch of women to lie with him at night, commissioning a larger hut for them all to sleep in.

But just as it seemed everything had slotted neatly into place, Simon became aware of the rise of Anthony. He'd claimed a special place in the compound's narrative by stumping up for everything around them, and gradually he'd become quite the mentor. He wandered the gardens like a contented monk, and he was a skilled interpreter of Simon's teachings.

One terrible morning on his way to the jog, Simon passed Anthony's hut as he emerged with a recently arrived young woman, Adele. They were so immersed in one another that they didn't even notice him walk by. It rocked him to the core, and his morning run was spoilt with forgotten feelings of rejection. He spent the day aloof from the community, and he cancelled prayers.

That night as he strolled to the mess hut, he passed by Anthony, again sitting with the same girl. Their hands were folded together, and they were speaking in hushed tones. He overheard Adele say, 'I love you. I want to be with you. You're my lover and my sage.'

Simon was rabid. He marched Anthony into the bush and called him on his treachery.

At first Anthony thought it was a joke, but when Simon took a fistful of his shirt and demanded he confess his ambition to his face Anthony folded at the knees like a newborn calf.

'You are my saviour, Simon,' he choked. 'I would never do anything to hurt you.'

Simon was unmoved. 'You don't teach anymore, you understand? If I want a partner I'll tell you. If I want your help, I'll fuckin' ask.'

Anthony nodded mutely, and Simon believed his warning had taken hold. But less than twenty-four hours later, when Simon returned from a solitary bush walk, he found Anthony leading a service for Brutus, one of the compound's prized bucks, who'd nibbled too close to the edge of the pond and been found floating there hours later. He watched on as the gathering held hands and prayed, Anthony at their centre.

Simon's rage of the previous day gave way to a focused certainty. He'd seen the way the top dog in the nick had dealt with any challengers, and although it occasionally got ugly it taught people their place. Anthony had been a loyal and useful deputy, but this time he'd flown too close to the sun.

The next morning, Simon found Anthony before breakfast.

'We've become distant,' Simon said.

Anthony appeared relieved at Simon's reversal. He gave an uncertain smile.

'I don't want that, Simon, I promise,' he said.

'I want you to pack for a fishing trip. Just you and me. We haven't done one together since we first came out here.' Simon flashed him a grin. 'It's time.'

Anthony beamed and trotted away to gather his things while Simon packed the car.

All the way out to the deep water, Anthony chatted gleefully. When Simon was satisfied they were far enough from shore, he let the motor idle and began sorting through the equipment.

'It's so still today, Simon,' Anthony said. 'Look at that horizon.'

Simon straightened and stared into the distance. 'Perfect.'

'If we don't bring fish home today, I'm going to take it up with the Boss,' Anthony said.

'I thought I was the Boss.'

Anthony chuckled, but then stopped short.

'Well?' Simon said.

The boat bobbed in the gentle chop; Anthony grasped for something to say.

'Who were you talking about, Anthony?'

'You. I mean—I meant God. I mean God will bring us fish, but you're the Boss, Simon.'

Simon grinned. 'Glad to hear it.' And he went back to his work.

Anthony was silent now. Simon could imagine him sitting there bruised, staring out with hurt hanging off his chubby face.

'Do me a favour, would you?' Simon said. 'Take a look over the side and tell me if you can see any fish down there.'

Simon knew Anthony would oblige, so behind him

he calmly lifted one of the heavy oars and swung it down hard onto Anthony's head. The blow was brutal, and because his weight was already over the side of the boat Anthony toppled straight into the drink.

Simon watched as Anthony sank under the water. It was remarkable how quickly a person could vanish. When he lost sight of him, Simon plonked himself beside the outboard and started her up. He eased the throttle to full kick and bounced back towards the shore.

As he approached land, he steered the boat into a cluster of rocks. The impact sent him flying. His injuries were sufficiently convincing and the boat badly damaged enough for him to spin a tragic story of how beautiful, faithful Anthony had been killed in a terrible accident at sea.

A shrine was erected beside Anthony's pond in remembrance of what he'd given to their lives. Mourners left flowers and wept, and slowly, day-by-day, they let go of the man most regarded as one of the elders of the place.

Simon used this tragedy to swipe Adele from Anthony's nest and plant her in his own. It was his final act of snuffing Anthony out. But quite unexpectedly he began to crave Adele like morning cigarettes. Her scent reached above all the other girls in his hut, and he soon found himself intoxicated.

She, on the other hand, grieved long for Anthony and refused to have sex. She told him to his face she couldn't hear God through him, said she wanted to believe—ached for grace—but was lost without her "light". Who would believe it? Complex, oversleeping, curfew-breaking Adele? How had Anthony been able to get through to her when *he* could not? What kind of key would open her heart? He was her misunderstood prophet, and she his crown of thorns.

As Simon led the joggers through the breathtaking morning light, this wound was the only thing that dented the day's perfection. He knew that as they rounded the last bend before returning to the community they would find Adele, sitting in her usual place by the pond, mourning at Anthony's shrine. But today he had a plan to capture her heart. God had finally shown him the path he could walk Adele down, arm in arm.

Simon brought the group to a stop and assembled them within earshot of Adele.

'Take care what you listen to,' he intoned. 'By your standard of measure it will be measured to you; and more will be given you besides. For whoever has, to him more shall be given; and whoever does not have, even what he has shall be taken away from him. Mark 4.24.'

The followers nodded and in unison muttered their agreement. Simon noted Adele had looked up from her grieving.

'Because I heard Him, God gave us all that we have here. And he told me that one day we would take our faith into the world and teach others our way. That time is almost upon us, my hearts. He promised me a sign, and today that sign has come.'

Adele stood, now fully intent on Simon's words.

'I don't yet know the meaning of the sign,' Simon continued, 'but isn't that so typical of the Lord?'

The followers all shared the irony, laughing with open hearts.

'If the sign is a sword, I shall pick it up,' Simon said. 'If it is a river, I shall ride upon it.' The followers hooted their agreement. 'And if the sign is a star, I shall follow it.'

Even Adele seemed caught up in his words now. Simon could see her approaching. He raised his voice another notch.

'And if beneath that star I find a child—a lamb of God—I will pick him up, and I will take him for my own. For he shall be mine.'

5

Gail arrived dead on eleven, just as Nicole's confidence as a new parent began to splutter. With each passing minute, her fragile little human seemed to become more and more unknowable. Were all new parents this confused at the beginning, or was this only another complication that came with having a God-child?

Gail began by walking her through the basics— feeding, dressing, sleep times—but as she arrived at the part about nappy changing there was a knock at the door. She heard Tim volunteer to answer, heard him clomping up the hall and swinging the front door open.

'Aren't you going to ask me in, you rude, hairy man?' Nicole heard Clare say.

Nicole noted Tim's failure to respond. An unusual feeling cut through her, so she abandoned the changing table and went to see her mother.

'Mum,' she chirped, 'Gail's teaching me to—'

Nicole's eyes landed on her mother. Like the sight of

her baby's halo the night before, Clare's recovery didn't compute.

Absence meant that Nicole had been spared the full tragedy of her mother's decline. It was easy to imagine that over on the other side of the country she was still the same old Clare, so seeing her returned to health was simultaneously unbelievable yet strangely familiar.

Clare rushed Nicole, and the two of them laughed and cried and held onto each other in a rolling knot of celebration.

Gail edged out of the doorway, gazing on with astonishment.

When the disbelief abated, Garry collected everyone and steered them into the lounge room. Nicole and Tim took to the couch, while Clare bounced on her toes before them.

'I made Garry walk over, poor bugger. We might take a leaf out of your book, Gail, and never get into a car again.'

Clare giggled at her own joke, but it was far from a celebration for Nicole and Tim, who were studying Clare like an unexploded bomb.

Clare huffed.

'Oh, come on. It's not like I've been *run over* by a car.'

'No, Mum,' Nicole said, reaching for a positive tone, 'it's just … this puts it in a whole new context.'

'If it's true,' Tim added.

It seemed Clare couldn't believe her ears. 'If *what's* true?' she gasped. 'Look at me.'

'We don't know for sure it was Billy,' Tim said.

'Of course it was Billy. I felt something last night. When he took my hand I felt something.'

Garry made a move to shut her down, but Clare went on.

'How could it be anything else?' she insisted.

'Okay,' Nicole said, sensing Clare was not going to let it go. 'So what now?'

'Well, we know why he's here now, don't we,' Clare shot back.

Nicole and Tim glanced at one another.

'Err, no?' Tim said.

'It's obvious,' Clare continued. 'He's a healer. He's here to save us.'

Clare was racing way ahead of them. Nicole and Tim had barely come to terms with the simplest practicalities of having a new baby, let alone setting out his Holy purpose.

'Mum, can you imagine what would happen if this got out?' Nicole said.

'It's going to get out the moment anyone catches a glimpse of me isn't it? How do we explain that?'

'You had a miraculous recovery,' Tim said. 'It happens all the time.'

'It does not,' Clare snapped.

'Jesus,' Tim said, 'we have to think about this. I mean … we need to keep this a secret, right? We all agree on that don't we?'

'You can't keep him locked up forever,' Clare said.

'But we're not going to parade him through the streets either,' Tim said.

Clare had the evangelical look in her eye of someone who'd had their life changed forever and who wanted everyone else in the world to share their experience.

'I don't think this is entirely your decision,' she said.

'Who else's decision could it possibly be?' Tim said.

Garry jumped out of his chair and stepped between them.

'Okay, okay, stop.' He turned to his wife and, with a single glance, dampened the flames. 'They're right, Clare. We have to think about how we manage this.' He turned to Nicole and Tim. 'If you're going to keep this a secret then you're going to need a plan. How will you keep him out of sight? Your friends, for example. They'll want to see the baby sooner rather than later.'

'Garry's right,' Tim said, 'we need to be selective. We should only include friends we know we can trust.'

'And the rest?' Nicole said, fearing where this was heading.

Tim shrugged. 'Right now all I can think is that this needs to be the world's best kept secret.'

Gail, who'd been silent, stood. 'Forgive me,' she said, 'but I think you need to talk to the Church.'

All eyes turned to her.

'The Church,' Tim repeated flatly. 'Didn't that end badly last time?'

'Clare is right when she says this is bigger than all of us,' Gail continued. 'The Church has experience in these things. They'll know what to do.'

Tim took a calming breath. 'Gail, that's exactly what we're trying to avoid. Can you imagine how badly they'll want to get their hands on him?'

'God has sent him. He must have a plan.'

'Yeah, he dumped him on couple of clueless atheists. Excellent plan.'

As the temperature threatened to rise again, Nicole felt the answer land inside her. She got to her feet and called for quiet.

'Listen,' she said, 'this is what I think. For two weeks we do nothing. We carry on like any normal family who's just had a baby. No visitors. No friends. No church. Only us. And then in two weeks—'

'This whole halo thing might have gone away,' Tim said.

'Hardly,' Clare said.

'Possibly,' Tim snapped.

'Then in two weeks,' Nicole said, claiming the room back, 'once we've had time to figure this out, Tim and I will make a decision about what we're going to do.'

Nicole's tone made it clear this wasn't a suggestion, but a plan. One by one they all fell into line—except Gail.

'What you're asking would be reasonable in any normal situation—' she began, but Nicole cut her off.

'Two weeks, Gail. I need you to promise.'

Gail looked bitten. She rose to her feet and headed for the door.

'Very well, I give you my word. We can revisit this in two weeks.'

But Nicole wasn't satisfied. 'No, Gail, you misunderstand. Tim and I will decide what to do.'

Gail paused at the door. 'Then I'll finish up and get out of your hair.'

She turned on her heel and headed off down the hall. Nicole turned to Tim.

'Was that too much?' she said.

'No fucking way. How is this her decision?'

But Nicole felt bad. She couldn't leave it like that with Gail.

'Can you ask her if she needs a lift home?' Tim looked as though he'd rather stick pins in his eyes. 'Please?'

Tim dragged himself off the couch and headed down the hallway. Nicole heard the front door close firmly and then Tim reappeared.

'Well?' said Nicole.

'What the fuck. I offered her a lift, but she just walked out,' he said.

***

Bishop Neil took Father Jim's call like he'd been interrupted from a game of chess. Usually it was Father Jim on the receiving end of a call from the Bishop, weaving and ducking his rebukes for being too outspoken, too controversial, not enough of a team player.

'To what do I owe the pleasure?' the Bishop said tightly.

Father Jim was nervous, but he had to keep faith with what had driven him to make the call in the first place. 'You're really going to have to go with me on this one, your Excellency,' he said.

Father Jim sensed the Bishop was already tiring of him.

'Go on,' the Bishop said flatly.

'I've had a visit from a parishioner that I need to talk to you about.'

He began a preamble about the giant star and the speculation surrounding it, but the Bishop cut him off and told him to get to the point, so Father Jim repeated the story Gail had told him about the miracle child. Even as the words left his mouth he knew how improbable they sounded.

There was a prolonged silence on the other end of the line.

'Bishop Neil?' Father Jim tested.

'You say this woman gave birth to a baby with a halo,' he said, finally.

'No, no, she delivered it. She's a midwife.'

Again the line went silent. Father Jim heard the old man sigh heavily.

'Father. This star has brought a lot of loonies out of the woodwork—'

'Your Excellency, with respect, she's asked me to come and visit him to see for myself.'

'And you plan to go?'

'Of course.'

'Then you're as crazy as she is.'

'Shouldn't we at least investigate?'

'It's prudent to keep a distance from fanatical behaviour, Father Jim. If you encourage this kind of hysteria, you very quickly taint the name of your church.'

The Bishop leant on this last sentence, reminding him how often he'd been accused of this before.

'Then what should I do?' Father Jim said.

'Counsel her to seek reason in the one true saviour, our Lord, Jesus Christ.'

'I think if you spoke to her—'

'I assume you've rung for my advice?'

'Yes.'

'Then you've heard all that I have to say on the matter.'

Father Jim was still smarting from this exchange— pacing the vestry with a queasy feeling of dread for how Bishop Neil would almost certainly use his phone call against him—when the phone rang again. He took his time answering it and was relieved to find it was Gail on the other end, and not someone further up the ecclesiastical food chain calling to finish him.

'I have some news,' she said.

'Please go on.'

'Things have changed. The couple wants two whole weeks to themselves before they make a decision about what to do. I'm afraid you can't meet the baby yet.'

Father Jim felt the ground shift beneath his feet. What little credibility he had to back this story up had now vanished.

'Ms Alverez,' he began, his tone infused with frustration. 'You understand this makes your whole story begin to seem a little doubtful.'

'Doubtful!' she snapped. 'Father Jim, there is nothing doubtful about what I have told you.'

'That's precisely the point. I'm relying on your word and nothing more.'

'This very morning I witnessed the child's grandmother stroll into the house—healed—after years of chronic multiple sclerosis. This was the child's doing! He has already performed a miracle, and he's less than a day old!'

'But it's all speculation unless I can see for myself.'

'And you will. I will hold to the family's request of silence, but the minute their two weeks is up you will accompany me to their home, and you will see for yourself, Father. Do not turn your back on the most important religious event in two thousand years.'

Father Jim was too uneasy to speak. He wanted to say that she'd set him back on the path again—that he would come and visit the child. And he wanted to assure her that she could trust him to keep the family's secret. But he couldn't. He knew all too well that, by now, the Bishop would be leveraging favour with the Archbishop by spilling his cynicism to him about Father Jim's story, and right now it would be a wildfire cutting a swathe through the upper echelons of the Catholic Church. There was nothing he could do to stop it.

6

How do you plan for a journey when you're travelling with a divine spirit? Could you even know which direction to take? Nicole felt powerless and confused. She'd claimed a golden fortnight to get to know her child, but where on earth would she start? The very act of claiming their ground meant that only she and Tim could decide where to begin.

The first step demanded they keep Nicole's parents at arm's length. As much as Clare had promised to abide by their wishes, she couldn't help but offer her opinion on just about everything, and it made her visits super intense. Their quest for simplicity was paramount, and Clare threatened to bring it undone.

On more than one occasion, Garry had steered her out of the house when things went off the rails—and returned only when supplies and home cooked lasagna were needed.

Some days, Nicole envied Tim's dislocation with his

family. He called himself an orphan—brought up by his Uncle Billy when his mother died too young and his father had submerged the pain in alcohol. When Tim had moved from Brisbane to Melbourne with his band, he'd cut ties with the entire clan forever, and they'd seemed to forget he was on the same planet with them. Nicole had never even met them.

Their friends presented the greatest threat to their solitude. Nicole's phone rang off the hook. Most of the time she let the calls go through to voice mail, or the answering machine in the hall would pick them up. She weakened at times though, desperate to hear familiar or loving voices. On the occasions she answered she'd fib and tell her friends she hadn't had the baby yet, but that fib almost came perilously undone when Billy gave a cry right in the middle of one call. All communications had to stop. The friends would have to be dealt with after the golden fortnight was up.

The most logical place to start the journey before them was to reach for a book. Tim announced he was going off to tackle the Bible, while Nicole took a more down to earth approach with titles such as, *Know your Baby*, and *What to Expect the First Year*. These books gave beautiful insight into how her baby would grow and how her relationship with him would develop—and she devoured this information because she was after all his mother, and at the end of the day what she cared about most was that he was loved, and cared for and happy—but these books assumed you hadn't given birth to the Messiah, which was the one complication that made understanding her child uniquely tricky.

Tim surfaced from his research looking like he'd been down the rabbit hole.

'There's some crazy shit in here,' he said.

Nicole couldn't help but laugh. The thought of her

husband studying the Bible struck her as a good reality TV show format.

'Listen,' he went on, sitting her down on the couch next to him. 'There's this story called the binding of Isaac where God tests this guy by telling him to kill his own son to prove his faith. I mean listen to this: "And Abraham stretched forth his hand, and took the knife to slay his son. And the angel of the Lord called unto him out of heaven and said, Abraham, Abraham"—he said it twice—"lay not thine hand upon him: for now I know that thou fearest God".' Tim sat back. 'I mean, really? That's just batshit.'

Nicole trod down a smile.

'That's the Old Testament. It's a parable.'

'Sure, but you have to admit, it's a pretty disturbing concept. I mean are we going to be asked by some heavenly voice to do something nuts? And look—there's all this cloak and dagger stuff too. Like the Pharaoh commanding that all Hebrew babies be killed because the Hebrews were beginning to take over the place. Sound familiar? And then Moses, who was actually one of those babies, was spared by the Pharaoh's wife and she brought him up as her own. But when he grows up he kills an Egyptian because that Egyptian smote a Hebrew brethren.'

'They're Bible stories.'

'Yes, but the point is it's not just Christianity. It's all religions. People do crazy shit because they believe they're serving God.'

'That was two thousand years ago.'

'But have things changed that much? All it tells me is that now we don't need to go from house to house slitting the throats of children, we can just drop a fucking bomb. And we do. Or strap one to our bodies. All in the name of God. I mean, how does that even make sense? Why does religion inspire this fucking thirst for blood? And who is going to be the first to slip a knife into our child because he doesn't represent the "correct" faith?'

Tim's distress landed on Nicole hard. She secretly swallowed against the unease it swelled inside her.

'Religion also teaches love,' she said.

Tim rolled his eyes.

'So they say. So why is there this tribal antagonism? Isn't God, God? We know he — she — exists now. So surely there's nothing to fight over.'

'Idiots and psychopaths. They're the cause.'

'Correct. And it feels like they're everywhere. How do we protect Billy from that? How do we protect him from what he is?'

Typically, Tim's outlook was darker than Nicole's, so she chose not to join him on his voyage into the shortcomings of religion. Instead she doubled down on being the best mother she could and nothing more. As far as she was concerned Billy was hers, and hers alone. He didn't belong to any church, or to the world at large as some kind of saviour; he was just her sweet little boy. He needed her for the basics of life, and she was happy to provide them. She learned to nurse him the way any mother would. She chatted to him and washed him, lay with him to get him to sleep. Without another child to compare him to, Billy seemed to behave like any ordinary baby.

Occasionally, his divinity shone brightly though, and Nicole was reminded in no uncertain terms what she was dealing with. Sitting by his cot one day she looked up to find a ring of butterflies circling in formation above his head. First they flew horizontally, then like aerial acrobats they broke and reformed, flying perpendicular to him. After around five minutes Billy waved a hand, and they broke from the formation and flapped out of the nursery window.

Another thing she was forced to acknowledge was that the overwhelming feeling of love she'd experienced on the night of his birth wasn't just your run-of-the-mill joy of bringing a child into the world. Billy projected love like light. It was a feeling of genuine wellbeing that directly corresponded with her proximity to him.

Nicole ran an experiment with Tim, testing the range of Billy's transmitter, inching towards him from the back of the house until they felt the first beams of it reach into them. There were chalk marks up and down the hall. If you ignored their cackling it was very close to a scientific experiment.

Eight days into their fortnight, and after a thousand unanswered phone calls, Nicole looked up to find Tim easing himself into the nursery, clutching a piece of paper.

'What's this?' Nicole said.

'A list,' he said gingerly.

Nicole's face darkened.

'We had to make one eventually,' he said. 'They're not going to stop calling.'

Nicole reached for it, but Tim tugged it away again.

'Hey,' she said, slightly annoyed.

'Let me explain first.'

'Explain what?'

'My criteria.'

Nicole didn't like where this was heading.

Tim sat next to her by the cot. He took a deep breath before continuing.

'Friends made together,' he said finally.

'As in—'

'As in friends we've made since we've been seeing each other.'

Nicole was now alarmed. This had to mean no "old" friends. No school friends. No friends she played with as a kid and talked with about the days when they would nurse their babies together.

'What about Carrie?' she said quietly.

Tim shrugged sadly. 'There's nothing wrong with old friends. I really like Carrie. But for a secret this big…' he paused to find exactly the right words, '… I feel like it needs to be shared with friends formed in partnership, you know? That we've made together.'

Nicole reached for the list again. This time Tim let her take it. Nicole looked at it and then looked straight back at him.

'There are seven names on this list,' she said sharply.

Tim nodded.

Nicole couldn't speak. What could she say? How do you reduce your world down to such a pathetic scrap of paper? She got off her chair and walked out of the nursery. Tim followed her into the lounge where she was studying the list. He approached silently and sat beside her.

'Nic, this was never going to be easy.'

'I know. But *seven*.'

'It's what we talked about, yeah? Who else but these guys?'

Nicole knew he was right. She rested her head onto his shoulder.

'When should we start calling them?' she said.

'Today,' Tim said decisively. 'We'll ask them over for a morning tea, and we'll spring him on them.' Tim grinned at her. Nicole could just picture the scene, and it made her grin too.

'Okay,' she said, her mood picking up. 'Let's do it.'

***

Stephanie already felt like the ringleader. Perhaps because she was the only single one of the coupled friends chosen to meet Nicole and Tim's new baby. Or perhaps it was because Nicole had emailed her the list prior, making her promise not to let it leak to any of their other non-invited friends.

Being a self-confessed social media tragic, Stephanie had created a closed Facebook group with only those selected for the visit, and on it they'd debated why they had been the chosen ones. Trent and Justin were nursing friends of Nicole's who adored her, but warned her that if Tim ever turned they may kill each other to have him. Jake and Sonia, a singing duo Tim played with from time to time, held Nicole and Tim up as mentors for how they wanted to be when they grew up. And Louise and Guy were both police officers who'd met the couple at one of Tim's solo shows, taking pity on Nicole who was sitting like a band-widow by the bar. None of their histories made a link for Stephanie as to why this otherwise disparate group should end up taking the honour of being the first to meet Billy.

Stephanie had posted a time and a place to meet before they arrived. Over the course of the Facebook correspondence, the ugly thought that something was tragically wrong with the child had taken hold, and as an act of solidarity they assembled a street away to synchronise their arrival, so whatever issues Nicole and Tim were facing they'd only have to give the painful explanation once. Stephanie saw it as her duty to soften the blow.

As they arrived at the front door, she took it upon herself to remind everyone that this wasn't about *them*. 'Whatever they're facing,' she said gravely, 'they're going to need our support.'

The group nodded grimly.

Stephanie knocked. Footsteps pounded down the hall towards them, and the door flew open to reveal a woman who looked impossibly like Clare.

'Hello!' the beaming woman cried.

None of the friends moved.

'It's me,' she said. 'Clare!'

Stephanie's mind made the comical adjustment that this was a joke being played by another family member: maybe Clare had a sister. But before she had time to wipe that thought, Clare was shooing them down the hall to the lounge where, rather than finding the atmosphere of Juliet's tomb, the family met them with open smiles and colourfully iced cupcakes. Nothing added up.

Nicole and Tim kissed them all and made sure everyone was seated before Tim launched into what seemed like a delicately prepared preamble.

'Hi, everyone. Thanks for coming,' he said.

His smile seemed genuine, if a little nervous.

'Faark. Sorry we've made you wait so long till we got you over.'

Everyone chuckled stiffly.

'We love you guys, but we weren't sure how to approach today. I mean it's big for us. God, big in so many ways. You know what I mean?'

Stephanie was nodding, but she didn't really know what he meant. Her queasy feeling of dread had returned. Was this upbeat reception simply a despairing family putting on a spectacularly brave face?

'You guys are the first people to meet him,' Tim said, 'and for the moment, the *only* people who are going to. We need you to promise that you will not tell *anyone*—not a single soul—what you see today. Can you do that?'

No one spoke. No one even breathed.

'What?' Stephanie finally said. 'You want us to promise … now?'

'Yes.'

'Oh. Well, sure. I promise.'

One by one the friends made their bewildered oaths.

Tim swept away to get Billy. A hush fell in his absence. Smiles were passed around the group, but none of them seemed to land with any confidence. And then Tim arrived with the baby.

Stephanie gasped when she saw him. And she wasn't alone. In the single moment of clapping eyes on him, seven belief systems were scattered to the winds. She could hear everyone's voices becoming shrill. Her heart pumped faster with the panic of being part of something incomprehensible.

She jumped to her feet and went to Nicole, who had stood to absorb the crush of friends coming at her.

After appealing to the group not to make it about *them*, Stephanie burst into tears and made a full-throated inauguration as a new believer.

Nicole was crying too. She held Stephanie to her, and they stood squeezing each other with joy and astonishment.

While so many things made no sense, others now became clear.

'Is this why your mother isn't sick anymore?' Stephanie said. 'Did Billy heal her?'

Nicole nodded happily, and Stephanie couldn't help but laugh out loud. There was an uncontrolled feeling of joy in the room. Was that it? Joy? Or was it pure love? Stephanie didn't understand that either, until Tim offered for her to hold the baby.

When she took Billy in her arms, she finally understood. The heady feeling became overwhelming— to the point where she thought she might pass out.

Looking at Nicole and Tim, she recognised how accustomed to him they had become, how this sensation seemed to be routine to them now.

When she passed the baby on, she saw acceptance creeping over the friends like fog as they gradually hailed the impossible, and Billy worked his magic on them too.

For an hour the celebration rolled on, until their designated time came to an end. Like a good ringleader, Stephanie took it upon herself to call time. The invitation was for an hour, and an hour it would be.

She led the friends back up the hall to the front door where the family hugged and kissed them before they scattered into the day. Stephanie had the feeling that their Facebook group would quickly become a place of refuge for them as they tried to come to terms with being witnesses to what felt like the dawn of a new human race.

***

Once the friends had gone, the family collapsed back into the couches, exhausted.

'Holy crap we did it,' Nicole said.

'I thought Stephanie was going to seriously lose her shit,' Tim replied, and they all laughed.

Nicole wanted this moment to last longer than it did. She felt satisfied because their friends had supported them. It was like the inner circle had grown, and now there was more of them ready to take on what was waiting for them out there in the world. But the moment couldn't last because it was time for Garry and Clare to head back to Perth. Even on Garry's reduced roster, patients were piling up.

This was the part Nicole always found the hardest. It wasn't so much the guilt of being separated from her mother while she was ill that was hard, it was knowing how much she'd miss them both when they were gone.

Nicole had suffered a benign sense of guilt about her mother's condition. In ordinary circumstances it would have been easy to feel shame for deserting her, but Nicole didn't. Without knowing it, in leaving Perth she was simply following a path that had been carefully laid down before her. She didn't realise she'd been played until long after the ruse had been executed.

Nicole remembered a childhood spent wafting through hospital wards — a pint-sized Florence Nightingale — ghosting her mother. From school she rushed into nurse's training, impatient to become the real thing, just like her mum. When Clare was diagnosed it coincided with Nicole's final year of training, and Nicole was so distraught she practically gave up her studies to devote herself to her mother's care. Unbeknownst to her, Garry and Clare were observing how much her socialising plummeted. She remembered them constantly encouraging her to get out of the house, which made her feel like she was being a nuisance and not helping in any practical way. So she just tried harder. When she graduated, she endured the humiliation of her father flipping through old contact books to solicit a placement for her across the country in Melbourne.

At the time, Nicole didn't understand her parents were merely trying to spare her the inevitable misery that lay ahead. Choice had been quietly extracted from the equation, and they were shaking her out of the nest and setting her free.

Meeting Tim was the major event that helped her finally put roots down in Melbourne. She and Tim joked that as a pair they were like a couple of refugees with only each other to turn to. And it was only then that she realised what this giant act of love had been all about.

All along her parents had known it was in her nature to care, and they saw it as their duty to save her from herself. It broke her heart to know how much they loved her and what they gave up for her happiness.

This time as her parents kissed her goodbye, Nicole still felt a familiar tug of pain, but it was tempered by the sight of her mother dancing down the driveway and slipping effortlessly into the back seat of Tim's car.

She waved them off and returned to the cleaning up. With Billy sleeping peacefully and Tim on the airport run, she floated around the kitchen, washing the bone china and wiping crumbs from the kitchen bench.

She felt stronger for sharing her secret, and incrementally less lonely.

As the last plate went onto the dish rack, she heard a knock at the door. Her first thought was that Tim must have forgotten something, and she trotted up the hall to answer it. But as she reached the door something made her pause. The previous two weeks had taught her caution, so she pressed her eye to the peephole.

To Nicole's astonishment, she saw Gail standing there. And beside her was a priest.

***

Father Jim had become uneasy. He noticed the approaching footsteps falter. There was a presence behind the door, but then suddenly it was gone again. Something wasn't right.

He turned to Gail and tried to read her expression. Was it defiance?

'They *are* expecting us,' he said.

It was a rhetorical question, because Father Jim hadn't imagined in his wildest dreams that they wouldn't be.

'No,' she said plainly. 'They wouldn't have seen you if I'd told them.'

At first Father Jim thought this was a joke, but Gail's stony face said otherwise. Suddenly his need to leave became overwhelming, and his feet were already on the path back down the driveway.

'Stop!' Gail commanded, snatching at his arm. 'We'll go around the back.'

Father Jim protested, but Gail frog marched him down the overgrown path by the side of the house.

When they reached the back door, through a window, Father Jim could see Nicole hiding behind the sofa.

'It's me,' Gail said, jettisoning all politeness and barging inside. 'Nicole, I'd like you to meet Father Jim.'

Nicole gaped as Gail edged the Father towards her.

Nicole looked past him to Gail. 'What happened to our agreement?' she said coldly.

Gail was unflinching. 'You said two weeks, and the two weeks are up.'

'You promised to keep this a secret!'

Father Jim was finding it all unbearable. He made a faint attempt to break in. 'Gail. I think I'll be going.'

Gail grabbed him by the arm again, but Father Jim tugged it away.

'I will not do anything to cause this woman distress,' he said.

Without a word, Gail marched out of the lounge room. Father Jim feared she was going to get the child herself. Nicole sprinted after her, calling out for her to stop.

Father Jim was frozen to the spot, impotent with shame and confusion. He could hear Nicole demanding that Gail 'Leave him alone', but then footsteps were pounding back down the hall towards him. That's when he saw Billy for the first time. In slow motion, he sank to his knees, and almost involuntarily he reached out to touch Billy's hand.

The moment their touch connected, Father Jim seemed to swell. His head swayed and he groaned deeply, and before he could stop it coming he had the overwhelming desire to dredge up a secret so deeply buried that it hadn't seen the light of day for over fifty years.

He was back in his childhood—in Ireland—sleeping in the dank closet of a room at the end of the hallway of his father's pub. He could sense the door opening, as it would night after night. The horrible stench of the monster that visited him filled his nostrils.

Father Jim could feel Billy peeling off this scab—the years of denial being torn from his body. For a moment he felt a cavity so raw that it ached with exposure to the air, and then in the next moment the pain was gone. The ancient grief that had so haunted him his entire life dissolved, and for the first time Father Jim was free of it.

The priest's body slackened. Tears ran down his face, and slowly he rose from his knees.

'Nicole,' he said, gasping for breath, 'I believe. I believe in what your child is. He has taken away my pain. I want to help you. Please let me help you.'

***

The moment Tim swung open the front door he could tell the energy in the house had shifted.

As he passed by the nursery, he noticed that Billy wasn't in his cot. Then he heard voices coming from the lounge room. One of them sounded male.

When he reached the lounge room, he saw Nicole sitting on the couch with Billy, flanked by Gail, and beside Gail was a priest.

Nicole looked up and leapt off the couch, reversing him back into the kitchen.

'What the fuck is going on?' he snapped. 'Did you know about this?'

'Of course not. Gail brought him.'

Tim looked past her. His eyes narrowed on Gail.

'Calm down and listen for a moment,' Nicole said, touching his face like he was a baby. 'I know we didn't invite him, but he's here now, and we may as well speak to him.'

Tim was silent.

'Tim?'

His eyes returned to hers, a gesture of capitulation. The two of them returned to the lounge room united, and sat on the couch together.

'Father Jim, this is Tim,' Nicole said, like she was introducing two heads of state.

The priest rose to shake Tim's hand. There was no doubting he had a way about him. His eyes seemed marinated in kindness.

'I'm guessing I'm not what you expected to come home to.' Father Jim grinned, and Tim nodded his firm agreement. 'I'm sorry for invading your home. Believe me, my deepest wish is to help you.'

'And how do you plan on doing that?'

'Let me start by giving you some context for all of this.'

'Please.'

'Since 1673, there have been thirty-eight reports of the Second Coming of Christ that have been seriously investigated by the Church. These are documented cases where appointed representatives were sent to either authenticate, or reject the claim.'

'Thirty-eight,' Tim repeated. 'How many turned out to be real?'

'None. None of them proved to be Christ, reborn,' the Father said.

Tim felt his spirits rise, and they well and truly soared when the priest went on to describe these children, who could allegedly move objects, summon spirits, and spontaneously conjure fire. Tim was now anticipating this priest was about to absolve them of their problem.

'What about Billy?' he said.

Father Jim held his eye.

'I believe he is Christ, reborn.'

Tim involuntarily shrank.

'Why does he have to be Christ?' Tim said, taking a tone. 'I mean, couldn't he just be one of these children with an ability?'

'Because he has a halo,' the priest said. 'No other child has ever had one. And his birth was heralded with a star. Then there was the miracle with Clare, and I had my own experience with him today. It's only my opinion, of course. I'm not qualified to make a definitive call on it. The appropriate representatives of the Church need to come and assess him.'

'And where are these "appropriate representatives" from?' Tim said.

'Rome.'

Tim swallowed hard.

'No way. No way in the world,' he said. 'There's no fucking way I'm letting a bunch of goons from the Vatican come and probe my child.'

'It's too late,' Father Jim said, quietly. 'They're already on their way.'

7

Father Jim knew his explanation had to be good. For the past fortnight, the feeling of people wanting to take a piece out of him had become routine, and observing the look on Tim's face assured him nothing had changed.

He'd anticipated the couple's response to his revelation about the imminent arrival of the Romans, so he'd rehearsed an account of the events that had led up to the day.

'Please hear me out,' he began. 'The reason we're at the point that we are is because of a fatal mistake I made two weeks ago.'

Nicole and Tim sat forward. The priest could see he'd bought himself some time.

'When Gail first told me about the child, I had an unfortunate rush of blood; I made an error of judgment and reported it to my Bishop.'

Nicole and Tim bristled.

'Believe me it was before I knew you wished to keep

Billy a secret,' he went on quickly. 'If I'd known, I would never have made the call.'

Father Jim went on to explain how he'd barely slept the night of the dreaded phone call. He'd tossed and turned imagining the kind of damage he'd done.

At six in the morning, drained and nauseous, he took a phone call from the Archbishop. 'I hope I haven't called at a bad time,' he said.

The call revived Father Jim like a feet-first drop into a plunge pool.

'No, no, not at all,' he replied.

'I had a call from the Bishop this morning,' the Archbishop went on. 'You two had an interesting conversation last night.'

'We spoke, yes.'

'I'd like to revisit that conversation, if I may.'

Father Jim waited for the mother-of-all-rebukes. He sat up in bed, his nightshirt clinging.

'Tell me more about this woman who claims to have delivered a baby with a halo. Why haven't you investigated it further?'

'Bishop Neil counselled me not to.'

'I see. But you said you felt it worth pursuing?'

'I know it sounds a little crazy—'

'Yes, yes, you don't need to concern yourself with that. I want to know why you think she seemed genuine.'

'Your Grace, I think we need to be open to the possibility. I mean … what if we were witness to the Second Coming and did nothing?'

The line went silent. Father Jim had the terrible feeling he'd gone way too far.

'We both know Bishop Neil is a curmudgeon,' the Archbishop said, and Father Jim sensed the door opening very slightly. 'The Church may have been quiet on the matter of this star, but I've been reflecting deeply on it. I've studied the videos. There's no doubt there is something unearthly about it.' The door opened another inch. 'I like to think of myself as rather forward-thinking in this kind of thing. It's where you and I are alike, Father. We share a desire to see the possibility in things.'

The priest's heart was thumping. Was the Archbishop actually taking *his* side?

'Have we not been waiting for this very thing for centuries?' the Archbishop said.

Father Jim quickly agreed with him. He wanted to pursue how it epitomised the obstinance of the Church that Bishop Neil had so easily dismissed it, but the Archbishop went on, peppering him with questions: was there a substantial fire in the vicinity of the child's birth? Was the family Catholic? Was there any mention of a virgin birth? And, most importantly, had the couple told anyone else about the baby?

Father Jim had no answers, but he could reliably state that the family had chosen to keep the baby's birth a secret. This made the Archbishop delirious with excitement. He showered praise on the priest's shrewd choice in bringing it to his attention, and then he directly asked him for the family's home address.

Father Jim smelt a rat. "We'll take it from here" was ringing like a bell in his ears. It was now crystal clear where this phone call had been heading from the start. False alarm or not, the Archbishop was determined to get his hands on the baby before anyone else did. In all likelihood, Bishop Neil was currently languishing in Siberia for being so stupidly shortsighted the previous night.

Father Jim assured him he had no knowledge of where the baby was, but His Grace was way ahead of him.

'You will easily find out,' he fired back.

'It's a little more complicated than that. I gave my word to Gail that I'd honour the family's wishes that they be left alone for two weeks while they come to terms with what they're dealing with. As you can appreciate, I have no desire to go back on my word.'

The line fell silent.

'I understand your position, Father,' the Archbishop went on stiffly, 'but you understand what's at stake here. How would you feel if the family had a change of heart and contacted another denomination? If this child is what the woman says he is then we *must* be in control of the situation. You do understand that, Father?'

'I do, but what am I worth as a priest if I cannot keep my word?'

'If you choose not to cooperate, I will be asking that very question,' the Archbishop said severely. 'Let me be clear. You have to decide whether you consider this is an issue large enough to be the final straw for you.'

Father Jim felt an icy blast. He knew the Archbishop had possession of a dossier heavy enough with his misdemeanors to end his career at will.

The priest repeated the Archbishop's question in his head. Was this the issue that would finally end him?

Yes, was his answer. 'I gave the woman my word, and I will honour it.'

The line went silent again. Father Jim sensed he'd won the first round.

'All right,' the Archbishop went on, 'here's what I suggest. I will call you again at noon tomorrow. That will give you some time to reflect on this matter more deeply. Please don't make a choice you will regret.'

With that the line went dead.

Father Jim fell to his knees. Prayer felt comforting, a chance to surrender his decision to God. If he was guilty of pride by keeping his word, God would show him his error. But surely, staying the course made him the stalwart person God had chosen him to be.

Hours of prayer only toughened his determination. Whatever the cost, he would not betray Gail.

Rather than call at midday, the Archbishop arrived in person — clearly a ploy to intimidate him. Father Jim listened to his threats, then calmly laid out his own plan.

'I will visit the family as promised. And if I find the child to be genuine, I will counsel his parents to speak to the Church about what to do next.'

The Archbishop was unused to hearing the word no, and the priest could see the fury turning inside him.

'I have already called for representatives from Rome to come,' he spat. 'They will arrive expecting to examine the child.'

'And they will in the fullness of time.'

'Do you see the embarrassment this will cause me if they arrive and I have nothing to show them?'

'I understand, and I apologise. I will give them the child's location the moment I have agreement from the family.'

The Archbishop stormed out of the vestry. Father Jim was tossed in his wake. He couldn't believe he'd just stonewalled the Catholic Church—his home, his family. He should have felt only dread, but his spirits soared because he'd kept his word to the family.

'I get that this has caused you trouble,' Tim said, 'but all kinds of shit is going to rain down on *us*. What the fuck do we do now?'

Father Jim took a long breath.

'Start by putting your trust in me.'

'Forgive my cynicism, Father, but as I see it the Catholic Church would gladly mow us down to get their hands on our child,' Tim said.

'Any faith would,' the priest replied evenly, 'which is why I want to be here for you. I have my own battles with the Catholic Church. We are not perfect. But I promise to be on your side.' Father Jim sat forward on the couch. 'Whether you realise it or not, Billy's arrival has bound you to the tradition, the history and the mysticism of the Church. You are now a part of it—part of its narrative. Your journey is entwined with ours. If you let me, I will be your champion and help you come to terms with the incredible gift God has bestowed upon you.'

Tim and Nicole sat silently for a moment, glancing at each other.

'When would they come?' Nicole said.

'That is entirely up to you,' Father Jim replied.

'Where?' Tim chimed in.

'Here, if it suits you. It's your choice.'

Again, Tim and Nicole swapped glances.

'Monday?' Nicole said.

Tim agreed. 'It'll give us time to recover from today.'

'We introduced Billy to our friends today,' Nicole added, giving a tired smile. 'It's been a big one.'

'I'm sure it has.' Father Jim smiled. 'So I think it's time we got out of your hair.'

8

Simon could have killed for a cigarette. His nerve endings snapped like carnivorous plants at the thought of that heavenly nicotine. Only recently, he'd abandoned his fitful attempts at sleep and escaped to the cooling, friendless air, where he was content to wait—silent as an assassin—for Adele to come home.

To calm his rage, he tried laying out all his triumphs like cards in a game of solitaire, but it did little to dull the feelings stirred up by Adele's most recent betrayal.

She'd been gone all afternoon and now into the night. Unacceptable. The community knew it, and he knew it. Add to this her absence at morning runs, breaking curfew, skipping prayers; people were talking. Anything but a severe punishment tonight would make him look spineless.

The past two weeks had left him feeling humiliated. After his proclamation that God had sent them a sign, God had been silent. The brothers and sisters were hungry for the next phase. Every day he rose anticipating the boom of God's voice to guide him towards his destiny, but it hadn't come. Day after day, he'd sent Charlie to Garnerville to fetch the newspaper, but he returned with nothing Simon could use to pump up the community's sagging belief.

Adele had been sleeping in his hut for weeks now, but it was as if God was teasing him with her, knowing that revealing His true purpose would be the one thing that would finally convince her to give herself to him. He beseeched God for another sign, one that would show him the way, that would bring Adele to him and set her on the path beside him forever. But God was silent.

Leaves crunched on the path leading up from the pond. Simon stood and observed Adele's pace dwindle as she caught sight of him. He left her to stew for a moment before asking where the fuck she'd been. Avoiding his eye, she picked a leaf from a nearby shrub and twisted it in her fingers.

'Walking,' she mumbled.

'Where, exactly.'

'I think that might not be any of your business.'

'In this community there are rules,' he said evenly.

'Welcome to Guantanamo,' she said.

Simon's fist went through the flimsy bark of his hut, surely waking one of his beauties sleeping inside. It caused Adele to look up from her leaf.

'We are a family,' he spat. 'It hurts us all when you misbehave.'

'You treat me like a fucking child,' she said tightly. 'What if I want to go out walking at night? What if I need to, just so I can breathe?'

'It's not allowed.'

'Well, it's fucked!'

'Don't speak to me like that.'

'Or what, you'll take *me* fishing too?'

In another time Simon would have flown at her and taken her by the throat.

'You'd better explain what you mean by that,' he said darkly.

But Adele withdrew again. Simon could see she was pushing back on some vast emotion. She turned to escape, but Simon grabbed her by the wrist, and that was all it took to release the floodgates.

'I miss him so much I can hardly breathe,' she wept, and Simon felt his feet land on some solid ground for the first time in days.

'Anthony?' he said softly, choking on his own envy.

She nodded sadly. 'I feel so … so empty that I don't know what to do.'

Simon realised he still had her by the wrist, and it was hurting her. He recoiled and let her rub it while he searched for the right way to scoop her up.

'We all miss him,' he said. 'The whole community does.'

But this didn't help. Adele's shoulders continued to heave. Simon took his shot and drew her into him, and she rested her head on his chest.

'My life is one giant fuck up,' she sobbed.

'Shhhh…'

'I've only ever had two good things in my life, and Anthony was one of them.'

Simon felt his spirit soar. Two good things in her life. Surely the other must be him. He ached to hear her say it.

'And the other?' he crooned.

Adele looked up at him and wiped her eyes.

'I can't tell you,' she whispered.

Simon flinched. 'Of course you can, my heart.'

But Adele remained silent. He wondered if she needed a more intimate backdrop to unlock her secret, so he gently steered her back down the path and sat her on a sleeper by Anthony's pond.

'It's time you got it off your chest,' he said. 'I want you to tell me what the other good thing in your life is.'

Simon was grinning too widely. He intended it to be encouraging, but he could sense it was sending Adele back into the bush.

'You don't know this about me,' she said, 'but before I came here I belonged to another group.' Simon's smile wilted. 'They were my family before this one. It was where I was the happiest in my life before I met Anthony.'

'Okay?' he said, reaching for a supportive tone.

'We were called Light Up,' she said and smiled at the thought. 'It started when I was at art school. Fuck, I was completely lost.'

Her words bounced off him like he was the Man of Steel, and he found himself grasping at only half heard threads of her story: the dead-shit boyfriend, drugs, an overdose. None of it included him. It took him until the part about her moving in with a fellow art student, Jackie, before he was fully back on track.

That's when religion had come into her life. Jackie had dragged her to church, kicking and screaming, and like so many recovering addicts before her she felt it. In amongst all the chanting, the speaking in tongues, the hand waving, suddenly, there was Jesus Christ. It was the best drug she'd ever tried.

Adele could have been describing an old lover as far as Simon was concerned. Jealousy reached its fingers deep inside him as she described how someone else had impregnated her with the ecstasy of God. He longed to be her first, to be her only. No wonder she was so fucking unreachable.

'I wanted to celebrate my saviour, Jesus Christ, in my art,' he heard her saying. 'He belonged to me now, and I wanted to share him with everybody else.'

She described waking in the middle of the night with an inspirational idea. She hammered on Jackie's bedroom door until she let her in, and she blabbed at her till dawn, and the two of them plotted how to turn her idea into reality.

The idea was to create a flash mob—a subversive, human installation that would be fleeting and unforgettable. Hundreds would turn up at some public place and create a human sculpture as a devotion to Christ. Then they would disappear again like it had never happened. But the big thing—the kicker—the thing that would really seize the world's imagination, was that everyone involved would be naked.

Simon felt himself gaping at her. It was genius—sexual and subversive—and it stung that he hadn't thought of it himself.

'Amazing,' he stammered.

'I know, right? It was off the scale. Our first installation got about thirty people, but it connected so hugely that by the time we ran our second one over one hundred people showed up. It was just ridiculous.'

If he closed his eyes he could picture it. All that gathered flesh, defiant in the indifferent crowd. What a spectacle to run into in your lunch hour. How many people had returned to work with that incredible vision of God seared into their mind?

'It was so intense,' she went on. 'People abused us, or applauded. Some people even joined in.' She exploded with laughter. 'You never knew what was going to happen, and it just kept getting bigger and bigger.' She rested her head on Simon's shoulder. 'I started a

Facebook page which made Light Up go international. Installations popped up everywhere: Hungary, Britain, New York. We were everywhere on YouTube, and the more *we* posted, the more random people *out there* posted. It was huge.'

Adele's face suddenly darkened, as though being separated from her great love had exhausted her. She was silent for a moment. It allowed Simon time to catch his breath.

'Why did you leave and come here?'

Adele lifted her head from his shoulder.

'Jackie was murdered,' she said. Simon felt himself gasp. 'On the way home from an event. She was stabbed in broad daylight.'

Simon finally understood the pain Adele had been holding on to. It stripped him of his self-absorption. This tragedy had sent the poor girl tumbling through space until she landed at the gates of the compound, only to be treated to another tragedy. He wanted to mend her, to be the one who put her life back together.

'That's where I go,' she said quietly. 'When I go missing. I go to find out what they're up to.'

Simon spluttered. 'You leave the compound?'

She nodded.

'I dug a hole under the fence, and from there I walk to the highway and hitch to the hotel in Garnerville, and I go online.' She gripped his arm. 'Oh, Simon, you should see it. The Facebook page has exploded. There are installations going off all over the world.'

Simon was still recovering from the revelation that Adele had dared to leave the compound. She could be banished for that, yet she was actually confessing it to his face. Simon couldn't have adored her more if he tried. Her passion washed through him. He feasted on her intensity. He longed to inspire the world the way she was inspirational. He wanted all of that, and he wanted Adele.

'Show me,' he barked. 'Right now. Take me to Garnerville and show me your Facebook page.'

'Now?'

'Yes!' he cried. 'Let's hitch there right now.'

'You'd break your own fucking curfew?'

Simon grabbed her hand and dragged her towards the track.

They raced to the top of an incline, and Adele steered Simon off the path towards the perimeter fence. There she tossed aside a pile of bark to reveal a ditch.

'I don't fucking believe this,' he said. 'We run past here every morning.'

Like a commando, Adele rolled under the fence and emerged, grinning, on the other side. Simon tried duplicating her fleetness but emerged covered in dirt. Once he was back on his feet, Adele yanked him by the hand, and they made a crazed dash through the bush.

As they ran, foliage caught Simon's foot, and he tumbled into the scrub taking Adele down with him. Before he could struggle to his feet again, Adele was on top of him, laughing and clawing at his shorts. She dragged them down to his ankles and took his penis in her mouth, and Simon lay back, brimming with intoxicated joy.

All his anger was drained. There was only Adele in the world. Now she was on top of him, guiding him inside her, her blonde curls tumbling down her shoulders, and her lips on his, kissing him thirstily. She'd finally come home to him, and as they fucked in the hooded moonlight, for now, Simon wanted for nothing in the overflowing world.

9

By the time Clare and Garry's cab pulled up outside their manicured garden, the afternoon had turned golden. Clare jumped out and began tugging the carry-on bags from the back seat, while Garry helped the driver with the suitcases.

Clare turned to wheel her suitcase inside, but across the road the neighbour from two houses down was gawking at her from where he was holding a hose on his garden. Clare felt his eyes on her. She gave him a quick wave and hurried to the front door. Garry lumbered up the rear too slowly, and she snapped at him as he fumbled with the keys.

'Quick, Garry. Hurry.'

'Give me a moment.'

Once inside, Clare raced to the window in the lounge room and peeped out through the curtains. The neighbour hadn't moved; his gaze was still set on their house. Clare realised her astonishing news was now bound to become gossip. Somehow, she'd have to weave an explanation that would put distance between her recovery and her miracle grandchild.

Garry arrived to find her gazing out of the window.

'Clare. What's up?'

She struggled to find words. Two profound emotions were at war: the joy of being well, hammering against the despair of its denial.

'I don't know what I am,' she said at last.

***

That night, Garry sat with her until she was asleep. Finally, he had a quiet house and he could organise himself for the working week ahead. At 10.00 pm his head hit the pillow, and he slept like the dead until 4.00 am when he awoke to find Clare missing from the bed.

He sat up, listening. The house was far too quiet for someone to be moving around out there. The sun was still a long way from coming up, and the bedroom was bathed in the soda yellow of the streetlight.

He crept into the lounge room and found Clare sitting on the floor by the window. She didn't turn as he approached. He squatted beside her and placed a gentle hand on her shoulder. She was frozen, so he wrapped the blanket from the couch around her shoulders.

'Why did you want to marry me?' she said softly.

Garry sighed and sat onto the floor beside her.

'How long have you been up?' he asked.

'You must have regretted it more than once.'

'Clare. Come to bed.'

Clare ran her hands through her hair and twirled it into a knot behind her head. She pulled a hair tie from the breast pocket of her pyjamas and slipped it over the knot. Her hair fell into a ponytail that made her look like a teenager in the dim light, spilling in from the street.

'My illness was given to the wrong person,' she said sadly. 'I had no idea how to be sick. I tried to be strong and happy, but I was just *so* depressed. So unbelievably sad. I wanted to get out of your way so you could have your life back.'

Clare began to sob.

'Why did you want to marry me?' she repeated.

Garry took a long time to answer. This wasn't the first time he'd had to account for himself. In the terrible small hours when Nicole was a baby and wouldn't feed, or when Clare had had some accident with a bedpan early on in her illness, she would lose her footing on her brittle self-esteem and grasp desperately for anything solid as she fell.

'Before I met you, I couldn't ever imagine falling in love,' he said.

'Where did we meet?'

'This again?' Garry said, twisting a smile. Clare nodded. 'Okay, it was in surgery. You were an intern nurse.'

Clare smiled. 'It was my first day.'

'It was your first day.'

'I thought you were so forward,' she said, mocking outrage.

'Ah, but I'd never done anything like that before I met you, see? I wanted to get you before someone else did.'

'There was never going to be anyone else.' Clare turned to him. 'You were so calm and serious. It was my mission to make you laugh.'

'And you did. And you do every day.'

Clare sank into his embrace. They sat in silence for a moment, then she straightened up.

'I'm well again.'

'Yes.'

'So why do I still feel sad?'

'That will pass.'

'No. It's not the kind of sadness that *can* pass.'

'Clare, we can't explain this rationally. It was a miracle. You need some time to adjust.'

'No. That's not it. I'm sad because—' Clare faltered. 'I'm sad because … I'm not worthy.'

'Don't be ridiculous.'

'No, no, I'm not being … just hear me out. I can't help but think, why me? Why, out of the whole world of suffering, should it have to be me?'

'That's beside the point. Billy chose you and that's your blessing alone.'

'I can't live with that.'

'You'll learn to.'

'So many other people need him, Garry.'

She lay onto the carpet and drew her legs up to her chest.

'I don't know what I am,' she said again, softly. 'I'm either living proof of God's power, or I'm a secret that's too dangerous to share.'

10

Headlights appeared over the rise. Simon scrambled down the roadside embankment and disappeared out of sight. His pathetic desperation left Adele weak with laughter, so as the headlights hit her they revealed a woman barely managing to stay upright. The slowing engine roared again, and the car vanished into the night.

'This is your fault!' she wept. 'Stop looking so fucking scary.'

Simon emerged from his hiding place and circled her like some twisted ghoul.

'You're a freak.' She squealed and ran off.

Simon chased her and lifted her off the ground. Then they collapsed together, laughing helplessly.

Simon wrapped her in his arms and kissed her deeply. He was still trembling from their mad dash through the bush where they'd tumbled in the bracken and shrieked at the moon and made love. Her smell was still on him, and if he closed his eyes he could see her face flushed with desire as she rode him.

Adele shoved him off and got to her feet.

'Come on,' she said, businesslike. 'We've got to get to Garnerville.' She held out a hand to help him up. As Simon took it, she let go and he tumbled back onto the road.

This creased her over with laughter once more, and Simon told her how fucking hilarious she was. He would have sought revenge if not for the distant sound of tyres and the glow of headlights over the verge. He ducked into his hiding place again, and Adele stood ready to flag down the car.

The lights of a beaten up Toyota ute struck her, and miraculously the car slowed.

'Let me do the talking,' she said.

As the car pulled to a stop, she gave the driver a silken smile and slipped into the front seat before he could take off again.

'Thank you *so* much,' she said, 'we've been out here for ages.'

As the driver was processing the word "we", Simon materialised from the darkness. The driver turned to find him clambering into the back seat. The driver looked at him like a wet dog had just jumped in his car.

'Headed for Garnerville?' Simon said.

The driver gave Simon a reluctant nod, then pulled out onto the highway.

***

It was 10.30 pm when they hit Garnerville. The town was little more than a post office and a few shops. Being the gateway to the surf coast, it survived on a steady stream of backpackers and local farmers.

The Garnerville Hotel had been transformed from a

grand old country pub into a backpacker haven filled with threadbare couches and cheap beer. Rooms were stacked with tottering bunk beds and mattresses for the floor. At this time of night, the bar throbbed with hits of the 90s and was filled with sun-ripened youths planning their next day's safari.

Adele led Simon past the reception where a purple-faced man lit up when he saw her. She blew him a kiss as they passed. Simon gave thanks this woman lived with him in the compound, because dealing with her ability to effortlessly mesmerise men out in the real world would eat him like cancer. Deeper along the hallway was a converted lounge filled with computers. Each screen hosted a tousled haired kid staring intently into their Facebook page.

'You have to be patient,' she said. 'The connection speed here is crap.'

She parked herself in front of a vacant screen, and Simon dragged up a chair.

Adele shook the mouse and the screen came to life, prompting her for a password. A screen popped up and she clicked her way through to the Light Up page. A strand of messages and pictures unfolded down the screen.

'Look. These messages come from all over the world. See this one? This is from Georg. He heads up the Oslo group.'

Simon leaned into the screen. Georg's post crowed about a flash mob they'd performed the previous week. The tag read: "A depiction of the star of God", and there were accompanying photos of thousands of naked people making an image of the star. Next to them was a photograph of the actual star that had inspired the event.

'My God,' Simon said, 'there it is.'

Adele smiled. 'And look.' She clicked on a link to a video. Footage of the star—shot from a shaky handycam—began to play. The camera zoomed in and out as the photographer narrated. 'What the fuck? Are you seeing this, Adrian?' Other voices were calling out and laughing in amazement.

Adele scrolled again. There were other posts of the star from earlier in the week, uploaded from all over the world.

'Where was this taken?' Simon said.

'It doesn't say.'

'But was it *here*, in Australia?'

'I don't know. I guess.'

Adele pointed to the bottom of the video. 'Look at how many hits it's got.'

Simon didn't understand.

'See that number?' she went on. 'That's how many times it's been viewed.'

Simon gaped. 'Twenty-five million? How is that even possible?'

Adele turned to him, amused. 'You really don't know shit about this, do you?'

Simon was too absorbed to respond. Adele scrolled back to the top of the page.

'Look at this. Our membership has exploded. We've got 189,043 follows.'

The significance eluded Simon.

'Last time I logged on we had around 90,000,' she said. 'That was a week ago.' She pointed at the screen. 'Look here. Since we've been on the page, four posts have already come through.'

Simon swung his attention back to the top of the page, and at that very moment a new message appeared. It read: "OMG Jesus is reborn! You HAVE to see this. Bless the Lord!"

This drew them deeper into the screen. Adele moved the mouse across a link to a video and clicked on it. There was no sound on the clip, no voice narrating it, but what they saw stunned them into silence.

In a perfectly average looking cot—filled with blankets and soft toys—lay a perfectly normal, happy child—normal that is, except for the brilliant halo which floated in the air just above his head, illuminating the room.

Simon gasped.

'That has got to be a fake,' Adele said. She played the clip again. It was twenty-three seconds long. There were no tags to explain the video, and the title simply read: "This is real".

Adele said something about the video being posted only five hours earlier, but Simon wasn't really listening. He was too busy weaving the star and the child into his own narrative. Here was the path God had promised him. Finally, He had revealed it.

Simon felt the blood expanding inside his head. It thumped in his ears. The answer he'd been seeking had been hiding inside Adele all along. He'd made him wait before He chose the time to reveal it. Then Adele had led him along the path, and Simon had followed. And at the end of the path, God had revealed Himself.

Adele was the herald.

'Simon,' he heard her say, 'do you think this is the Second Coming?'

He turned to her, rigid with purpose.

'Yes. It is. And we need to talk to the person who shot this video.'

Adele snorted, which momentarily incensed him.

'It's a YouTube clip, dummy. It's anonymous.'

Simon wasn't following.

'Look,' she said, pointing at the screen. 'It's been

posted by "Hopeformorning", whoever that is. It could be anyone, anywhere in the world.'

But Simon didn't believe her. Nothing was anonymous. God would see to that. He was only sitting in Garnerville watching this video because God had planned it that way. It was His will that he should see it. This was the final fragment in the prophecy God had made when he was in prison—the prophecy that he would one day be a leader of men.

His mission now was to find "Hopeformorning", and he knew how he could do it too. And when he did, he would have that child.

11

Nicole collapsed onto the bed and wriggled into Tim's arms. It felt good to be alone with him after a day of unimaginable density: the friend's visit, the priest, the revelation of the Romans. With Billy asleep in the nursery, the house was theirs again—still and dreamy—and the bed felt like safe asylum.

She felt content in her exhaustion—the satisfaction of a job well done. With the present attended to, Nicole permitted her thoughts to turn to the future. She tested what it might be like to "come out" with her baby and reveal him to the rest of the world, but no feeling came to her. Normally she had an instinct about what was around the corner—a dim torch beam that gave a glimpse into the terrain ahead—but that had deserted her for now.

'Are we just stumbling from one place to the next?' she said.

Tim pulled away.

'What are you talking about, we're *totally* in control of our lives,' he said.

Nicole smiled. 'I have no idea what's going to happen to us.'

'Honey. One step at a time.'

The phone in the hall rang; it broke their moment of peace. Tim sat up to answer it, but Nicole grabbed his arm to stop him. He fell back onto the bed as the answering machine picked up.

'Hi … it's me…' a voice said, echoing down the hall.

It was Stephanie; she was crying.

'You've probably already seen it, but I wanted to tell you myself that it wasn't me. I'm so sorry, but it wasn't me.'

Tim leapt off the bed and skidded to the phone, but Stephanie had already hung up.

'What was that?' he said, and Nicole shrugged.

Tim grabbed his mobile and dialled Stephanie. She croaked a hello.

'Steph? It's me. What's going on?'

'Have you seen it?' she whispered.

'What?'

'There's a video of Billy on the internet.'

Nicole was angled into the conversation. Tim turned to her, his face serious.

'About fifty people have already posted it on Facebook. I can't believe it, Tim. I promise it wasn't me.'

Tim made for the computer in the study, Nicole following close behind.

'What's it called?' he said, wiggling the mouse. 'I'll have to have a look.'

Nicole felt a prickle of panic. Who would have so wantonly betrayed them?

'Tim? It's called, "This is real",' Stephanie said.

Tim typed in the title. In seconds, the clip appeared.

'I'll call you back,' he said.

Tim selected the video. Nicole leaned in to watch it—a shaky, twenty-three second clip of their child lying peacefully in his cot, looking up at the camera. There was no hint of who could have taken it, but the list of suspects wasn't very long.

'This can't be one of our friends, surely,' Nicole stammered.

'Nic,' Tim said, taking a calming tone, 'let's not lose our shit over this. Look at it. There's no way anyone can see that it's Billy, or that it's our place. It's completely anonymous. There's no way anyone can trace it.'

That's not the point, Tim,' she said, fury rising. 'Someone we trusted with everything has betrayed us.'

The hurt broke over her in waves. She leaned onto the desk to steady herself. Tears flowed.

'Nic, it's gonna be okay.'

'It won't, Tim. What are we going to do if we can't trust anyone?'

Tim put an arm around her shoulder. But it wasn't comfort she wanted now. It was answers. She pulled away from him.

'The person who posted that video was in our fucking house today. Doesn't that creep you out?' she said.

Tim was silent.

'It's so easy to do it. Any one of them could have posted that video. And now they've destroyed everything!'

'You're right,' Tim said. 'It's fucking unbelievable. Do you know what? I reckon it had to be Gail.'

'It couldn't be.'

'Why not?'

'Why would she do that?'

'Because she's a fanatic. I dunno. I'm going to call her.'

'No. Let me. I know how you'll handle it.'

Nicole grabbed her phone, and in moments she had Gail on the line.

'Gail, it's Nicole. I really need you to be honest with me,' she said. 'Did you film Billy today and put it online?'

There was a pause. Nicole thought the line might have dropped.

'Gail?'

'I don't know what you mean,' she said evenly.

'There's a video of Billy on YouTube. Did you put it there?'

'Nicole,' Gail said. 'I wouldn't know the first thing about how to do something like that.'

Thinking it through, Nicole could see that. Gail was feudal.

'What about Father Jim?' she said.

'When did he have the opportunity to take a video of Billy?' Gail said. 'He was sitting with you the entire time.'

Nicole closed off the call.

'I believe her,' she said. 'I don't think it was them.'

'I'm calling the others,' Tim shot back.

He picked up his phone. As Tim dialled, Nicole began tracking their movements across the morning, scanning for any hint of who could have done it.

'It could have been any of them,' she said bitterly. 'How can we see any of them again if they all deny it?'

Nicole stood next to Tim as, one by one, he went down the list without getting a single confession.

When the distressing job was done, Nicole returned to the bed. Tim followed and gathered her up.

'Nic, we knew this was going to be tough.'

'Yes, out *there!*' she exploded. 'I didn't expect our own friends to betray us.'

Nicole now had a sense of why she had no instinct for what was to come. The road ahead was so utterly unpredictable—so lacking in precedent—that plotting a course was impossible.

She wrestled with it all that night and all day Sunday, seeking counsel from her parents and comfort from her husband. For now, these were the only people she could truly rely on. As the day rolled on, the thought of letting go of her friends went from unbearable to a cold necessity. The bitter process of cutting them out of her heart had begun.

12

It was 3.00 am by the time Simon and Adele made it back to the compound. The road had been empty, and this tested the charm of their big adventure. If not for a broken-hearted surfer heading back to the city to lick his wounds, they might have made camp by the side of the road and not arrived back until daylight.

When they finally reached the hut, Simon grabbed Adele and dragged her into his arms. He needed to hold her one last time before they climbed back aboard the routine of the compound. His exhaustion made the euphoria of their furtive sex seem all too distant, and he ached to cling onto it for one more moment.

'You feel like my girl now,' he whispered.

Adele pulled away, studying him.

'I'm a bit funny about being someone's "girl".'

Simon was confused. His mouth was still wet from her kisses, and her smell was all over him.

'Not *anyone's* girl ... *my* girl.'

Adele had cooled towards him, and he couldn't understand why. What ingredient had God added to women to make them so unknowable. He longed for her to remain that mad girl who had pushed him to the ground just beyond the perimeter fence and fucked him beneath the stars. How could he capture that and keep it? There was only one way he could think of.

'You doubt me,' he said, 'but you shouldn't. I'll show you the depth of my feelings. I'll deliver to you the most profound act of love you have ever known, my girl. Then you'll understand what you are to me.'

Adele formed a tired smile, patted him dismissively on the chest and slipped inside the hut, making his attempt at gallantry feel like little more than a juvenile flourish. How could she crush him so effortlessly? He remained in the predawn air a moment longer, searching the heavens for the answer to her infinite mystery.

***

Morning brought rain. Simon led the jog through the steaming bush like it was a commando drill. As the rain pelted them, he urged them forward along the track, chanting slogans and loudly praising the Lord. He challenged them to drink in the Lord through the very pores of their skin, to let the drenching rain wash away their sins, 'For God is coming,' he cried.

When they returned to camp, Simon gathered them for a group embrace. As they stood, heads bowed in prayer, he could feel a special excitement crackling through them.

When everyone began to disperse for breakfast, Simon sought out Esben.

Esben had the look of a tethered dog aching to be petted.

Simon took him by the elbow and told him he needed his help.

'Simon, you know I would do anything you want me to.'

'Good,' Simon said evenly, and walked him further away from the straggler's earshot. 'Do you know what YouTube is?'

Esben laughed nervously.

'Err … YouTube? Yes. I know what YouTube is, Simon. It's a video sharing platform that—'

'Good. Esben, if I needed to find out the address of someone who posted a clip on that site, would you be able to do that for me?'

Esben's eyes glazed for a moment. Simon imagined the thoughts ricocheting inside his head. Synapses connecting with synapses chasing free-floating algorithms down distant pathways of his computer hacking youth. The boy was masterful. Simon pictured him as an artist in front of a blank canvas sizing up the masterpiece he was about to paint.

'You see, finding the email address of the person who posted the video is the simple part. That's a no brainer. Any newb could give you that. It's getting their address from the server that's the tricky part. It depends on their server, too. Offshore, onshore, big ISP, little ISP, private user, business user, all of it traceable and trackable and nothing that I couldn't handle, and if I couldn't handle it, I could certainly find someone who could.'

He stood there blinking at Simon, his smile filled with just a touch of terror.

'Good. We're going to Garnerville right now. Get some dry clothes on, and I'll meet you at the car.'

Simon strode back to his hut to change. He could feel everyone's eyes on him, and he could tell they were bristling with anticipation for what was to come.

Once he was dry, Simon found Charlie and took him aside.

'There's a good chance we'll be off on a raid today,' he said. 'I want you ready.'

Charlie hesitated.

'Yeah, it's two weeks before the next one's scheduled,' he went on, 'but this is big. Get Duck, Rob and Aamir. Two cars. And load the weapons. We'll leave the minute Esben and I are back from Garnerville, understand?'

Charlie grunted in the affirmative and started off.

'And Charlie?' Simon added. 'Don't tell anyone.'

Simon piled Esben into the SUV. As he drove out of the compound he could feel Esben gazing at him—desperate to begin some kind of interaction.

'What?' Simon said.

'I love you, Simon,' Esben blurted. 'I mean … it's been months since I've seen the other side of that fence, but I don't care. I just want to be with you.'

'You are a true disciple, Esben. You will be rewarded for this.'

This was enough to keep Esben quiet for the entire rest of the ride to Garnerville. When they pulled up outside the hotel, Simon saw Esben give a junkie's shiver of anticipation at what he was about to do.

Simon drew a couple of chairs up to a computer screen and went to hand him Adele's password, but Esben was already into the system. He opened YouTube and turned to Simon for the name of the clip they were after.

'This is real,' Simon said.

Esben's fingers flew across the keyboard. The clip began to load, and finally there was the shaky footage of the baby with the halo. Now Esben understood why Simon was so charged. He turned to him in wonder, and

Simon nodded back at him, confirming the size of the prize.

Esben knew where to go next. He typed a long thread of characters into the address bar and hit enter. The screen filled with hieroglyphics. Somehow, Esben sifted through this mess and followed a link into another page. Now they were flying through a Milky Way of seemingly unconnected symbols, which spun them deeper into the void. At times, he stopped and concentrated on a specific strand of code, interpreting it, unpacking it, and then using it to fly off through cyberspace once more.

Finally, he landed on a page that made him sit back and grin.

'There's your email address,' he said, beaming.

Simon noted his voice had a different tone to it. Authoritative. Confident. A touch of mischief. Was this how he addressed his peers rather than his spiritual hero?

'Can you get a street address?'

Esben sat back and cracked his knuckles. 'Does a bear shit in the woods?' Esben caught himself. 'Sorry.'

Simon gave him a tender whack. 'Off you go then.'

Esben hit the keyboard again, disappearing back into the unknowable digital world. Soon he was locked out of an IP's webpage and three attempts to crack its defenses failed. He cursed under his breath, egging himself on. He tried several other ways around it, muttering solutions and swearing at the perpetrator who had momentarily foiled him. Finally, he pumped a fist and told his imaginary nemesis to suck his cock. Then he turned to Simon and grinned.

'Got a pen?'

***

Simon and Esben roared back down the dirt track towards the compound. Charlie was waiting for them and dragged the gates open.

Simon opened the window and stuck a head out.

'We're on,' he said.

Charlie needed to hear no more and charged off to gather the others. Simon turned to Esben.

'Great job, brother.' He leaned into him. 'Don't undo all your good work by telling anyone what we found, understand?'

Esben nodded, his look of terror returning.

'Don't worry about me. I'm good,' he said.

Charlie returned with Aamir, Rob, and Duck. With their tattooed necks and knuckles, they could have belonged to a bikie gang as much as a religious sect. The men lugged bags and weapons into the cars and climbed aboard. Simon approached Charlie, who was in the driver's seat of one of the SUVs, and passed him the torn piece of scrap paper Esben had scrawled the address on. Charlie gave it the once over.

He turned to Aamir in the passenger seat.

'Get comfortable,' he said.

Simon jumped into the driver's side of the other SUV. The engines roared, and the cars bounced out of the compound in a display of military muscle. The gates closed behind them, leaving rows of brothers and sisters clinging to the wire, wondering where on earth they were headed.

The cars turned off the dirt track and onto the highway, heading south. They drove through Lismore and then to Grafton. Day turned into night. As the road stretched out before them, Simon unveiled their mission.

'We're going to the address where the clip of the baby was uploaded from. It doesn't mean he actually lives there, it's just a place to start. If it turns out the baby's not there, the people who live there will know where he is. I don't want any fucking around, boys. Do what I say and let them know we mean business. Whatever happens, we're coming home with that baby.'

***

They drove through the next night, only stopping for petrol and food. In the dawn they reached Albury, and the breeze through the open windows became noticeably cooler and drier. It didn't seem long after that that they passed through the satellite villages out of Melbourne, carved into land that only recently was pasture. They hit the ring road, plunging deeper into suburbia. They crossed town—squeezing through the morning gridlock—slowly finding their way to the inner suburbs.

At 11.45 am, the two SUVs approached the address Esben had extracted from deep in cyberspace. If God was on their side they would find the baby there, barely metres from their grasp.

13

When Tim met Nicole he was almost entirely a full-time guitarist. Butterfly Kiss, easily his most successful band to date, was flirting with the big time—or so they had thought.

Their move from Brisbane to Melbourne seemed to have paid off spectacularly. Their gigs were packed, and their first EP, *Get Some,* had found airplay. Belief was high inside the bubble, and there was a swagger in the band that only comes with the sense of momentum.

With all that buzz orbiting him, Tim felt famous for the first time in his life. He loved the attention he commanded whenever he entered a venue. Having all those eyes on him made him walk taller.

It was before the band's success began to decline that he met Nicole. Scanning the audience from the stage one night, he picked her out of the crowd. She was standing with friends, wearing a clinging summer dress that showed off her perfect figure and put an unusual splash of colour into the mostly black-wearing crowd. With her blonde hair, she stood out a mile as the only woman he wanted to go home with that night.

After the gig, he perched under a blaring house speaker and shouted an introduction.

'I like your dress,' he said.

'Sorry? What?' Nicole yelled back.

'I like your dress!'

'My *dress*? What about it?'

'I like it.'

'Oh, … thanks.'

Nicole shared a giggle with her friends, who outnumbered him three to one. He had no interest in engaging the others, so the trick would be how to elegantly extract her from them.

'It's so fucking loud here!' he yelled. 'Can I ask you something?' and he led her away to a quieter part of the club. 'What are you up to?' he said.

'Now?'

'Yeah. Fancy a drink? Somewhere quiet?'

Nicole spent a full ten seconds evaluating him.

'You don't waste any time,' she said at last.

He grinned. 'On the contrary. I've been waiting to ask you that all night.'

This statement contained just enough cheek to get her over the line.

He took her to a bar with dimmed lights and retro sofas, where he offered to choose a drink for her. He returned with a seductive looking cocktail in a tall glass. Away from the gig, he didn't feel the need to be so self-consciously "on", and he sensed she liked that.

When they returned to his car, she threw her arms around his neck and kissed him. It was a completely unexpected forwardness that was neither cheap, nor bossy. Tim found the way she abandoned herself to the kiss devastatingly erotic, and his mind tumbled forward to what it would be like to make love with her. When she drew away from the kiss, she suggested they do just that.

Her apartment was on the third floor and overlooked the river. It was a nest of white cushions and wicker baskets. The walls, floorboards and furnishings were all white, and the door handles were dressed with white tassels. It was heady with an essential oil that Tim recognised but couldn't place.

Nicole dropped her bag at the door and in one effortless motion glided over the back of the sofa and landed stretched out horizontally on the cushions below.

'Come here. I want you to see something,' she said.

Tim made his way over, making no attempt to copy her moves. He rounded the arm of the sofa and sat on the edge, looking down at her.

'No, here,' she said, waving him towards her.

Tim lay beside her on the couch. She grabbed a pull tie by the window and gave it a tug. The curtain in front of them opened to reveal a tree-lined vista of the river, drenched in moonlight. The view was dramatic—but one you might fail to notice unless you weren't tuned in to it. Tim got it. They lay together taking it in and enjoying the quiet dancing between them.

Then he turned to her and kissed her. This kiss was gentler than the one they'd shared earlier. He felt Nicole surrender to it, and he eased himself on top of her. She cupped the back of his neck with her hand and drew herself deeper into his lips; her other hand drifted along his back and slid inside his pants.

Tim had never known anyone with such an erotic touch. He could feel himself falling into her. It was unstoppable. He held her tighter to him, and they began to move together on the couch.

For the next two months, Tim and Nicole spent every night together. Tim rearranged the squalor in his apartment so she could stay over at his place too, and the love affair went from whirlwind to astounding.

Nicole had become Tim's first true love. Prior to meeting her his connection with a woman usually lasted for about as long as her presence in the room, so when he found himself thinking about her constantly, even when she wasn't there, he was taken by surprise.

Nicole had been an early starter, having had her heart broken good and young. She identified Tim as an innocent, so as much as he thought he was a man of the world his heart clearly hadn't experienced the real thing yet.

Without acknowledging this insight to him, Nicole managed his spectacular fall into the abyss with tenderness. She was his nursemaid. He was like a child learning to walk. Nicole held his hand until he got his balance right and was able to stand by himself.

Falling in love broke him with reality so completely that at first he didn't notice the terrible decline of Butterfly Kiss. To be fair, it happened in barely discernible stages.

First they lost their Friday night gig. Then the bass player joined a funk band that had already signed with Sony. Months passed before they could permanently replace him, and when they finally did they chose badly, ending up with a kleptomaniac who stole from their wallets in the band room and who wouldn't turn up to rehearsal. Then another residency fell. And another. Soon they found themselves with one weekly gig that paid a hundred bucks in the hand and netted around thirty punters.

The promising *Get Some* had suddenly become cold in the eating. A&R guys at the record companies were no longer taking their calls, and replied to emails with a superficial upbeat tone that promised nothing.

This implosion happened over the course of a year. Tim, being high on love the entire time, hadn't put the pieces of the collapse together. He was the only member of the band to be surprised when their singer, Stevie Sweet, tearfully announced he was leaving the group.

That was the end of it. Butterfly Kiss was dead. It shook Tim to the core. He went to Nicole and emptied his heart of all the injustices the music business had perpetrated. They talked until dawn, by which time it seemed the only solution for his broken heart was for them to move in together.

They debated the best place to put down roots. Tim made a case for the north of the river, while Nicole lobbied to be by the bay. This sent them on a confused search, which ended in a visit to the back streets of Malvern. Tim found the area exotic in its conservatism, and the houses there offered the kind of spaciousness reserved only for grown-ups. This was the trajectory he felt they were on, so when the little house at the end of the cul-de-sac offered a room for a music studio, a backyard big enough for bocce and an outdoor dining table, as well as a spare room for visitors—and what the hell, maybe a nursery one day—he was all in. It would be a fresh start. The year to come would be devoted to reinvigorating his musical dreams and hanging out with the girl of his dreams.

Living with Nicole brought home to Tim how settled into her career she was. She'd already found her calling and she revelled in it daily. She'd rise at 5.30 am and head off in her white district nurse's Corolla for her shift of aged care, where she'd lift and wash the elderly, listen to their complaints, and nurse their aches and pains. While Tim always felt the things *he* wanted were just out of reach, Nicole was already immersed in hers. At the end of her day, she didn't continue her work into the evening, dreaming up a catchy hook, or scheming a strategy to attract the interest of the record companies. Where she could switch off and relax, Tim's head was always set somewhere in the future, always obsessing about what else he could do to "make it". He envied her the place of sanctuary she'd found.

Once his studio was set up, Tim began writing some material and seeking out players for a new band. With three songs to begin with, he started with players at the top of his wish list, but he soon found that their reputations made them targets for everyone else looking to set up a band. Tim couldn't sustain them. Things weren't moving quick enough, and his music was not astounding enough. Down and down the list he went, until the band he ended up with was a workman-like outfit with members who lacked imagination and who fitted music around their day jobs.

The year finished as it had started, with Tim craving some kind of momentum, and the next year began as the last one had finished. Gigs were hard to come by, and there was zero interest from the record companies. Frustration built, and he began looking back with regret to the good old days of Butterfly Kiss.

One day, a creeping feeling took hold. It reached up from the dark of his subconscious. He observed that everything had begun to go wrong after he'd met Nicole. He swatted the thought away as ridiculous, but once the seed of that idea had sprouted he couldn't tear it out. In his darkest hours—when Nicole had gone to bed, and he was sitting in his studio, grasping for killer hooks— he'd trace the demise of his career back to the white apartment by the river. He began to wonder if you could actually have love *and* success. Maybe the two were incompatible.

A queasy undertone seeped into his feelings for her, completely unnoticed by Nicole. Tim worked hard to hide it from her, aware that she was the best thing that had ever happened to him. He knew the sweetest, the most 'good' person he'd ever met was his lover, and she did not deserve the blame for his escalating failure. But he couldn't prevent the idea from tainting the way he saw her. For the first time there was a tiny chink in her perfection. He woke to find crop circles left by the meanest part of him that read: 'Nicole has jinxed you'. As a result, a small part of him withdrew from her. A secret part. The part that said he was entitled to way more than he currently had.

One night while playing one of his rare gigs to a crowd of around twenty people, a young woman who'd braved the dance floor alone chose to sway through the last three songs of his set without taking her eyes off him. It drenched him with a burning feeling of danger, and when he locked eyes with her, he could feel himself getting hard behind his guitar. Something had taken him over. That another woman had looked at him with that intensity of desire again flicked an override switch, and by the end of the gig he was no longer in control. Sweaty and nervous, he abandoned packing up his gear for a barstool next to the girl, and although she breathed pure bourbon and her eyes struggled to remain completely open, he was already desperate to fuck her.

It took him less than five minutes to get her into the back of his panel van and less than ten to get her back out again.

He took a lingering detour around the city on his way home, feeling both euphoric and nauseous.

He wouldn't see Nicole until after work the following day, so he had hours to cycle through the feelings of remorse, self-justification, and guilt. It was an uneasy day, spent absently performing random chores and imagining all the ways this could play out. When at last she finally arrived home, he was surprised at how easily he could partition his actions of the previous night as an event that had nothing to do with her and was best consigned to history. He said nothing and gave away absolutely nothing.

The worst part of him argued that this small taste of his former life would inject him with some much-needed luck that Nicole had been eroding. But that was wrong. His new band bit the dust. Rather than start again, he tried his hand at producing, which also bore little fruit. In the end even Nicole began to quietly suggest he should get some kind of job to help with the bills that she had been consistently picking up for the last few years.

His audio engineering skills led him back into the studio, although this time it was behind the desk. Through a series of fortunate events, he found himself in a full-time job, mixing TV commercials and corporate videos.

At last he was getting a taste of what Nicole had experienced for so long: the ability to arrive home at the end of the day and switch off, unburdened by the perpetual need to "make it". It was a revelation. And it made room for him to accept the most profound and life-changing choice: it was time to have a child.

Without noticing, Tim quickly settled into a routine. With the time-sucking rigors of the new job, Tim found himself ensconced in a completeness, where almost all of his time and energy were spoken for. He barely had the bandwidth to look back at his previous life with regret—until the video of the star appeared on YouTube.

Suddenly he felt a familiar stirring—like the feelings that are revived when you play an old song. It broke him from his mould. When the world became obsessed with the star video, Tim felt like he'd become some kind of anonymous rock star. He was at the centre of something again. No one was specifically watching *him*, but nevertheless, he was that guy living under that roof in the clip everyone was talking about. He liked it. It felt exciting and rare. It aroused him, and he wanted more.

When the spell of the video began to wear off, Tim couldn't help himself from perpetuating the frenzy. He needed to sustain that euphoric feeling of worth. So the moment Gail and Father Jim had slunk out of the house on that Saturday afternoon, he crept into the nursery and made a clip of Billy on his phone. He created a new YouTube account—*Hopeformorning*—especially to hide his tracks, and he uploaded the clip.

Such was his lust for the splash it would make that he didn't even consider what the fallout with Nicole might be. He hadn't given any thought to how deep her hurt would go. All he'd considered was how to make sure the video remained anonymous. As long as there were no clues to the baby's location they were safe. The world could be spellbound by it, but it would remain just out of reach from them, and he would still feel that delicious tingle of fame.

But Nicole's open and trusting heart meant that just the suspicion that their friends had betrayed them was terminal for their friendship. Tim suddenly found that he now had to double down on the lie and sideline their friends—or confess.

Tim chose self-preservation and kept quiet. Better to lose their friends than to lose his wife. He partitioned the secret off into the same hidden place he'd put his infidelity. It could lay there alongside the drowsy eyed girl forever more.

14

Sunday rolled like a ship on the open sea. Clare's moods tumbled from joy to despair: one minute the stereo was belting out 'Miss You', by The Rolling Stones and she was throwing herself around the lounge room with abandon, the next she was curled up on the couch sobbing. She knew Garry was attending to her the best he could, but Nicole needed him too—to calm her fury about a video of Billy that had been posted online by her friends. Tim also needed a piece of him. So, as usual, Garry was the emotional switch board for the family, keeping everything from falling apart.

On Monday morning, Clare awoke to hear the front door close softly behind Garry. She lay there fighting off the empty feeling of being left behind. Still confused about what she would be to the world when she came out as cured, she stared out at the soft, early morning through a crack in the blinds and shuffled through all the possible activities that might drag her out of bed. In the end, it was one of the mandarins Garry had bought at the market on Sunday morning—which he'd described as one of the sweetest things ever grown by mankind—that finally tempted her. When she peeled the skin away and broke open the fruit nothing could make her put it into her mouth. She had no appetite and no will to do anything more than lean over the kitchen bench and stare down at the cold marble. Garry would be at work. He would be consulting with patients, backed up from their two weeks away. He would be in surgery. He would be striding the hospital corridors with the authority of a man returning to take back control of his domain.

Garry's work days were her loneliest during the final stages of her illness. Three days a fortnight she had had to endure what she referred to as a babysitter, as Garry set off for his professional conquests. They were long slow days. Days of tag-teamed carers, whose gentle voices only plunged her deeper into despair.

After an hour of trying to reassure herself that everything was different now, she gave in to her loneliness and set off for the hospital. She didn't bother with makeup, or dressing for her role of well-equipped surgeon's wife, because she merely planned to be an anonymous figure lurking in the background until she found a moment to distract him from his patients and share a sly ten minutes with him. She slapped a baseball cap on her head for disguise and headed for the bus stop.

When she arrived and approached the front entrance, she had the strangest feeling of retracing her own steps as a different person. These were the ramps she'd been wheeled over so many times. It was a well-worn path that led up to the fifth floor and the depressing physiotherapy ward.

116

She stepped into the lift and reached for the button for the second floor. Her hand hovered. The doors closed, and the lift began to ascend voluntarily. If she pressed the button now she could still interrupt the climb and hop out at the second floor, but her hand didn't move. Buttons lit up, as the lift sailed past floor three, four and five, right up to the ninth floor, where the doors opened to reveal an ashen-faced man, his hollow eyes betraying some terrible personal tragedy. Clare slipped past him into the cancer ward.

Closer to the nurse's station, a wheelchair was parked facing away from her. Just tall enough to be seen over the top of the seatback was the bald dome of a child's head. Clare approached, and she caught a glimpse of the little girl who was occupying the wheelchair. She was wearing floral pyjamas and holding a bag of fluid from which tubes snaked around her lap and then disappeared under a bandage on her forearm. Her face had the texture of a corpse, but she was looking up at the nurse with clear, hopeful eyes, giggling happily at something the nurse had said.

Clare felt the air being sucked out of her. She fought back tears. The little girl's mother was standing by her, chatting cheerfully with the nurse, ignoring the obvious, raging death that had taken hold of her daughter. They were all carrying on in such a matter-of-fact way—in a manner of such warm-hearted acceptance—that it broke Clare's heart cleanly in two.

What was she doing here? Why did she even get out of the lift?

Unnoticed by the group in front of her, Clare walked deeper into the ward. She had no idea where she was going, but her legs compelled her forward.

The ward was quiet, apart from a few distant voices, and the conspicuous starship hiss of the air-conditioning.

She passed by rooms of all sizes: rooms recently emptied, shared rooms, rooms with ominously closed doors, and rooms containing single occupants, wheezing like living corpses.

In a corner room with the blinds thrown open, bathing in the naked sunshine, was the figure of a child, eight or so years, lying on her own. She was plugged with tubes, and she stared out the window into the distant blue day. Clare paused in the doorway and watched her for some time.

Finally, the little girl turned to her.

'Hello,' she croaked.

'Hello,' Clare said. 'What's your name?'

'Philadelphia.'

'Oh, my. What an auspicious name.'

'Mum calls me Philly.' The girl smiled. 'What's auspicious?'

'It means fortunate. Prosperous.'

Philadelphia turned away, back to her blue sky.

Clare's regret hit her like a kick in the guts. How could she have been so stupid? She hovered, embarrassed, not fully grasping why she was standing there at all.

'My name's Clare,' she said at last.

Clare approached and sat on the bed. She searched for something to say to repair her gaff, but what she really wanted was to change Philadelphia's miserable fortunes. If only she could upload her sickness from her—trade places. If a trace of Billy's healing remained in her somewhere, maybe she could pass it on.

In a moment of insanity, she reached out to the girl.

'Here,' she said. 'I want to try something.'

Clare took Philadelphia's hand and wrapped hers around it. She closed her eyes and focused on the feeling she'd had when Billy touched her. She visualised the healing he gave her like it was a physical entity inside her, and then she sent it surging into Philadelphia, like an imagined wave of elixir.

When she was done, Clare opened her eyes and glanced at Philadelphia, who was looking at her with a polite, composed sympathy.

'How do you feel?' Clare asked.

'My mummy does that all the time,' she said kindly. 'Except she puts her hands on me here.' She broke her grip with Clare and placed them on her stomach. 'Nothing works.'

Clare heard herself gasp. Tears flowed. She rocked forward and sobbed into the prickly blanket draped over Philadelphia's bed. In her mind, she reached out to Billy, pleading with him to take away this poor, little girl's illness.

There was the sound of footsteps. Clare looked up to see a woman standing in the doorway. By the alarmed expression on her face, Clare judged her to be Philadelphia's mother.

'Excuse me, but what do you think you're doing?'

Clare had no answer. She could only back away from the bed and repeat, 'Sorry, sorry, sorry,' over and over.

This caught the attention of a passing nurse who stopped to ask if everything was all right. Clare insisted it was and hurried from the room. But she ploughed straight into the neighbouring room and knelt at the bed of the little boy. He was barely conscious, rolling his groggy eyes towards her. She pressed her head into his blankets and muttered to herself. The nurse, who'd followed her in, rushed over to remove her, but Clare sprang to her feet and raced out. The nurse pursued, only to see her disappearing into the next room.

'Excuse me,' the nurse called. 'Excuse me.' But Clare

didn't respond, instead kneeling by the bed again, taking the patient's hand.

The nurse called out in a professionally even tone that someone should call an orderly.

'You need to come with me,' the nurse added firmly.

Clare looked up, wide eyed, and then pushed past her back into the corridor. Two nurses had already approached, but rather than run from them, Clare wilted, curling into a ball on the floor. She remained there, sobbing.

'Does anyone know who she belongs to?' one of the nurses asked, and the rest gave a bewildered shrug. 'Let's get her up then.'

At that moment an orderly dashed around the corner.

'This is her, huh?'

The nurse nodded.

'We were just getting her up.'

'Okay,' he said. 'I got her.' He reached down to lift Clare from the floor when suddenly he recognised her.

'Mrs. Sharp?' he said, astounded. 'Is that you, Mrs. Sharp?'

15

A pall of silence had settled over the lounge. The priest and Gail were just sitting there, waiting. Nicole's face was open and kind as usual, but Tim could read the nerves lurking below the surface.

Father Jim had given them all a heads up about his bruising couple of days leading up to the Roman's visit. Tim appreciated his honesty.

Once the video of Billy had appeared online the Archbishop had latched onto the priest like a catfish in the muddy shallows, raging at him that he risked losing Billy to another denomination, and threatening him with excommunication if he didn't bring the meeting forward. But Father Jim had refused, making a point of telling Tim and Nicole that he'd stuck to his word.

When his story was over, silence had descended. A silence no one was capable of shifting. Gail seemed content to let it play, like she could endure it endlessly. But the priest kept taking stabs at reviving the flat-lining chat with sentences like, 'Gail had me walking here today … can you imagine?' and, 'It's nice it's not raining.'

But now even Father Jim had ceased trying.

Mercifully, there came a throaty rumble from the street. Everyone broke urgently for the window. A black Maserati Quattroporte with tinted windows pulled up outside the house. It sat glinting in the sunshine like it was posing for a brochure shot. In unison, the doors swung open and two unusually handsome men stepped out. Tim noted they were wearing sharp suits and dark sunglasses. Their jet-black curls were groomed flat to their heads, and they wore their side burns long.

Tim shared a glance with Nicole. Where were the deacons swinging incense and wearing white robes? They watched on as the two men perched by the car and scanned the area. They pointed towards the burnt out house, and then began down the cul-de-sac towards it. One of the men seemed to be limping.

When they reached the house, one took a camera from his breast pocket and snapped some shots, while the other made large paces, measuring the distance between the fire and the Blake's house.

This done, they marched back up the cul-de-sac.

In unison, everyone pulled back from the window.

'I'm guessing they would be the Romans,' Tim said.

A knock at the door soon followed. Without making any formal agreement to do so, they all hurried out of the lounge to answer it.

Nicole opened the door to reveal the two men standing there like a couple of misplaced Armani models.

'Ciao,' one said, loudly. 'I am Maurizio. And this is Armand.'

Armand was the one with the limp. He was smaller

122

than Maurizio and stood slightly behind him. His face, which appeared perfectly chiseled from a distance, was actually quite scarred and pockmarked.

'We are here to see the child,' Maurizio went on, and he looked past Tim to the priest. 'You are Father Jim McGuire, no?'

The Father offered his hand, but Maurizio ignored it.

'You are a lot of trouble, prete. May we come inside?'

And with that, Maurizio slipped past them and headed down the hall, Armand following behind.

Nicole narrowed her eyes.

'Stop!' she said firmly.

Maurizio turned to her, puzzled by her tone, and Armand fell in behind him again.

'That wasn't very polite,' she snapped.

Maurizio shrugged indifferently. 'Si. As you wish.' He thrust out a hand. 'You are Nicole. You, Tim,' and he shook their hands firmly. 'And you must be the Gail. You don't want us here, but if you want some polite, we'll be polite. Prego. Now. Can we see the child if you please?'

The two Romans stood there, waiting expectantly.

'What are we missing here?' Tim said. 'We just opened our house to you guys.'

'Si. After we wait for days,' Maurizio said. 'When you may have The Christ under your roof! You think this is a game?'

Gail marched up to him and needled a finger into his breastbone.

'Listen to me,' she hissed. 'Don't be an asshole. I don't know what you've been told, but your visit here was delayed because Father Jim kept a promise to this family. They insisted on a period of privacy. You need to respect that too.'

'His Excellency says you try to escape us. He sent us

hunting for you. We drive around everywhere looking for you.'

'No, that's not right,' Father Jim said. 'I told him last week I would not let you see them until today. He's lied to you.'

Maurizio turned to Armand. They spoke very quickly in Italian, and then they turned back to the group. Maurizio gave a deep bow.

'Mi scusi. Sometimes they treat us like dogs.'

Tim couldn't believe these guys were actually deacons sent by Rome. They seemed to think they were rock stars, not priests.

'Perhaps we should just get on with this,' Tim said.

'Please,' Maurizio said, smiling politely. 'I would like that very much.'

Tim led them down the hall to the lounge and offered them a seat.

'Billy's in his cot,' Nicole said. 'Shall I get him?'

'Grazie,' Maurizio said, now unleashing a dazzling grin.

Armand stood by the back door. Tim noticed him trying the handle, checking it was unlocked. When he found that it was, he gave Maurizio a private nod, and began prowling around the lounge room. As he moved, he pumped his chest out with sharp, uneven breaths, and his shoulders popped back and forth spastically.

Tim caught Maurizio's eye, and he gestured to Armand.

'Is everything all right?' he said.

'Armand is Il Lottatore. A fighter. If there is trouble with "the balance", he is here to take care of it.'

'The balance?'

'Where there is God, there is also Satan. If your baby is God, Il Lottatore will keep us safe while we inspect him.'

Tim had no idea what he was talking about. 'I haven't seen any trouble with the balance round here,' he said dryly.

'You wouldn't,' Maurizio shot back. '*We* would. The fire for instance. The fire has marked out Satan's presence. When your child was born, for God to bring him here? It would not escape the attention of the Devil. He makes himself known with fire. In the case of your child—if he's what we think he is—he's a phenomenal act of God, so we were looking for a significant fire.'

Tim's mind went back to the night of the birth, the smell in the street as he drove out to pick up Gail. If what Maurizio was saying was true, it was already happening. Nicole was singing, and God was all around them. And Satan was there too, putting his own mark on the event. Tim shivered. This was the kind of mumbo jumbo he'd scoffed at all his life.

Nicole's footsteps approached from the hall. Armand flipped in the air and landed hard on his back. In an instant he was on his feet again. He reached down and adjusted his leg, which had twisted at an ugly angle in the fall. Tim heard it crack, as he clicked what must have been a prosthesis back into place under his Italian strides.

Nicole appeared in the doorway carrying Billy; the Romans caught sight of him and instantly fell to their knees. Armand convulsed violently as though fending off blows to the stomach; Maurizio sobbed and mumbled in Italian.

'Sono venuto qua come un ipocrita,' he blubbered. 'Pieno d'orgoglio. Ti prego, aiutami.'

He bowed forward, tipping his head to the carpet.

Armand's convulsing intensified. He flew backwards, like a kick had connected with his face, and he landed on his back with a sickening thud. Maurizio broke from his reverie and turned on him.

'Portalo fuori,' he roared and stabbed a finger towards the back door.

Armand obeyed. He wrenched the back door open and threw himself into the garden, where the bizarre brawl continued. Armand was a child's toy, tossed from one side of the garden to the other. Every time he hit the ground, he was up again, fighting on.

Maurizio turned his attention back to Billy, his manner now becoming more intense.

'I have never seen this before,' he said insistently. He reached out and ran his fingers through Billy's halo. 'It is truly a miracle.' He toyed with the dazzling light, testing it. Then he took Billy's hand.

The moment he touched it, he appeared to become dizzy. He took a handful of Tim's shirt to steady himself.

'Mi scusi,' he mumbled. 'I feel his power intensely. It is very strong with him.'

He took a steadying breath and then turned to Tim. But he seemed to look straight through him. His eyes had become possessed, like he was overcome by some powerful spell.

'We must take him to the Vatican,' he said urgently.

'What?' Tim said.

'He needs to come with us to Rome.'

Tim and Nicole turned to each other.

'Err, you know that's not going to happen, right?' Tim said.

'We must. It is only there that he can be safe. Il Lottatore can only fight for so long.'

Tim felt the blood pounding in his head.

'No fucking way.'

'You have to understand. He needs to be protected.'

'He's been perfectly safe here,' Nicole shot back.

Maurizio snapped out of his funk.

'No,' he commanded. 'That is not so.' He gestured to Armand. 'You see him fighting? You understand he is protecting us?'

Armand was on his back, swinging his meaty fists at the thin air above his head.

Tim shook his head in disbelief. 'This is insane. You're not going to take our child!'

'You'll come too.'

'There's no way he's going anywhere.'

'He must. For his own good.'

Something snapped inside of Tim.

'Okay, get the fuck out,' he barked. 'We didn't invite you into our house so you could abduct our child.' Tim jabbed a finger at Father Jim. '*He* told us you were coming here to help us, for fuck's sake.'

Father Jim was on his feet. 'He's right,' he said. 'I promised them.'

'This child has work to do,' Maurizio beseeched. 'He must come with us or the Devil will come for him.'

'He's a baby!' Nicole cried. 'He is staying with us. Here. In this house.'

'No!' Maurizio exclaimed.

Tim had heard enough. He stormed from the room and dragged a baseball bat out of the cupboard in the hall. When he returned to the lounge room he was holding it above his head, ready to swing it.

'Both of you,' he snarled. 'It's time you left.'

16

Simon killed the motor. It felt good to sit for a moment in silence. All around him the pristine gardens vibrated with health. Geometric shrubs burst proudly through even lawns, and deciduous trees hung onto the season just long enough to fulfill their design task. Nothing here was like the compound, where the very air heaved with life, and the trees drew their shade of green from the earth, not a bottle.

Charlie's SUV still chugged behind him. Simon gave him a wave, and Charlie turned off the motor.

'Wait here,' Simon said into his two-way. 'That's the street right ahead of us, but it's a dead end. I'm gonna do a cheeky drive-by to see what's on offer. Safer if only one of us goes.'

Simon started his car and cruised around the corner. The stillness of the neighbourhood had to be to Simon's advantage. There were no kids playing in the street, no asthmatic whir of leaf blowers, no eyes anywhere to be seen.

Simon headed towards his target at the far end of the street: the little California bungalow. Sitting outside the house was a gleaming new Maserati. It caught Simon's eye, like an unusually beautiful woman.

As he drove towards it the front door burst open, and two men in suits scurried out of the house chased by another wielding a baseball bat. Simon found himself driving headlong towards them. He had a split-second decision on his hands. Continue on down the cul-de-sac and get tangled up in this scrap, or abort?

To his right was a burnt-out house. It had to be uninhabited. With less than an instant to process, Simon spun the wheel and bounced into the driveway of the house. It was mercifully long and would serve well as a temporary shelter. He stopped and leapt out of his car. Rob and Duck followed.

Up the street, shouts cracked the silence of the neighbourhood. A car door slammed. The throaty rumble of the Maserati started up.

Simon ducked for cover by the side of the house. He could hear Rob and Duck closing behind him as he peered out to the street. The man with the bat swung it into the car's perfect duco, leaving an ugly dent. The car jerked and peeled out of the street, onto the main road. The man with the bat stomped back inside.

Simon tried to interpret what he'd seen. This guy was defending something, and there was little doubt in Simon's mind about what that could be. He felt a shiver of excitement as he pulled out his two-way.

'Stay where you are,' he said. 'Something's going on.'

'What was with the fucking car?' Charlie said.

'Give me some time to sort it.'

Simon led Rob and Duck into the house through a collapsed wall. Inside, the walls were quilted with charcoal, and daylight pierced the crumbling ceiling in thick shafts. Even without the heat, it smelled of metal and steam. Simon squelched his way across the soggy carpet and squatted next to the window. All was quiet up at the California bungalow. He said a little prayer of thanks for avoiding detection. As always, the Lord had his back.

***

Tim stood in the doorway dangling the baseball bat in one hand. He could feel his heart pumping against his chest after chasing the Romans out. He must have looked scary, because Gail and Father Jim were backing away.

'You. You. Out,' he said.

Father Jim shuddered to life.

'Tim, I'm so, so sorry,' he pleaded.

'Go!'

Gail gave the priest a nod, and they made a break for the front door. Tim was clearly in no mood to argue.

Tim slammed the door behind them and turned to Nicole. 'We need to go,' he said.

'Go?'

'They want our baby, Nic. You think they're just going to walk away? My guess is they've already called for backup, and they'll be here in ten minutes with the cavalry.'

Nicole sighed.

'You're right. Where do we go?'

'I don't know. We just need to be away from *here*.'

'What about my parents' place?' We could drive there.'

Tim scanned the possibilities, the long road across the Nullarbor. 'I'll call your dad. You pack.'

'Great.'

Nicole raced to the nursery to pack, as Tim snatched up his phone to call Garry. Very quickly, he gave his father-in-law a picture of what had gone down.

'Come to us,' Garry said without hesitation.

'That's what we were thinking.'

'It's best. Make sure you don't leave any clues to where you've gone. I'll hire an apartment for you. Somewhere close by. You won't be able to stay here. It'll be the first place anyone will look.'

Tim loved how light Garry was on his feet.

'Thanks, mate. Better go.'

'And, Tim.' Garry lowered his voice. 'I need to warn you about something.'

Tim braced himself. Had something happened to Clare? Was she sick again?

'Clare isn't entirely behind the secrecy you both want for Billy. She's been finding it difficult. I'm giving you the heads up.'

'Thanks.'

Tim closed off the call with an enhanced feeling of dread. Didn't the outside world present enough of a challenge without having to worry about their own family too?

He raced to the bedroom to find Nicole zipping up a suitcase.

'Ready?'

'What did Dad say?'

'He's awesome. He'll have it sorted for us by the time we get there. Let's go.'

They threw the bags into the boot of the car and strapped Billy into the baby capsule for his very first car ride.

'Let's go,' Tim said.

***

It was time to send in some eyes. The house had been quiet for long enough. But as Simon turned to give the order, the house coughed up another surprise. A priest and an old woman burst out of the front door and hoofed it down the street.

Simon tried to get a good look at them, but they were setting a cracking pace, and they were soon obscured behind the front wall of the house. He crept back through the charred lounge room to keep sight of them. As they passed, the priest glanced his way. It was a fleeting glance, but enough for Simon to wonder if he'd been seen.

Simon's two-way crackled.

'Are those two interesting to us?' Charlie said.

Simon took a moment. Even a hint that the priest had seen them would put the old man in an early grave.

'No,' he said at last. 'Let 'em go. I'm gonna send Duck over to the house for a scout. Hold your position.'

Simon skittered back through the rubble.

'Duck. I want you to go take a look.'

Duck visibly swelled. 'Yes, boss.'

'Go and see who's in there—if the child's there— understand? And see what the guy with the baseball bat is up to.'

'Right.'

Duck went to scamper; Simon grabbed him by the arm.

'Do not get caught.'

'Yes, boss.'

Simon hung on.

'I mean it, Duck. Don't get caught.'

Simon watched Duck make a loop around the cul-de-sac then edge his way along the side of the house. Simon lost him from view.

The wait for him to reappear seemed interminable. Simon didn't relish swooping in to save him if he chanced upon the guy with the baseball bat. That would guarantee the guns would come out sooner rather than later, and Simon had hoped for a bloodless extraction.

Finally, Duck emerged, his steps quickening as he headed back around the cul-de-sac. His head was bowed, and his fists were plunged deep into his pockets. When he reached the burnt out house, he tumbled through the collapsed wall to report in.

'One man and one woman. Maybe a baby.'

'What do you mean, maybe?'

'The woman was talking to a cot, but I couldn't see inside it.'

Simon breathed through his frustration.

'So we can assume the baby is there. What was the man doing?'

'He was on the phone.'

'The man with the bat.'

'Yes.'

'Where?'

'In the kitchen.'

'And the woman?'

'In the baby's room. Talking to the cot. She was folding clothes.'

'No one else?'

'No one else.'

Simon pulled out his two-way. 'Charlie, we're going in. I'll take the SUV up to the house, and you be ready to roll when we come out. Send Aamir up to me now.'

'Roger that.'

Simon turned to Rob and Duck.

'A quick prayer, boys.'

They knelt in the rubble.

'Dear Lord,' Simon said. 'Keep us safe and deliver us our prize. All we do, we do for you. With this child safe in our keep, we will do great things in your name. Amen.'

'Amen,' repeated the others.

'Right, Duck? You're driving. Rob, you're coming inside with me. We're taking the guns, but no shooting unless we have to. Understand?'

Rob nodded, cool as Elvis.

Duck was sweating. This was no usual raid. There was no cover of nightfall—and all the millions of eyeballs in the big city surrounded them.

'Let's move,' Simon said.

But just as they got to their feet, the silence of the street was broken by the metal-on-metal grind of a garage door on the rise. Simon darted to the window to see a car pulling out of the garage.

'Fuck.' He spat and put a foot through the scalded wall in front of him. 'They're on the move. Get to the car.'

As one, the men raced out of the house and under the police tape towards the SUV. Aamir was already jogging towards them down the driveway.

'Into the car,' Simon barked. Then he pressed his lips to the two-way. 'Charlie!'

'I see 'em!'

'Don't let them out of your sight. I've got Aamir. We'll be right behind you.'

Simon threw his car into reverse and flew backwards down the driveway. He reached the street and rammed it into gear. Tyres chirped as they roared out of the cul-de-sac.

'Fucking hell, Duck!' he bawled. 'Folding washing? She was packing, you moron!'

Up ahead, Charlie was tailing the Toyota to where the

road ended at a T-intersection. Simon planted his foot and caught up to them. The cars reached the intersection and stopped, waiting to turn.

'Stay in touch with them,' Simon said into the two-way. 'When we find ourselves on a quiet stretch we'll move in.'

The lights changed, and the convoy rolled along the main road. Simon and Charlie kept a safe distance behind.

'Rob, when we stop, I want you to take their car,' Simon said. 'We may as well take it home with us. If we leave it here it'll cause too much interest. Duck, you go with him. Aamir, you get the husband. He can travel with us.'

Up ahead, Tim turned off the main road. Charlie followed.

The street was lined with poplars and had a golf course to one side. On the other side, a cyclone fence caged an industrial complex with endless rows of parked truck cabs. This was as quiet a street as Simon was going to get.

He planted his foot and raced past Charlie, drawing level with the Toyota. Gradually, he squeezed their car over to the side of the road.

Tim's mouth was wide with surprise as he pounded on the horn, but Simon edged in closer, forcing him onto the stony shoulder and cutting him off.

Charlie came up the rear, and suddenly the Toyota was trapped.

Tim leapt out, ready to give Simon a mouthful—but stopped when he saw the guns. He jumped back into his car, but Simon was ahead of him, ripping the door open and dragging him out.

'Oh, no you don't,' he barked, and threw Tim against the side of the SUV. He patted him down for a phone.

When he didn't find one, he gave him a shove towards Rob.

'Put him in the back.'

Rob towered over him. He gripped Tim's shoulders and folded him into the back seat of the SUV. Charlie stood by to guard him.

Simon ripped opened the back door of the Toyota. As he leant in he caught sight of Billy for the first time. His breath caught in his chest, and he was too overcome to move. The world turned in slow motion. His head was high and skinny, swimming in the love that Billy radiated.

'Oh, my God,' he stammered. 'Lord, God, look at him—beautiful.'

Nicole was cowering. 'Don't hurt us,' she sobbed. Her face was wet with tears, and she clutched Billy to her in terror. 'Please. Please don't hurt my baby.'

Her cries snapped Simon out of it. Raids weren't usually this hostile.

'No one's getting hurt,' he said, calming himself. 'Where are your phones?'

Nicole didn't understand why he'd want them, but she pointed to the dashboard. Tim's phone sat in a cup holder. She opened a bag at her feet and handed him hers. He opened them one at a time and ground the SIM cards onto the road with his heel, and then he stomped on the phones as well. He collected the broken pieces and pocketed them.

'Duck,' he said.

Duck knew what to do. He rushed over and jumped into the back seat next to Nicole. Rob got behind the wheel.

'These two are going to look after you,' Simon said. Then he checked up and down the street for traffic—for any eyes—but there was nothing. He pounded the roof of the car and turned a finger in the air.

'Let's go!'

Engines roared. Simon jumped into the SUV and threw it into gear. He turned to Tim, who was twisted around, trying to catch a glimpse of his wife.

'Hey!' Simon barked. Tim spun to face him. 'You're not going to give me any trouble are you?'

He said it like it was a question, but it wasn't a question. And this man understood the situation. Not so brave without a baseball bat in his hands. Not so brave with a gun pointing at his belly.

Tim shook his head and turned away.

Gail's Dream

Climbing the terracotta stairs, she notices it's quiet. Too quiet. Flavia, the nanny, likes to play music and only stops when Cielo is asleep. And it's not her sleep time yet. The traffic is a roar coming up from the street far below, and the humidity seems to hang off her. She pauses at the top of the stairs to catch her breath and take out her keys.

She calls out to Flavia in her singsong way, but there's still no answer, and the door doesn't swing open for her. The first key she picks out is the heavy iron one that looks like a tiny barbequed skeleton. She rattles it inside the old security door and hauls the door open. Not so much a door as a portcullis, always locked, inside and out, day and night. She swings open the heavy wooden front door beyond and calls out once again. When no answer comes, her heart begins to pick up pace.

Sun spills in through the magnificent bay windows that offer views out over La Paz. The palatial balcony gleams in the late-morning heat—the recent sun shower still steaming up from its brilliant white marble.

Flavia has left things tidy as she always does, but where could she be? And where is Cielo?

The apartment sprawls before her. Any of her neighbours could fit three of their apartments inside hers. And nearly all of them would gladly smash through that iron door and leave with armfuls of treasures if not for the knowledge of who her lover is.

She's aware of the sound of her heels as she clicks across the marble floor towards the bedrooms. They're dark, as they are when Cielo is napping. As she approaches, she lets her bag slip to the floor, and without understanding why tiptoes the last few feet to the door.

She pauses, her pulse beginning to race. A single glance around the doorway might break her heart. She's pictured this scenario many times before. She's seen the menace in Alejandro's eyes when they've fought. She's even planned an escape strategy in case he ever sprung something like this on her.

She surprises herself by how contained she is as she rounds the doorway and enters the room. It's been gutted. No cot. No chest of drawers. No hanging toys. Just a vacant space where once there was the quiet warmth of her baby.

She feels as though she's going to faint, so she consciously anchors her feet to the floor as her body begins to sway. She's aware that her mouth is gaping, and she can taste the tears that are now streaming down her face. Dumbly, she begins to take in the room, and the bareness it has now become. On the far wall, in the space where the colourful posters once were, she sees a single sheet of paper with one word scrawled across it. She approaches. It reads, "olvidala"("forget her"). This is something she knows she will never and can never do.

She already knows her next move. Before she's really aware of following a strategy, she's in her bedroom, inside her bedside drawer, fishing out her passport. She goes even deeper to find an envelope folded into a tiny square. She unrolls it and tears open the paper. Inside is a key. An artifact buried deep, out of caution, for emergencies such as this.

She slips the passport into her bag and flies down the steps to the street, leaving the apartment open to the will of her neighbours. She has her car key at the ready as she rounds the corner at the bottom of the stairs and finds the Mercedes still warm from her morning outing. She leaps into the driver's seat and squeals out of the little cobblestoned street onto the main road.

As she speeds towards the hills, she tries to imagine Alejandro's wife as she receives another child into her home. This will make seven. Only three of which are her own. Will she offer resistance, or will it be a simple matter of the servants taking orders to clear out another room?

She knows the trip she's taking could well be suicide. But she doesn't care. How could she do nothing? And, anyway, it would only be a matter of days before someone came to escort her from the apartment back to the YWCA—or the airport. Or the morgue. Her time here is up, and she knows if she ever wants to see her baby again she has to do the unthinkable. She has to snatch her from the lion's den. She feels strong because Alejandro wouldn't, in his wildest dreams, imagine she would dare do such a thing.

The hills are steep and luxurious, and there is only one house off the highway. She stops her car and makes the last leg of the journey on foot. She heads for the scrub at the rear of the house. This is where she will be shot. This is the place they will cut her throat and bury her where no one will ever find her, she thinks.

She slows her step as she approaches the gate to the towering perimeter wall. She takes the key from her pocket and whispers a prayer in Spanish as she lines it up with the keyhole. Miraculously, it slides in and she turns it. It clicks. So loudly in the quiet breeze. If only it were pouring, as it will be come late afternoon, it would drown out the sound of her.

She pushes through the gate she has never entered before expecting to be greeted by a guard dog, or a man with a gun, but she can only hear the sound of children playing. This is a good sign. They will be a distraction for any adults.

If she knows her Cielo, she'll be asleep now. Sleep time like clockwork at noon. Where would they put a sleeping child?

She nears the back of the house, open to a manicured garden and sculptured fish ponds. No sign of life. She imagines the adults smoking and drinking café on the balcony at the front of the house overlooking over the city.

She creeps inside. Quietly, quietly. The voices of children getting louder. She's in a kitchen. Brown-haired children bobbing in and out of sight above the counter as she creeps by, but they don't see her. Ahead is a staircase heading to God knows where. She's sweating and shaking with fear. Even a child's squeal could spell her death now.

She launches at the staircase and finds herself on a carpeted first-floor landing. Rooms head off in all directions. It's eeny meeny miny mo. All the doors are closed. A game of Russian roulette. Which door? The door with my child behind it, or the door with my angry, now-ex-lover wielding a gun? She closes her eyes and tries another silent prayer, but random thoughts interrupt her.

How on earth did she end up here? Why did she choose Bolivia, for God's sake, when her travelling buddy stayed back in Peru?

She steadies herself, pushing back at the loose thinking. Stay focused. Pick a door.

The second door on the right speaks to her. It draws her in. Without questioning, she's turning the handle and opening it. A cot. Tiny breaths. Her little Cielo. She scoops her up and is back out of the room in a heartbeat. Children's voices become louder as she creeps down the stairs. She can hear the blood pounding in her ears as she moves back through the kitchen and into the garden once more.

It's a quiet Sunday afternoon, and Alejandro is either calming his Maria, or cowing her. The servants have scattered. The muscle is spread far and wide.

Gail reaches the perimeter wall and slips through. Hardly believing her good fortune, she quietly closes the gate and disappears into the scrub.

In a moment the heavens open. The afternoon rain has come early, and Cielo wakes to the wet on her face. Gail shushes her as she slips and slides down the hill towards the car. She reaches it and piles inside. She guns it with Cielo in the passenger seat next to her. No time to strap her in. Any moment there'll be shots. Any second a car will loom like a shark in the rear-view mirror.

The highway is wet, and the corners sharp, but the Mercedes holds firm. She sweeps along the road too fast, heading for the embassy back in the town. She checks the mirror constantly. So far so good. How long will it be before baby Cielo is missed? Will an unlucky nanny be the one to break the news, or will Alejandro find out for himself when he's had enough of Maria's petulance?

She reaches the town without slowing. Danger could be lurking in any side street, around any bend. Any luxury car could contain her killer, who'll already know where she is heading with the baby.

The traffic begins to hold her up. Her eyes dart. Ahead is the turn off to the tree-lined boulevard of the international embassies. The cars ahead are pulled to a stop. Her patience is at breaking point. She pumps the horn, but it makes no difference. She pulls out of her lane and takes off along the outside of the traffic as fast as she can, racing the oncoming cars. Miraculously, she reaches the turn safely but cuts off a car coming out of the street in the opposite direction. She spins. The wet road offers no traction as the world turns, and she loses her grasp on which way is which.

The rear of the car in front connects with the passenger side of hers. The world is in slow motion. Gail reaches out helplessly for Cielo as the steel bumper emerges through their front door, taking Cielo with it. Like an explosion, glass shatters into Gail's eyes, and she only gets the slightest impression of her child flying past her on the way to the wet street beyond.

The car stops spinning. Gail clears the glass from her face, screams out for her baby. She tries to open the door but realises her arm isn't working. She tries her other arm but finds that the door is not working either. There's shouting. A man wrenches the door open. Is he her killer? Suddenly, she's outside the car, on the *ground. Rain is soaking into her eyes and her hair. Blood pours down her head and into her mouth. It's brassy and thin with rain.*

She can see Cielo on the road. Two people are kneeling beside her. They are crying. They keep looking towards her from the baby. Gail lifts herself off the ground and staggers towards them. Her legs shake, and she wants to be sick.

The people clear for her as she lifts Cielo off the ground with her good arm. She staggers away from them. They call after her in Spanish, wanting to know where the hell she's going.

But Gail doesn't stop. She staggers onwards, the trailing onlookers all calling after her to stop—to hand over the child.

She continues on to the embassy and pushes the buzzer. She doesn't know what she's said, but the gate swings open, and she knows she's home.

She collapses onto the pristine lawn in the rain and holds Cielo tight to her. A crowd from inside the embassy forms around her, prompting her politely, yet urgently, to tell them what has happened. She doesn't understand their words.

She only wants to hold her child and to sleep. She looks down at the baby in her arm and realises that she's not holding Cielo at all. The bloodied child in her arms is Billy.

17

Gail was aware she was crying even before she woke. As the dream receded, she could feel her pillow warm and wet beneath her face. Forty years on, and the same dream still cracked open her sleep. Forty years on, and her heart still broke for Cielo.

She sat up in her bed and reached for the picture frame on her bedside table—her only snapshot of Cielo. She studied the yellowing picture—a face emblazoned in her memory. So many details of her remained: her breath on her skin as she fed, her smell, her tiny fingers grasping one of her own. They all left an indelible imprint, which simultaneously agonised and warmed her.

This kind of grief was impossible to shift. And the desire to let it go was often outweighed by the need to hang on to it. So the pain never left. It lived in the form of tributes: like shaving her head on her child's birthday. Like never driving a car again. Like shopping for faiths that might soothe the pain. Like dedicating herself to the pursuit of bringing life into the world.

This time the dream had an ominous spin though: Billy's face had appeared in Cielo's bloodied swaddling clothes. It woke her with a start. Like opening a drawer to find a spider inside. She understood Billy was on her mind, but why in her dreams?

She forced herself out of bed, ready to tackle the day. After one of these dreams, it was easy to retreat to the blankets indefinitely. One lost day would turn into another, and a whole week would pass before she managed to go outside the house. But this was not going to be one of those weeks. She was now filled with a sense of destiny. For the first time in years she would peel the dream off like a sodden overcoat and get on with things.

Her first destination was the AM radio in the kitchen. The voices of talkback strangers were always the perfect underscore to her morning ritual of eating rice porridge, tending the vegetables in her garden, and feeding the goldfish. Gail liked nothing more than to pick a tomato, ripe from the plant, and slice it onto an unbuttered piece of home-baked sourdough.

By the time she'd showered and dressed, the muscular sting of the morning news rang from the kitchen. She wandered through to pour her tea and listen to the outside world.

But this morning, the headlines were delivered with all the hysteria of the outbreak of war. Overnight the Vatican had issued a statement claiming to have confirmed that the child with the halo in the now-infamous video was genuine. The baby had been examined by representatives of the Church and was deemed to be the Second Coming. A discovery—it was at pains to point out—that had been made by the Catholic Church.

All the blood drained from Gail's body. The secret was out. It was as exciting as it was frightening. What awaited the Blakes now? And how would the world react? Would citizens prostrate themselves in the streets, or give a doubtful shrug and go back to their lives? And what about other faiths? Would they hitch their wagon to the hysteria or rail against it?

The Vatican was shrewd enough to keep the whereabouts of the child to themselves. Gail guessed they had no choice but to make the announcement immediately, otherwise they risked being beaten to the punch by someone else.

Her mind turned to Nicole. Had the Romans returned and convinced them to go with them to the Vatican, or had they employed more forceful tactics?

Heart pounding, she reached for her phone and dialled Nicole. It went straight to voicemail. She tried Tim. No answer. She tried their landline, only to get the same message bank designed to keep the world at arm's length.

She snatched up her bag and marched out, and she didn't stop until she reached the house at the end of the cul-de-sac.

The street was as she'd left it the day before: no news cameras or religious fanatics jostling for a spot in front of the house. The only addition was a large black sedan, which occupied the driveway. The car doors were swung open, and two men sat with their legs dangling out, smoking cigarettes.

When Gail approached they snapped to attention. They were both middle aged with the look of hard men gone soft.

Gail's first guess was that they were from the Church, posted there to guard Billy. As she approached, neither man made a move. Gail assumed they expected her to stop and engage them, but she marched straight past.

The men shared a confused look, like she'd snipped both of their neckties in half on the way past.

'Excuse me, Madam, but I can't let you—'

Gail ignored him, heading for the front door.

'Ma'am!' one shouted. 'There's no one home!' Gail was at the front door knocking by the time he came to his senses. He bolted up the driveway after her. 'Excuse me, but what is your business here?'

Gail ignored him and bellowed at the front door, 'Tim! Nicole! It's me!'

'Nobody's here,' he barked. He had the look of a man who was losing control of the one situation he'd been instructed to take charge of. Gail gave him a withering glare and headed towards the back of the house. She glanced in each window as she passed, pushing through the overgrown foliage on the way to the back garden. The man followed helplessly behind.

When she reached the rear of the house she pressed her face against the lounge window. There was no sign of life.

The sickly residue of her dream rose like bile in her throat. Where was the family?

'I would like you to tell me who you are and what your business *is* here,' the man insisted.

Gail spun around sharply.

'No!' she spat. 'I want you to tell *me* who has sent *you* and what you have done with the family.'

The man stepped backwards like Gail was about to eat him.

'I—I—I don't know what you are talking about,' he stammered.

A wave of insight crashed over her. With their big announcement, the Church needed to parade Billy to the world. It was the only way to validate their claim. So if they *had* taken him, why hadn't the parade already begun? What were they waiting for? Without the child, they'd set themselves up for worldwide ridicule. Doubters would be lining up to shoot them down. If Tim and Nicole had taken off, the Church would be on a frantic search to find them, so these guys were mere grunts, posted here on the slender chance the family might return.

She dearly hoped they had taken off, but the queasy feeling persisted. Her dream was reaching out of her subconscious and speaking to her—warning her that Billy had been abducted. But if not by the Church then by who? Who else even knew where to find him?

She pushed past the man, back around the side of the house. She heard his footsteps shuffling heavily behind her. When she reached the front of the house the other man was standing in the driveway, blocking her path. Clearly, he was the more senior of the two and was not going to apply the soft tactics his underling had.

'Hold your horses,' he said quietly. 'I need a name.'

'Fuck off,' Gail said and pushed past him. The man grabbed her hard by the elbow, surprising her with his roughness. 'Do you want me to scream?' Gail warned, keeping the menace in her voice.

'Do what you like, but I want a name, and I want to know how you know the family. You're not a parent, we've already spoken to them.'

Gail knew she'd hit the bull's-eye. If they'd spoken to Garry and Clare, it could only be to find out where Billy was. These guys were no more enlightened than she was. Gail tugged her arm from the man's grasp.

'How long have they been missing?'

'How do you know they're missing?'

Gail spelt it out like she was speaking to a moron. 'I was with them yesterday. Now they're not here.'

'I don't know anything about that,' he said.

'You *know* who they are—who their child is.'

The man remained silent. The other man approached. They swapped a glance.

'My name is Miriam,' she said, deliberately calming her tone. 'I live around the corner, and I was here yesterday until about midday. If you tell me when you arrived then we might be able to work backwards—find out what their movements were. I could help you find them.'

The promise of a result switched a light on in their eyes, like they were about to get something that would finally earn them some love from their boss.

'Please,' Gail said. 'We need to find them—for their own sake.'

'We arrived at twelve hundred and thirty hours,' one man blurted.

Gail did her math. The Romans must have come straight back with some muscle but were too late—the family was already gone. What had happened in the half hour between her leaving and these grunts arriving at half past twelve?

'Stay here,' she said firmly. 'If you stay here and wait for them, I'll see what I can find out. Between us we're sure to find them.'

The men stared blankly at her, nodding as if she was now assisting them in some oblique but important way. She took out her phone and dialled Father Jim.

'Hello?' he said.

'It's Gail.'

There was a long silence before he spoke again.

'Oh, Gail, have you seen what they've gone and done?'

'Never mind about that. I need to see you. I'm coming over.'

***

Gail was crunching her way up the gravel path towards Father Jim. He was relieved to see her. Even though he barely knew her, she was the only person he could truly share his conflicted feelings with.

How could they be so selfish, so stupid? The Catholic Church—his family—behaving like a greedy child wanting to possess Billy at all costs.

'Have you seen them, Gail?'

'No,' she said flatly. 'They've vanished.' She pushed past him.

'Vanished?'

Father Jim turned and followed her inside.

'Yes. Your mob has had the house staked out since we left yesterday. They haven't seen them either.'

Gail sank into the deep leather chair by Father Jim's writing desk. The priest arranged himself anxiously on the desk in front of her.

'Have they spoken to you?' she asked.

'The Archbishop? No.' Father Jim buried his face in his hands. 'Oh, I can hardly believe this. Do you think they've taken them?'

'No, I don't. They're looking for them, so they can't have taken them. If they had Billy, they'd be showing him off by now.' Gail looked up at him gravely. 'I think they've been abducted.'

Father Jim was beyond distraught, and typically wracked with Catholic guilt.

'No!' he blurted. 'Surely, they've just decided to disappear. That would be the smart thing to do.'

'They've been missing since yesterday. That's *before* the announcement. The men keeping watch at the house told me they arrived at 12.30 pm. In the half hour between us leaving and the guards arriving, I believe someone took them.'

'Why would you think that?'

'Because I had a dream,' she said. There was a challenge in her tone. Would he dare question why a dream would give her such certainty?

The priest held her eye, waiting for her to explain herself, but Gail remained silent. Somehow her conviction was beyond reproach. The priest had no choice but to accept her assertion for the time being and move on.

He turned his mind to the scene directly after they'd left the house. Someone must have come. Was there anything unusual? Was someone watching and waiting? Did he see anything? Tim had chased them out. Gail had raced ahead carrying on about Tim's misjudgement of the situation. They had passed by the burnt-out house.

That's when the answer hit him.

'I saw a car,' he said. 'Parked in the driveway of the burnt-out house.'

Gail's eyes lit up. 'Go on.'

'Well, why would a car be there? The place is derelict. TOY078. That was the number plate.'

'What? How could you possibly know that?'

'It's my curse remember? I notice things, and I store them away up here.' He tapped his head with a crooked finger. 'Maybe they were in that house waiting. Perhaps they saw us leave and then they pounced.'

'If we can find out whose number plate it is then we can find Billy,' she said.

'I'll call the police,' Father Jim shot back.

'No. We can't involve the police. Remember who we're looking for. If the police are involved it'll take ten minutes for Billy's identity to be all over the news. I bet the Church hasn't gone to the police.'

'Then how on earth do we track down that number plate?'

'We hire a car,' Gail said, grinning.

***

Even though the relationship had only lasted eighteen months, Alejandro had schooled Gail in some of the family's ways. The police in La Paz were easily bought, but some things weren't worth the money. For more inconsequential issues, Alejandro had myriad scams to get what he needed without having to pay for them. Identity theft was one. Occasionally, in an unguarded mood, he'd share these family secrets with Gail. They'd lie in her enormous bed, and he'd feed her crime stories and brag about the fixes he'd pulled off. It was thrilling, and Gail felt like she was living in a crime novel. It aroused her. Being held by this fearless, impenetrable man made her feel bulletproof. His reward, when the monologue finally came to an end, was Gail crawling on top of him and quenching the desire the stories had built up in her.

It was with this intelligence that Gail called a car hire firm and placed an order on her credit card. She and Father Jim passed the time waiting for the car to be delivered by listening to the frenzied talkback on the radio. An endless stream of listeners voiced their opinion about the validity of the Church's claims and speculated on the child's whereabouts. No other news counted. Politics was set aside. No one cared about the markets. World leaders eagerly engaged in the discussion, desperate to be associated with the astonishing revelation.

The Church still hadn't revealed the identity of the child though, which had callers baying for blood. "If they have the Second Coming, why won't they show him?"

The hire car was delivered within the hour. A skinny young man in a cheap suit handed the keys to Gail and gave her a form to fill out. He seemed strangely overcome by Father Jim's presence, barely making eye contact with him. He kept stealing sideways glances as Gail initialled boxes and ticked off clauses.

Finally, he revealed what was eating at him. He lowered his eyes and turned to Father Jim.

'Your honour?' he said softly. 'I've never been inside a church before. Is it too late for me?'

Father Jim smiled kindly and took his hands.

'You have always been welcome, and you always will be.'

Gail joined them beside the car. She'd already guessed what was going on and could see the devotion set in the kid's eyes. It was an opportunity too good to pass up.

'Do you have a card, young man?'

The kid sprung back into his role of hire car guy and whipped a card from his breast pocket. He handed it to Gail but addressed Father Jim.

'The card I just gave your wife has my number on it,' he said. 'Anything you need, please call me personally.'

Gail thanked him.

The young man jumped into the collection vehicle, grinning all the way back down the driveway.

Gail turned to Father Jim and took his hand.

'Well, husband, so far so good.'

Father Jim winked at her. 'I thought you couldn't drive,' he said suspiciously.

'I said I *didn't* drive, not that I couldn't.'

'Fair call. What now?'

'Give it an hour or so.'

'And then what?'

Gail didn't answer. Sometimes she enjoyed being oblique, and it amused her how serious Father Jim became as he tried to extract her plan from her.

Finally, she picked up the phone and dialled the number on the young man's card.

'Hello, Ahn speaking.'

'Ahn? It's Gail Alvarez here. You dropped a car to us at the church?' She paused to let him catch up with her. 'I'm afraid we've had a slight accident.'

'Oh, my God!' he blurted. 'I mean … I hope you're okay.'

'It was only a very minor accident. Not our fault. We're both fine, but I'm afraid we've had a bit of bad luck. I swapped my details with the other driver, but I've somehow misplaced the piece of paper I wrote them down on. And I neglected to get my licence back from them.'

'Oh, I'm so sorry, that *is* bad luck.'

'I have the registration plate of the car though. If I gave you the number, I wonder if you could let me know their address so I can at least get my licence back?'

'Oh, that's something we can't do, Mrs Alvarez,' Ahn said gravely. 'We could never give out other driver's details.'

Father Jim hovered closely, wearing a look of astonishment.

Gail turned on the tears.

'But you must help us, Ahn,' she wept. 'I need that licence to get the Father to his extremely important sermon tonight. A sermon celebrating the very special baby that has been born.'

This sent the poor boy into a spin. He weakly repeated that it was company policy, which made Gail's sobs even louder. In moments, he cracked completely and handed over the information she needed.

154

She hung up the phone and gave Father Jim a grin.

The car belonged to an Anthony Bezinger, but had been out of registration for over eighteen months. Gail turned to Father Jim and pumped a fist. The first place to start was the internet.

Gail hovered over Father Jim as he opened up his browser.

'How many Anthony Bezingers can there be?' she said.

'You'd be surprised,' he said, as he typed the name into the search engine. 'Let's have a look.'

Gail was dazzled by how fast the search results scrolled in. Pages of hits led them to everything from Saint Anthony to houses for sale in New York State, in Bezinger Avenue. But as Father Jim scrolled through the suggestions, something caught Gail's eye. She stopped him and pointed to the entry.

Adeleblanche: why him: Anthony Bezinger - my friend how can
www.balanceblogspot.com/tagged/adele#21233664
This is testing my faith. To escape the hurt I felt when Jackie died, only to lose someone else I love. Beautiful Anthony Bezinger. Why do the people I love die?...(more)

Father Jim followed the link to a blog page. Gail had no idea what she was looking at. It was an entry that sat among many others and was dated from two months earlier:

We buried Anthony today. Not his body, but his memory. We stood in the bush, and Simon said a prayer. We threw flowers onto a statue Joanne made, and we all spoke about how we loved him, and we told stories. This is testing my faith. I escape the hurt I felt when Jackie died, only to lose someone else I love. Beautiful Anthony Bezinger. Why do the people I love die? Why does tragedy follow me? Doesn't God want me to find happiness? My heart broke when you didn't come back to the compound my love. Now I don't know if I should stay. How can I? The community is not the same without you. I don't want to follow Simon, I want to follow you. Do I follow you to the grave? Tonight I will sleep here at the hotel. I don't care if they miss me. If I miss curfew. This is my time out. This is my time to honour you Anthony. Sleep well my darling. I love you. Adele. XOX

'What *is* this?' Gail asked.

'It's a blog.'

'It looks like a diary.'

'Yes. Like a public diary.' He leant in and studied the entry. 'Adele Blanche. If this is the same Anthony Bezinger, he's clearly on the wrong side of the pearly gates.'

'She makes him sound like some kind of religious leader.'

'She does. And this Simon. He sounds like the big boss.'

'She's part of some kind of religious community.'

This was throwing up more questions than it answered. How did Anthony Bezinger's car come to be parked in the driveway of the burnt-out house? What was the connection?

'We need to read her whole blog. From the beginning. And we need to find out where this girl is blogging from,' Father Jim said.

They went back to the start of the blog. She'd written a lot about 'the community' and 'the compound'. She spoke about the isolation she endured, but never about her location. The last entry was dated only two weeks prior. It described an escalating tension between she and Simon that was, in her words, driving her to despair. As was life in the compound.

156

Gail and Father Jim tried to connect the pieces of the jigsaw: an isolated religious group who were mostly self-sufficient? Thematically it seemed to fit. If they weren't behind the kidnapping, maybe they knew who was. Or maybe this Adele would.

But how on earth did these guys find Billy?

Father Jim tossed up another idea. He closed out of the blog and opened Facebook. He typed 'Adele Blanche'. Multiple listings filled the page. It was anyone's guess who was their girl.

'Any thoughts?' Father Jim asked.

'Most of them are French,' she said. 'Let's focus on the ones that live here.'

Gail studied the listings, narrowing them down to the local girls—trying to picture in her mind which face matched the angst in the blog. This girl was young, vulnerable, lost perhaps. She dug down into her instincts and picked a face.

'Her,' she said.

Father Jim clicked on her link. In moments they knew Gail had hit the bull's-eye. There was religious discussion all over her timeline. Her posts linked-up to another religious group called Light Up. There was no question. This *had* to be her.

They zeroed in on one of the posts that pleaded with her to explain why she'd disappeared off the face of the earth—and where she'd gone. Her reply finally gave them the direction they were after.

Adele Blanche

I'm at the Garnerville hotel. Just here to pick up msgs and then I'm back to the compound for the night. I'm ok. Don't fret. Send love to Kath and Tom. I miss u guyz. XOX

Like   Comment   Share

Father Jim turned to Gail.

'What now?'

'We go to Garnerville.'

18

Nicole was shaken awake as bitumen became gravel beneath the SUV's tyres. She instinctively reached for Billy, who was sleeping in her lap, his tiny lids shut against the dawn. His even, peaceful breaths warmed her skin as they bounced through the storm of dust kicked up by the SUV in front.

Overnight, the fierce man who seemed to be in charge had kept them all separated—she and Billy with him, Tim with the other men.

He was no fool, this man. He noticed everything. Nicole saw how careful he was to keep them out of sight, and he effortlessly dominated his underlings like they were under a spell.

The most frightening thing about the group was the disconnect they had between their aggression and their religious zeal. It didn't add up. Tattooed men, prowling restlessly, all the while giving blessings to the Lord.

Regularly through the night she'd asked to see Tim.

They'd only permitted it once. During a rest stop the boss man marched him over as if to persuade him his wife and child were unharmed. Tim's eyes were pleading and helpless, making Nicole want to run to him. But once he'd identified them, without a word, he was shoved away again. That was the last time she'd sighted him. For the rest of the night it was endless road, and the bounce of the car.

When the dirt road deteriorated into little more than a track, the cars came to a stop. Nicole tightened her grip on Billy as fear rose inside her. After all of these miles, had they merely brought them here to kill them?

The boss waved a hand through his window, and the engines died. The doors of the car in front swung open, and Nicole saw Tim shoved out at gunpoint.

'What are you doing?' Nicole cried.

The panic in her voice made the boss turn to her from the front seat.

'Relax. No one's gonna get hurt,' he grunted. 'Just get out of the car.'

The younger one was already out and opening Nicole's door. He seemed to tower over her. Nicole didn't move for fear.

'Get out,' he barked.

Losing patience, he dragged at her, and she found herself standing by the car surrounded by the rest of the men. One of them shoved Tim towards her, and the men looked them over with a kind of macho curiosity.

'Right,' Simon said, 'we're nearly there.' He gestured to his men. 'This is Rob, Aamir, Charlie, and Duck. My name's Simon.' He gave Nicole and Tim a self-satisfied smile—like the very mention of his name should explain everything to them.

Simon turned his gaze on Tim.

'You are?'

'Tim,' he said quickly. 'This is Nicole and—'

'Baby Jesus,' Simon butted in.

'Billy,' Tim said.

'Baby Jesus,' Simon repeated.

Nicole gave Tim a look designed to stop him going on with it.

'We really only want the child. But we understand he needs you both, and we're not animals here. So if you don't give us any trouble, everything will be sweet. In fact, I believe you'll like it here.'

Tim and Nicole stared mutely.

'Nod your head so I know you understand what I'm saying,' he pressed.

Tim and Nicole nodded.

'Good.'

Simon turned to the men and gave them a nod. They sprang into action, making for the vehicles. Tim and Nicole were the last to realise everyone was leaving, and they were now permitted to travel together.

They climbed into the SUV. Simon was already in the driver's seat, with Duck riding shotgun.

'Can you please tell us where we're going?' Tim said.

Simon glanced at Tim in the rear view mirror for a moment—long enough for Tim to understand he wasn't going to answer his question—then his eyes flicked back to the road ahead. He drew in a long, deep breath and burst into song.

Jesus is on the main line, tell Him what you want...'

He sang tunelessly but with abandon. Duck joined in.

Jesus is on the main line, tell Him what you want. Jesus is on the main line, tell Him what you want. Call Him up, and tell Him what you want.'

***

The vehicles slowed as they arrived at the towering perimeter fence. Simon thumped on the horn. Charlie joined in the honking from his car, and it soon drew a crowd, who rushed out to greet them. The gates swung open, and the cars crawled along the uneven path into the heart of the community. Simon's eyes blazed with triumph. Followers rushed to touch his hand as he cruised by.

'Straight to church!' he cried. 'Everyone. Straight into the prayer hall.'

As the procession continued deeper into the compound, he searched the crowd for Adele. He longed to see the expression on her face when she finally accepted what he was capable of.

The cars came to a stop outside the prayer hall. Simon laughed out loud as his followers danced around the car like revellers at a medieval feast.

Simon turned to Nicole. 'Keep him wrapped up tight,' he instructed. 'I don't want anyone seeing him yet.'

He dashed around the car to help her out, assuming the role of doting assistant. Tim was edged out of the picture as Simon escorted her inside. He guided her through the crowd and up to the altar where they assembled, ready to address the followers.

Simon looked out over the hall. An expectant hush descended, but Simon remained silent, his eyes searching the eager congregation. He couldn't start until Adele had arrived, and she was nowhere to be seen.

As a ripple of impatience crept through the congregation, he saw her edge in behind the crowd at the back of the hall. Their eyes met. A shy smile crossed her face, like she was relieved he was home and in one piece. But then her gaze shifted to Nicole—and the tiny package she was nursing—and her expression changed.

Simon hadn't expected this response; it filled him with panic. How could she not be awed by his triumph? With the crowd becoming restless, he had no other choice but to sail over his unease and address them.

'My loved ones,' he announced. 'Today I have returned to you with the greatest gift a shepherd could bring his flock. Today not only will you feel God through me, but you will also see Him. I have brought Him to you in the flesh, and He belongs to *us* now.'

Simon reached over to take Billy, but Nicole pulled away. Simon was so impatient he almost snatched him.

'Give me the baby,' he said firmly, and Nicole handed him over.

Simon held Billy up and drew the blanket back to reveal his face—and his beaming halo.

The crowd gasped.

'No longer will we worship mere symbols. From today, we have our very own son of God.'

It was like he'd turned a hose on a pit of primates. The prayer hall erupted. They wailed and spoke in tongues; others fell to their knees and waved their arms madly.

Simon noticed Adele recoiling from the chaos. She stood staring at the rapture around her for a moment, and then she slipped out of the prayer hall. The clamour around Simon fell silent; there was only a heavy pulse in his head. There was so much to celebrate, but his mind could only go forward to the time when he could find Adele and hear her explanation of what had gone wrong.

Simon sidelined Nicole and Tim and allowed the congregation to form a line so they could touch the baby, but he quickly grew irritated, and his head was elsewhere. Before the entire congregation had had the chance to engage with Billy he swept Nicole and Billy out of public sight. He escorted her down a path on the outskirts of the community to what would become her own hut.

'In you go,' he said, nudging her forward.

The former occupants had left in a hurry. There was still the odd piece of clothing left behind, and a few dog-eared paper backs dumped in a corner. A futon sat on the ground, draped with rugs and old blankets.

'This is your hut. Or you can sleep with me and the girls in *my* hut.' Nicole didn't appear to understand. 'I have a larger hut that I share with five others,' he went on, spelling it out. 'You can be part of that arrangement, or you can stay here. It's up to you.'

Simon's explanation seemed to sink in.

'Where's Tim?'

'He has his own hut. For the time being I think it's best.'

'For who?'

Nicole's bluntness almost got a rise out him.

'I understand you're going to need some time to get used to this,' he said. 'Don't fight us. You'll find the community is full of love.'

'We're only here because you kidnapped us,' Nicole snapped. 'Don't pretend it's anything different.'

'You're exactly where the Lord intends you to be. He delivered you to us.'

'How do you figure that?'

'Because you were so easy to find. How else do you think *we* found you before the rest of the world did? God showed us the way.'

Nicole was momentarily silent.

'Did you find us through Gail?' she asked.

'Gail?'

'Did she tip you off?'

'We found you because of the video you posted.'

'Well, that's impossible,' she shot back, 'because we

164

didn't post it.'

'It was uploaded from your house.'

'It was *shot* at our house, but then whoever did it—'

Nicole stopped dead. Simon saw her physically deflate before his eyes, as though the breath had been sucked out of her. She sat on the futon pulling Billy tighter to her.

'You're upset because this is news to you,' he said. 'Don't be. It was God's will alone that led us to discover you. And it's God's will that we brought you here.'

Nicole lay down and turned away. She pressed her face into the futon and sobbed. Simon watched over her for a moment, wanting to respond, but there was no guessing what had upset her so much. Her apparent tragedy had been his opportunity. It was the beacon that had led him to her. In time, God would show her that she and the baby were exactly where they were supposed to be.

Without a word, he slipped out of the hut and left Nicole to her grief.

***

Adele sat by the pond and watched as the brothers and sisters returned from the prayer hall, still ecstatic from meeting the Baby Jesus. She knew it wouldn't be long now before Simon came looking for her. Her instinct was to take off, to seek solace in the bush, but she needed answers, so she knew she had to face him.

Soon she saw him, ambling along the path towards the mess hall. He caught sight of her and stopped. She could tell he was weighing up what to do next—probably trying to calm his rage.

Finally, he abandoned his destination and joined her. They sat together in silence for a moment.

'You took off,' he said at last.

Adele sighed and looked at her feet.

'Adele?' he pressed, 'where did you go?'

'I didn't leave the compound. You'll be happy to hear that.'

'Hallelujah.'

Simon's face twitched, like he was tramping down a surging tide of emotion.

Adele took a breath and gathered all her courage. 'It's like you dropped him at my feet like a dead bird.'

Simon gaped.

'Isn't that what cats do when they bring in a prize from the bush?'

Simon searched the heavens. 'You are the hardest person on earth to please, aren't you.' Adele braced for what was coming. 'I deliver this community the greatest miracle in history and what do you compare it to?'

'You told me you'd deliver me the most profound act of love remember? Is this what you meant?'

Simon snorted. 'I have brought Christ to the compound!'

'You kidnapped them.'

'God led us to them.'

'Did you snatch them at gunpoint?'

'Adele, you were there when we saw that video pop up. Can you honestly say that our whole trip to Garnerville—the way that video happened to appear at that very moment—was a coincidence? Can you?' Adele turned away. 'You *saw* it. It was a sign. That was God pointing our way to the child. Am I right?' Adele remained still. 'Am I right?'

Adele nodded.

'So if that was a sign from God,' he went on, 'then it was our duty to follow it and bring him here. I'm only following the path that God has laid out before me.'

'Then why do I feel that it's wrong?'

'Because you're still resisting me. You've been searching for Christ for years, and finally I have brought him to you. Stop being afraid.' Simon took her in his arms. 'The time has come for you to release your fear and truly devote yourself to me.'

***

Hours had passed since Tim had seen his family. He lay on a dirty mattress and weighed up all his options. Should he wait until dark and hunt out an escape, or should he plan an attack? Maybe he could steal a car and go for help.

But any option he came up with was thwarted by his fear of how fanatical this group was. Would they answer any attempt to rescue Billy with a firefight and wind up killing them all?

By sundown all Tim's planning had come to nothing. He craved some momentum, so he sat up and demanded to see Nicole and Billy.

Charlie—who had been instructed to guard him—was sitting cross-legged in the doorway. He looked up from his Bible and regarded Tim suspiciously.

'What for?'

'She's my wife. I want to see her.'

'Can't do it.'

Tim began to boil. 'Fuck you,' he grunted and headed for the door.

Charlie stood, blocking his path. 'Simon told me to keep you here. And that's what I'm gonna do.'

'Go and tell Simon I want to see my wife.'

'No.'

Tim's instinct was to throw a punch, but he could see Charlie was waiting for that. Maybe even hoping for it.

So he backed down and sat on the mattress.

It was then Tim realised what he should have done hours ago. The hut was made of bark. The walls were paper-thin in places. The only thing keeping him inside was his own perception that he was imprisoned. Charlie wasn't armed, so when he eventually got caught all he risked was a beating, and he was happy to risk that if it meant sending Simon a message.

He scanned the walls for the most vulnerable place to make an escape. Slowly, he drew himself up off the floor, then threw himself at the bark and crashed through it.

Tim had no idea which way to go to find Nicole. He chose a direction and ran. He could hear Charlie behind him bawling for him to stop.

He raced past bewildered members of the compound, flashing by hut after hut, past vegetable gardens and then a pond.

Soon he found himself on a track that led out of the main part of the community and into the bush, but Charlie was on him now, tracking him closely. He dived forward and pushed Tim into the dirt. Then he was on top of him, an elbow at his throat, panting bad breath into his face.

'Bad idea,' he croaked. 'Very fucking bad idea.'

'I want to see Nicole.'

'Didn't you understand when Simon said everything would be sweet if you cooperated? You want to get yourself killed?'

Charlie took Tim's shirt in his two big fists.

'Now, when I let you up, you're going to behave, you understand?'

'No. You're going to take me to see Simon.'

'Or what?'

'Or it's going to be a long night between us.'

Charlie's size suggested automatic compliance. Being challenged seemed extremely confusing for him. He dragged Tim to his feet and eyed him menacingly.

'Let's go,' Tim said.

Darkness had settled around the compound, and the sweet smell of cooking meant it was mealtime. People were congregating. Charlie marched Tim past inquisitive eyes and towards Simon's hut. When they arrived, Simon was inside with three women. They were talking quietly, lying across an enormous bed on the floor.

Charlie pushed Tim into the hut.

Simon seemed bewildered. 'What's this?'

Charlie shrugged irritably.

Tim took in the relative opulence of the hut: the giant futon, the walls draped with colourful fabrics, the candles atop beaten metal stands, and the shelves laden with books. It had all the comfort of a genie bottle.

'Charlie and I have a problem,' Tim said. 'I want to see Nicole and Billy, and he tells me you won't allow it.'

Simon smiled a thin smile. 'I wanted you to get settled first,' he said. 'You can see them whenever you like.'

'Then I'd like to see them now.'

'I'll take you over there myself if you like.' Tim waited for the catch. 'Look, I want you to feel at home here. This is not a prison. It's a community of worship. The fences are for keeping people out, not keeping us in. Isn't that right, girls?' The girls nodded their agreement. 'Very soon you'll feel completely at home here. You'll get to know the way we live. The rules. I want you to feel that you can go where you like, see who you like, whenever you like.'

'As long as it's inside the fence.'

'Inside the fence, inside curfew. They're simple rules.' He turned to one of the girls. 'They've been known to be broken, but you won't do that. We have an understanding, right?'

Tim understood the menace beneath the words.

Simon headed for the door. 'Shall we go?'

The compound was transformed at night. There was a hushed romance about the place. When the heat of the day lifted, the evening brought people out, strolling together, arm in arm.

When they reached Nicole's hut, Simon stopped and leaned into Tim.

'Just so there's no misunderstanding. Don't fuck with me. I meant it when I said it's only Baby Jesus I'm interested in.'

Tim got it. He could see where the showman began and ended with Simon.

'Stay here,' Simon said. 'I'll let her know you're coming in.'

Tim wasn't thrilled to wait to see his own wife, but at least if he cooperated he'd be able to hold her in his arms again.

Simon disappeared inside, but after only a few moments he reappeared.

'She doesn't want to see you.'

Tim was stunned.

'Bullshit. Why wouldn't she want to see me?'

'I don't know. She's upset. She said to tell you to go away.'

Tim pushed past Simon and entered the hut. Nicole was on the bed with Billy. He could tell she'd been crying. A twist of fear ran through him.

'Honey. What is it?'

Nicole didn't look at him. 'Go away,' she muttered.

Tim moved closer.

'Has something happened?'

'Leave me alone. I don't want to see you.'

There was fury in her voice. Tim was shaken. How could she possibly be so angry with him? He went to the bed and rested a hand on her back, but she shrugged it off.

'Hon...' he faltered. 'Please, just tell me what's up.'

Nicole rolled towards him, eyes blazing.

'We're only here because of you. They only found us because of your fucking video!'

Tim recoiled.

'What have they told you?' he stammered.

'They traced the video to our house. That's how they found us.'

In an instant, Tim's shock betrayed his guilt, and it was writ large across his face, as if his past infidelity was now laid bare. All the lies and cover-ups played through his mind, turning him sick with shame.

Because no words would come, he reached out again, but as he did Nicole batted his hand away viciously.

'Get out,' she yelled. 'Get out!'

She rolled away from him and sobbed. Tim was frozen. There was no explanation he could think of to bring her back. No apology large enough to match her rage. His only option was to leave her to burn it out and return when the embers had cooled.

He rose from the bed and headed outside. Simon followed. Tim barely knew he was there. They walked in silence back towards the mess hut.

'You're probably hungry,' Simon said.

For the first time, Tim observed a note of genuine empathy.

'What?'

'It's mealtime. Are you hungry?'

Tim shook his head absently. 'I just want to go back to my hut.'

'Then you're free to go there if you want. Charlie will

join you in a minute.'

For an hour, Tim tried to calm the thoughts in his head. He kept assuring himself that in time, everything would be all right. Nicole would forgive him. He only had to remain strong and be there for her when she chose to.

At around 9.00 pm, minutes from curfew, Charlie looked up at Tim.

'Hey,' he said brightly, 'come with me.'

'Where?'

'I want to show you something.'

Tim didn't move.

'C'mon. I bet you've never seen anything like it.' Charlie went to the door of the hut, grinning. 'Coming?'

Reluctantly, Tim rolled off his bed and followed.

Charlie led him through the darkened compound, past huts illuminated from within by candles and kerosene lamps. Hushed conversations spilled from inside.

Charlie picked his way along the path with routine familiarity until they reached Simon's hut, which also glowed from within.

Charlie crept around the side, signalling for Tim to follow. When they reached the rear, Charlie peeled back a piece of fabric that was draped across a window and nudged Tim to take a look.

Inside lay five naked women. The warmth of the candlelight gave their skin a delicate luster. Simon was on top of one, making love to her very slowly. Another, lying beside them, was kissing him deeply. Two more knelt alongside him and gently stroked his back with their hands, rubbing him with oil, their long hair falling across him. Another lay beside them, watching, waiting for him.

Soon, Simon rolled off the first girl and moved

towards the next. The girls reached for him, dragging him delicately into them, but he chose the girl who had been waiting patiently and entered her. She groaned softly. The others took up new positions, folding themselves into him, touching his skin and kissing him.

Tim had never seen anything so erotic. His heart beat faster, and a rush of what felt like pure adrenalin went straight to his groin. He could feel himself getting hard. The instinct to look away became lost in a fog of surging desire, and the harder he got the more he wanted to be inside that hut.

'Not bad, huh?' Charlie chuckled crudely. Tim glanced quickly back to him, broken from the moment.

Charlie winked and headed off into the darkness.

Tim took one last look at the picture inside the window before he followed. His heart was racing, and he could feel his body trembling. Where had these people brought him? For a terrible moment, Tim had absolutely no idea which way was up.

19

Twenty-four hour news channels were showing the cul-de-sac, awash with press. Media vans and television crews had turned the street into a kind of post-apocalyptic parking lot. Bored reporters lay on their backs in the sun or played hacky-sack as they waited for something—anything—to turn up. Garry had seen enough. He flicked off the TV.

It was no different to the circus that had assembled outside his own house. Reporters from all over the world were clamoring for scraps of what had become the biggest story on the planet, and this was their ground zero.

In the family's absence, Billy's identity had been revealed, and as it turned out it was Clare who'd blown the whistle.

After he'd salvaged her from the cancer ward, Garry had brought Clare home and put her to bed, thinking a nap would go some way to fixing her. But while he was distracted by the call from Tim—who was hatching a plan to escape from the Romans—Clare picked up the phone and called the local radio station and asked to speak on the talkback line. Billy's identity hadn't gone public yet. All anyone knew about him was the video that had gone viral, so you'd imagine a caller willing to confess their relationship to the child would stop traffic. But when Clare announced on air that she was the Godchild's grandmother, the talk-back host could scarcely believe his luck.

'That's fascinating,' he chirped. 'Budda's grandmother happens to be a pal of mine. I should hook you two up.'

'This isn't a joke,' Clare said. 'The baby is real. He healed me.'

'From a hangover?'

'Multiple sclerosis.'

'Sounds nasty. Does he have a cure for snoring? My wife'd be thrilled.'

'You're not taking this seriously.'

'Oh, I am, believe me. Stay on the line there, Clare, and we'll send round those nice men in the white coats.'

Clare had done her best to sound credible, but it was pointless. Too many fakes had already been on the airwaves before her.

Moments after she'd hung up, the phone rang. Garry took the call. It was a friend who'd heard the whole thing and was terrified it might be the same Clare Sharp that she knew.

'It can't have been *my* Clare,' Garry said, 'she's asleep in the bedroom.'

'Some crackpot just rang the radio station claiming to be her. She said her grandchild healed her multiple sclerosis and that he was the child of God.'

Garry's heart raced. Who could make that up?

He closed off the call with the promise to investigate.

Clare was sitting up in bed, sobbing.

'What have you done?' he said.

Clare buried her head into his chest, and he gently prised the story out of her. She confessed to calling the radio station and to sounding like a complete lunatic. She was so fragile that Garry's anger was quickly extinguished. If she'd come off as bonkers then at least their secret may still be safe. Maybe she hadn't done as much damage as he feared.

When Clare was settled again, he tried calling Nicole. He knew they'd have already left for Perth, but they'd need to know what Clare had done in case it blew up in their faces.

His call went straight to voicemail.

He tried Tim's phone, with the same result.

Garry spent the rest of the day waiting for the fallout to hit, but it never did. Strangely, the world seemed to have left them in peace.

Clare's mood settled, and by 9.00 pm they were both fast asleep.

In the morning they woke to the radio news trumpeting that the Church had confirmed they'd found the Second Coming. Garry was stunned. Billy hadn't been identified yet, but the world would be impatient for a name. He tried Nicole's phone again, but there was still no answer.

Not long after lunch, Garry looked up to see a news van scream to a halt outside the house. A news crew jumped out like they were navigating a war zone.

Garry froze. Finally, someone had joined the dots.

He knew Clare was way too unpredictable to let them get anywhere near her, so he raced out the front door to try and head them off.

A female journalist had a mic at the ready as she marched towards him up the driveway; a cameraman scrambled along behind her.

'Mr Sharp, your wife contacted a radio station yesterday claiming to be the God-child's grandmother. Is this true?'

Garry shoved his hands in front of the camera.

'Can you please turn that thing off. I'm not going to talk on camera.'

'Mr Sharp, your wife claimed—'

'I said I'm not going to talk about this. Now if you'll please get off my—'

'The world is searching for this child, Mr Sharp. Do you know where he is?'

Garry could see she wasn't going to back off. He was about to make for the safety of the front door when she lost all interest in him, pushed past him, and headed for the house.

Garry turned to see Clare rushing down the driveway towards them.

'This was me!' she cried, holding up a photograph. 'This was taken three weeks ago.'

The cameraman zoomed in on the cripple in the photograph, panning out to contrast it with Clare's now perfectly upright stature.

Garry tried to push the crew away, but they had the smell of blood in their nostrils.

'My daughter lives in Melbourne,' Clare went on. 'She's driving here with the baby as we speak. He will heal all who need healing, care for all who need caring—'

Garry broke through the crew and dragged Clare back up the driveway to the front door. He slammed it behind them.

'You're angry with me, I know,' she said.

'Angry?' he bawled. 'Why did you do that?'

Clare buried her head in her hands. 'I had to. It

simply had to be done.'

'Well, what now? How do we keep Nicole and the baby safe?'

Clare looked up to him. Even in her despair there was strength in her.

'We'll control it,' she said evenly.

'It's too late for that now, Clare.'

'He will save us all. You wait. That's his destiny.'

Clare was no longer talking about her grandchild; she was describing an event. In her narrative, Billy wasn't even a baby anymore; he was 'the saviour'.

Garry's head throbbed. He left her hunched on the floor and dialled Nicole's number again. The call went through to her voicemail.

'Darling. I wish you'd pick up,' he said. 'Something's happened here. It's not safe for you to come anymore. The media have your identity now, and they'll be waiting for you. Call me and we'll work out what you can do.'

Garry hung up. There was nothing more he could do.

20

Father Jim ached to get out of the car and stretch, but nothing could make him move. His entire body was numb—like a limb that had been slept on.

Next to him, Gail sat silent, petulant. The yellow and maroon of the motel's neon sign beat on her face.

Father Jim refused to look at her.

'There's no point giving me the silent treatment,' she said. 'We're alive aren't we?'

Gail was an impossible woman. A woman with an iron will, which constantly tested Father Jim's priestly disposition. Maybe in ten minutes he would calm down enough to speak to her again, but for now he didn't dare open his mouth.

'You're just unused to company,' she went on. 'You need to learn to work in a team.'

This almost lit the powder keg that was Father Jim's fizzing brain.

They'd left for Garnerville in such a hurry that the

Father had had no chance to change into civilian clothes and was therefore stuck in his priestly weeds for the rest of the trip. He hadn't even packed a toothbrush. Gail had insisted they were too far behind the kidnappers to give them any more of a head start, so any provisions would have to be picked up on the way. But when they'd stopped for those said provisions, Gail had returned with two chocolate bars and a map of the north. She'd tossed him the chocolate and hit the road, commanding him to plot their course for Garnerville.

Father Jim spread the map across the passenger side of the car like he was wrestling an angry, deep-sea creature. Gail swatted it out of her way and swerved hair-raisingly onto the wrong side of the road.

When they finally made it onto the freeway north, Father Jim discovered the kind of driver Gail was. One moment it was like she'd just sprung out of the blocks at Monaco, then the next she'd slow to a snail's pace so that any driver following would be forced to tailgate precariously. She'd roar past a car, only to slow down again once she'd passed them. Victims of this incomprehensible behaviour would blast their horns in fury, but Gail was oblivious.

As they buzzed north into the dusk, through smaller and smaller towns, Father Jim could see Gail was becoming increasingly exhausted.

'I think it may be a good idea to stop and rest for a while,' he suggested.

This made Gail grip the wheel even tighter.

'We need to get to Garnerville,' she insisted.

'You look tired.'

'Well, I'm not.'

'Well, I think you are.'

'I'm not, I'm not, I'm not,' she barked.

Father Jim backed off and intensified his focus on the

road ahead.

'What are we going to do when we get there?' he asked.

'We're going to find Adele. When we find Adele we'll find who took Billy.'

'How can you be so sure of that?'

'I can't. But it's our only hope. If we can find the community she mentioned then maybe they can help us find who took him. Maybe they know. Maybe *they* took him.'

'What if they object to us nosing around?'

Gail shrugged. 'We have to take it as it comes. If we need to go to the police then that's what we'll do, but to start with it's best for the Blakes if we protect their identities.'

'Even if it gets us killed?'

Gail turned to Father Jim, her eyes steely. 'I am prepared to do whatever it takes.'

Father Jim understood at that moment that he was too. Like Gail, he would risk everything for Billy.

Gail turned back to the road, and the little car buzzed on in silence.

***

As night closed in around them, Father Jim noticed the car beginning to swerve dangerously onto the wrong side of the road. He glanced over to find that Gail had nodded off completely.

'Gail!'

She looked up with a start and wrenched at the wheel. But her panicked corrections only sent it further onto the wrong side of the road. Just then, two blinding headlights appeared in front of them. Convinced Gail had lost control, Father Jim put both hands onto the wheel and dragged. The car jerked onto the right side of the road again, and the truck roared past, missing them by a coat of paint.

Now they were in freefall. The car hit the shoulder of the highway, and the rear spun out sending them sideways towards a ditch. They could only hold their breath and pray they would stop before they completely left the road. Finally, the tyres bit into the siding, and they slid to a stop inches from an embankment steep enough to send the car tumbling end to end.

They sat in silence, Father Jim's heart pumping.

Without a word, Gail collected herself and turned the car back onto the road.

'I think it would be wise to stop for the night,' Father Jim said evenly.

'We need to get to Garnerville.'

'You nodded off. Do you want to kill us both?'

'Then you drive.'

'I *can't* drive.'

'Who on earth doesn't drive!'

'I don't.'

'You're not much good then, are you?'

'Mary, Joseph, and Jesus!'

Gail withdrew.

When the outskirts of the next town appeared, Father Jim became restless.

'There's bound to be somewhere to stay here,' he snapped.

As they rounded a bend, a motel loomed before them, and Gail finally succumbed to her exhaustion, turned off the highway, and into the motel car park.

***

There was still plenty of road to come before they hit

Garnerville. After an early start, Gail and Father Jim drove hard all through the next day. When the outskirts of the town finally appeared before them, Father Jim opened his throat and praised the Lord.

Gail drove to the hotel in the centre of town. Adele had written in her blog that this was where she was staying overnight all those weeks ago, so it followed that someone there might know her.

Between her shaved head and his priestly weeds, Gail and Father Jim managed to turn every scruffy head in the bar as they entered. They made their way along the sticky carpet to an office where a man in his fifties emerged from behind the door.

'Can I help youse?' he said, looking puzzled.

'Hello,' Gail said, smiling shyly. 'My name's Angela White. This is Father Duncan. We're looking for my niece. She's been missing for some time, and we believe she's staying in the area.

'She got a name, Mother Bird?'

'Adele Blanche.'

The man laughed. 'Adele? She's in here all the time.'

Gail resisted an impulse to pump the air.

'What's this all about?' the man said. 'I'm sorry … I'm Eddie.' He reached across the counter and shook Gail's hand. Then he took Father Jim's.

'I'm afraid there's been a death in the family,' Gail said. 'We've come to bring her home for the funeral.' She leaned in closer. 'It's complicated. She hasn't replied to any correspondence for a very long time. I've brought Father Duncan along to help convince her to come home. He's our family priest.'

'Sorry to hear that, luv,' Eddie said. 'I can't tell you when she'll be in next. It's usually once or twice a week, and I never know when.'

'Do you know where she's staying then?' Gail

pressed.

Eddie shook his head gravely. 'She's out of town somewhere. In some kinda hippy commune. They keep well to themselves. Adele told me once she was breaking the rules even coming into town.'

Gail's heart sank.

'Oh, that really is a terrible shame. The funeral is set for early next week. Would anyone else know where the commune is?'

"fraid not. They're pretty hush-hush. All I can tell you is that it's somewhere south of here, off the highway. Not much help am I?'

Gail gave him a warm smile.

'Oh, you've been an enormous help.'

'What if we took a drive down that way,' Father Jim broke in. 'Would we find them?'

Eddie rubbed his stubble, scanning the countryside in his head.

'Could do. Can't say anyone has had any interest in looking until now. There can't be that many roads into the country down that way. If you took a drive up some of those dirt tracks off the highway you might run into them.'

'Then we'll set off first thing in the morning,' Gail said. 'You don't happen to have a room for the night do you?'

'Two,' Father Jim said.

***

After a good night's sleep, Gail and Father Jim were ripe for an adventure. They took the highway south, taking in all the picturesque country they'd missed in the dusk on the way up. They wound through meadow-covered hills, which rolled all the way down to the coast. They passed through towering old-growth forest so thick it filtered the glorious morning sunshine into twilight.

Half an hour into their trip they began searching for a track off the highway. The coast stretched out to their left, so the turn off for the commune had to be to the right. Forty minutes from Garnerville, Gail spotted a small driveway heading into the bush. She left the road and started up the rocky track.

They bumped and scraped along the track for twenty minutes before it came to a dead end at a derelict, old barn. Beyond it there was only an overgrown meadow and a dry creek bed.

'Back to the drawing board,' Father Jim said.

Gail returned to the highway and kept heading south. The next turn-off led them to a chicken farm. The one after that quickly turned into a winding goat track, which led off into the bush. But the next time they turned off the highway, they found themselves on what seemed to be a driveway. It was broken up, but without question it had been used recently. This had to be the way to the community.

After about half an hour on the track, a towering perimeter fence came into view. Gail slowed the car; the purr of the motor suddenly seemed very conspicuous in the isolated countryside.

As they neared the gate, people began to congregate. They stared out through the fence like this was the first car they'd ever seen.

Gail pulled to a stop.

'What now?' Father Jim said.

'I don't know. Get out and talk to them I suppose.'

It was hard to tell if they were hostile or not. Gail opened her door.

'Come on,' she said.

Father Jim climbed out of the car, and the sight of his

priest's robes drew gasps from the crowd. One of them peeled away from the fence and ran back into the community.

Father Jim turned to Gail.

'Is this really such a good idea?'

A car started up somewhere inside the compound. Then two men appeared at the fence holding rifles. One unlocked the gate.

Gail's eyes landed on the guns. She threw open the driver's door and clambered in.

'Get in!' she barked. 'Get in!'

Father Jim needed no convincing. He was barely in his seat before Gail planted her foot, and the car roared.

In the rear-view mirror, Gail saw the huge gates swing open. Moments later, an SUV hit the track, coming after them at speed. The driver was hunched over the wheel, and two others were crouched forward, shouting and pointing.

Gail's hands were welded to the steering wheel as she bounced down the rocky track at hair-raising speed.

Within moments, the SUV was on top of them, pushing hard at their rear bumper.

Gail's eyes were set on the track ahead of them. She was only just managing to stay in control as she thrashed their car onwards.

Dust exploded around them. Coins, trash, reading glasses tumbled around the cabin.

Gail hit a bend too fast, and the car lost its footing. The rear slid sideways, and Gail instinctively hit the brakes. It was the wrong choice. The car lurched and swung wide, spinning off the track and into a grassy siding that offered no traction at all. Suddenly it was like they were sliding on ice. The world spun around them.

Ahead, at the far end of the meadow, an embankment led down to a dry creek bed. The car rocketed helplessly towards it. They hit the embankment and plummeted downwards. The car smashed into the stones at the bottom, and Father Jim went crashing through the windshield and into the dirt.

An airbag slammed Gail back into her seat.

The SUV roared to a stop at the top of the embankment. Within moments, one of the men had scrambled down into the creek bed and was ripping Gail's door open and dragging her out. She screamed and fought with her fists, but she was no match for him.

Two other men stood over Father Jim, who was lying, twisted on the river pebbles. One of them held a gun in one hand and nudged at him with his foot.

Father Jim clutched at his chest, gasping for breath.

A man who seemed to be in charge sniggered. 'The old bastard's having a heart attack.'

The priest wore the confused look of a dying animal.

'He doesn't have long,' the man added.

He placed his boot onto Father Jim's throat and pressed down.

Father Jim cried out for God to help him—to save him—but all he could manage was a muffled grunt.

Soon, his struggling stopped, and he lay motionless on the stones.

'Get rid of him,' the man said. 'I'll take the woman up to the compound. Make sure the car disappears.'

Gail was standing by the car, crying out for Father Jim. The man who'd killed him approached and thumped the bonnet of the car next to her.

'Shut the fuck up!' he roared. 'He was dead when he hit the ditch.'

'No!' Gail cried.

He took her by the arm and marched her over to where the SUV was idling.

'You've got a lot of explaining to do,' he said coldly.

21

If there was one thing Alejandro had taught Gail, it was that information is power. As she was being marched through the compound towards the leader's hut, this was the one mantra she kept repeating in her head. The man couldn't know she'd seen him kill Father Jim; he was too busy killing him. And he couldn't know if she had any back up arriving.

She decided early that his aggression had to have been be inspired by the sight of Father Jim's clerical clothing. If they did have Billy, this suggested they thought the Church was coming after them and that they had to neutralise that threat—fast. What she couldn't work out was why they hadn't killed her too. Perhaps it was simply to get information, and if that's what they were after then it was information that would save her now.

There was no time to mourn Father Jim. The horror of watching him die so brutally had to stay sequestered inside her for another time while she planned a strategy to stay alive.

First she had to assess what kind of planet she'd landed on. The onlookers seemed bewildered and passive, not nearly as brutish as the welcoming committee. They looked the way you'd imagine the members of a religious community should look: meek and docile. These were the people she needed to find a way to reach out to.

The youngest of the thugs shoved her inside a hut. He marched her to the bed and sat her down.

The leader followed them in and prowled for a moment.

'What are you doing here?' he said.

Gail knew to answer only the question she wanted to answer, not the question she was asked.

'Please calm down,' she said. 'You think I've come here to harm you, but I haven't. I'm told you're doing amazing work.'

The man seemed startled.

'Who told you that?'

'I'm a religious person. Word spreads.'

'Why was the priest with you? What did he want?'

'He's a religious person too.'

The man stopped pacing.

'What have you heard about us?'

'That this is a paradise where you come to worship God in peace. So far that isn't my experience.'

'Why *specifically* do you say it's a paradise? What have you heard?'

Gail shrugged.

'What's your name?'

'Margaret. I've come here to see the work you do. To find peace and love. Please, I don't know what I've done to make you so upset.' Gail could see that appealing to his vanity had made a useful dent in his aggression. 'You may not know this,' she went on, 'but in the fringes, this place is spoken of as a kind of Shangri-la.'

'Are you alone? 'the man asked.

'What do you mean?'

'Did anyone come with you?'

'I came with the priest.'

'Besides the priest.'

'No.'

'Have you told anyone where you are?'

'No.'

The man knelt in front of her and gave her a hard look.

'Listen,' he said, lowering his voice. 'If I hear any vehicles coming up that track looking for you, you will be sorry you lied to me, do you understand?'

Gail held his eye, refusing to show him any fear.

'You have my word that I came here alone.'

The man got up and turned to the younger one.

'Keep an eye on her,' he said and charged out of the hut.

Gail could hear him pushing his way through the gathered crowd outside, fending off questions as he went.

The younger man seemed bewildered by the other man's sudden exit, and he looked as relieved as she was to have him gone. Gail pounced on the opportunity to bond with this slightly nervous looking youth.

'What's your name?'

'Duck.'

Gail smiled kindly.

'That's not a name that's an animal. What's your *name.*'

Duck looked embarrassed.

'Jack Waddel.'

190

Gail's smile grew.

'Let me guess, Duck for short.'

He nodded.

'What about him?'

'That's Simon.'

'What's he going to do with me?'

Gail slipped this in so fast that Duck had no time to formulate a lie.

'If he's going to present you to the community I don't think anything bad will happen to you.'

'Has he done bad things to others?'

'No!' Duck said quickly, defending Simon. 'No, I didn't mean it like that.'

'How else could you mean it?'

'It's just … well, you saw how mad he was. When I first came here I screwed up all the time. When I first went on the raids. Simon uses the knuckle to sharpen you up, that's all.'

'Raids?'

Duck dropped his head.

'Are the raids how you bring people to the community?'

Duck chuckled. 'No, it's how we get the food. Drive south and hit the stores.'

Duck mimed waving a gun around, and Gail played along, putting up her hands like she was being held at gunpoint.

'Are you here of your own accord, Jack?'

Her grandmother's tone seemed to woo him. He sat on the bed next to her.

'I love it here. If I ever set foot outside this compound I'd be back to me old ways.' He mimed sliding a needle into his arm. 'Simon saved me.'

'Simon?'

'He's our saviour.'

'What if someone came to shut you down?'

'I wouldn't let that happen. I'd kill for him.'

Gail could now see what she had on her hands: a puppy with teeth and claws trained to execute violence when needed. This was her insurance policy. Her goal now was to groom him to never lay a finger on her.

But before she'd got the job entirely done, Simon appeared in the doorway. It caught Duck off guard, and he leapt off the bed.

'Everything all right?' Simon asked.

Duck nodded unconvincingly.

Simon turned to Gail. 'The brothers and sisters are curious about you, so I'm going to present you to them in the prayer hall. Not a word about the accident, understand? You're a visitor who's come to worship with us.'

'That's what I—'

'We'll see,' Simon interrupted.

***

The path to the prayer hall was crowded. Gail could feel curious eyes on her, and she kept her head low as she walked. But as they intersected another path, Gail looked up and caught a glimpse of Nicole. She was carrying Billy, flanked by a couple of attendants.

Gail tried to duck her glance, but it was too late. Nicole had seen her, and she instinctively called out.

Simon turned to see the recognition between the two women, and it only took him moments to put it all together. Gail saw a fury rise in him.

'You fuckin' come with me,' he snapped, and he took her roughly by the arm. Then he turned to Duck. 'Bring Nicole to my hut right now.'

Simon marched Gail into his hut and threw her onto

the bed. Moments later, Nicole and Billy appeared in the doorway.

'Gail!' she cried and rushed over to her.

'What is this?' Simon growled. 'Margaret—Gail. Who the fuck is she?'

Nicole turned to Simon. 'She was my midwife.'

'What the fuck is she doing here?'

Nicole didn't answer.

'I came to find them,' Gail broke in. 'Nothing more.'

'And how did you do that?' Simon said.

Gail had to be careful. She couldn't implicate Adele. Adele might just turn out to be the ally they'd need to help get them out.

'I followed a dream,' she said hastily.

Simon narrowed his eyes. 'A dream.'

'I dreamt the baby had been kidnapped. So when the family disappeared I knew that's what had happened. I followed my dream, and it led me here.'

Simon began to prowl again. 'Bullshit.'

'I promise.'

'Who else knows you're here?' he snapped.

'No one. I didn't go to the police. I didn't tell anyone. I came by myself.'

Simon marched over and grabbed her by the shoulders. 'You are fucking lying to me!' he screamed. 'I will kill you myself unless you tell me the truth.'

Gail recoiled. Simon was moments away from tearing her apart. His eyes were blazing, and she could feel his fingers sinking into her flesh.

Just as it seemed like his next move would be to wrap his hands around her throat, Billy began to cry. The sound of it filled the hut and stopped everyone dead. Simon looked like he'd been punched. An expression of shock crossed his face, and his rage seemed instantly diffused.

He turned to Billy, suddenly calm. As if his job was done, Billy stopped crying and snuggled back into Nicole's embrace.

Simon now appeared completely undone. His eyes were distant, like he was processing something way beyond himself, like a massive insight had taken hold. Without another word, he released Gail and left the hut.

Duck fidgeted like an insect in a bottle.

Gail rounded on him. 'You go too,' she said.

He slunk away, and the women fell into each other's arms.

'Oh, God, are you all right?' Gail asked.

'We're fine,' Nicole said. 'We're fine.'

'And Tim?'

Nicole flinched. 'He's here.'

'Where?'

'I don't know.'

'Won't they let you see him?'

'It's complicated.'

'How?'

Nicole sighed. 'Tim was the reason they found us,' she said softly. 'They traced the YouTube clip of Billy to our house. Tim was the one who posted it.'

Gail squeezed her tighter. 'Oh, my darling. Of course he was.'

Nicole drew away. 'You knew?'

'Who else could it possibly have been?'

Nicole turned her back. 'We have to get out of here.'

'And we will. We just need to figure this mob out first.'

Gail put a hand on Nicole's shoulder, but Nicole pulled away. For a moment Gail was bewildered. Hadn't she risked her life to come here and save her? Hadn't she proved her loyalty?

'Nicole?'

'I feel bruised,' she said. 'Everyone wants to get their hands on him. On us. I'm pretty low on trust right now.'

***

When Simon reappeared in the doorway he was drenched from head to toe, and his hair was full of sand. His fury had vanished.

'Gail?' he said softly. 'I'd like to present you to the community now.'

Gail and Nicole shared a wary glance. What was he up to? Knowing better than to disobey him, they followed him into the prayer hall.

The community had already gathered, and Simon led them to the pulpit.

'My hearts,' he cried. 'We have a new sister in our community. Her name is Gail, and she delivered Baby Jesus into the world. She was blessed by this act, as we are blessed to have him now. We must show her kindness because she has suffered a great loss. Her travelling companion sadly passed away in a car accident this morning.'

Nicole turned to Gail with dread. 'Father Jim?' she whispered.

Gail's stoic exterior crumbled, and Nicole drew her near.

Simon's open-hearted welcome rolled on, but it only made Gail feel like more of a prisoner. To her, it was nothing more than a tender locking of the gates—a farewell to the outside world for as long as Simon saw fit.

She glanced around the crowd, seeking out a single pair of eyes that might understand this, but she could find only adoring glances anchored to their guru.

Then she noticed Tim edge into the back of the hall.

She watched his face fall as he caught sight of her. She saw Nicole catch a glimpse of him too and turn away.

Gail shivered. Nicole needed someone with strength at her side through all of this, and Tim had proved himself spectacularly unworthy. From now on, *she* would be the one to protect Nicole and Billy. This was her second chance at a rescue, and she swore a silent prayer to her Cielo that nothing on earth would stop her from succeeding this time.

22

Tim had given Nicole the night to recover before he had returned to mend things. It had been a night spent listening to the secret noises of the bush and tracking the course of the moon through the gaps in the hut's bark roof. On the rare occasion that he nodded off, his dreams lay waiting for him. One fragment in particular monstered him. He was back in the white apartment by the river, searching for Nicole. He roamed the empty rooms, finding nothing but memories. Eventually, he found himself at the window overlooking the river. In the dark of the slow current he caught a glimpse of Nicole floating face down in the water. This woke him with a start; the long night was determined to offer him no peace either sleeping or awake. Gradually, he put himself back together, and by the time the dawn came to draw the community out of its huts, Tim had reassembled himself sufficiently to take his remorse before Nicole one more time.

Charlie was no longer guarding him, so he dressed and headed out along the track.

When he arrived in the doorway of Nicole's hut, she was giving Billy his morning feed. She didn't notice him standing there at first, so he took the opportunity to watch over them silently. It was a painful picture of beauty.

After a moment, Nicole looked up. Her peaceful expression quickly became guarded.

Tim's heart sank. He'd never seen her look at him this way.

'How long have you been standing there?' she said flatly.

'Not long. A while.'

Nicole turned away again.

'Nic, I've been awake all night. I can't believe what I've done, I'm so sorry. It was stupid.' Tears welled. The apology he'd constructed over the course of the night sounded superficial and hopelessly inadequate now. 'You have to believe me, I had no idea anyone could possibly trace that video.'

Nicole exhaled. 'You lied to me.'

'I was afraid.'

'You blamed our friends. It's one thing to betray *us* but to accuse our friends, when all along—'

'I'll make it up to them. To you.'

'You sat with me and comforted me and told me we should cut them out of our lives.'

Tim had no explanation for this, only that the deeper he ensnared himself into the lie, the further it was to climb back out from it.

'You were so convincing. If you can look me in the eye and lie to me so effortlessly what else are you capable of?'

The haunting image the drowsy-eyed girl opened up

before him, deep and dark. He could feel the shame of it cross his face. Nicole had to have noticed.

'I want you to go.'

'Please, Nic—'

'Just go.'

'Can you forgive me?'

'You don't understand, Tim. It never occurred to me before that I couldn't trust you. It never entered my head.'

Tim searched for something to add—an explanation that would bring her back to him—but nothing came. As if in a dream, he dragged himself from the hut and staggered back through the compound. Nothing felt real. It wasn't possible that Nicole didn't want him.

He changed direction, headed for the scrub at the far side of the pond where a path led into the bush. He crashed through the overgrown branches that did their best to slow his pace. He tore at them, and it felt good to rip something out by its roots.

Eventually the path narrowed, and he found himself enclosed in a thicket far enough from the community to feel truly alone. He sat in the dirt, his hands bleeding and bruised, and he finally let his tears spill.

For the first time since Billy's birth had unleashed its chaos, he allowed the floodgates to open. It felt like he was erupting—pain spewing out of him like bile. Tears cascaded into his lap until he was sick of the sound of his own misery.

When he'd finally had enough and was ready to take his self-loathing elsewhere, he looked up to see Simon leaning against a tree, observing him.

Tim burned with shame that anyone would have observed his sickening self-pity. He shot to his feet and started off without a word.

'Don't go,' Simon said, 'I want to talk to you.'

He sat into the long grass and gestured for Tim to join him.

Tim turned to face him, ready for a confrontation.

'Please. We need to talk,' Simon said.

Tim stood his ground.

Simon shrugged. 'Have you worked out why yet?'

'Why I posted the clip?' Tim snorted. 'Because I'm an idiot.'

Simon chuckled 'No, I didn't mean that. You posted the clip because it was God's will that I should find you. There's no shame in what you did. Nicole will have to realise that eventually or she isn't worth your tears. No, what I meant was, do you know why God chose *you* to bring Baby Jesus into the world?'

'Well, for a start he didn't choose me.'

'Why do you say that?'

'Because it's obvious.'

'Why?'

'Because it was Nicole.'

'Why do you say that?'

'Because she's so fundamentally good.'

'Is she a Christian?' Simon asked.

'What's that got to do with it?'

'Is she?'

'No. Neither of us are.'

'So why would God give His child to a couple who didn't believe in Him?'

Tim smirked. Simon had a point. 'I guess we believe now.'

'So Nicole isn't any more qualified than you are, is she?'

'Can you cut to the chase?' Tim said.

'Look me in the eye and tell me Nicole is a better person than you.'

'That's easy.'

200

'Well, go on.'

Tim met his eye and repeated the statement.

'It's not true, Tim. You're judging yourself harshly because of something you were chosen by God to do. History is littered with heroes like you. You're God's instrument. It's not Nicole who was chosen to bring Baby Jesus into the world; it was you. And then you played your part in bringing him to us. Don't punish yourself for being part of God's plan.'

Simon's logic was so wacky Tim couldn't even manage a response.

'You need to adjust the way you see things,' Simon said. 'You're still seeing life through the prism of the world the way you knew it. But things have fundamentally changed for you. When you first came here I said you would grow to love and understand this place. I encourage you to do that. Why waste time resisting the beauty God is offering you? We live here as He intends us to, without the restrictions normally dictated by the conventional Church. That's the beauty of our way of life. We're the same, you and I. We're instruments of God. I want you to share what I have here. I want you to have what I have. You do understand what I'm saying, don't you?'

Tim did understand. How could he forget that beautiful tangle of bodies he'd witnessed only the night before? The idea of having it for himself crept with delicious dread through his whole body.

Simon stood and threw his arms around Tim.

'Don't look so serious,' he laughed. 'You're acclimatising. I'm only trying to accelerate the process. You'll surrender to it sooner or later, so why waste time?' Simon patted himself on the chest and grinned. 'I want you in here, Tim. And I'm impatient. I want it now.'

201

Tim was simultaneously repelled and drawn to Simon. As hard as it was to admit, Simon had managed to repair some small part of his broken heart. In Simon's world, Tim's betrayal was justifiable, and his words soothed the hammering of his guilt.

'When you're ready, come to me,' Simon said. 'When you want to talk, come to me. You and I will walk together. We'll pray. And soon your heart will be filled with light, and you will be freed from the shackles that weighed so heavily on you in your previous life.'

Simon walked Tim back to the community. They were silent the entire way. Tim kept trying to chase away the sense Simon was making, but it clung to him, hopeful and tempting. It was true that Billy had changed everything. The existence of God was now undeniable. Maybe Simon was right, God *had* brought them there for a reason, but they hadn't yet understood what that reason was. If Tim could understand the culture of the community, then maybe Nicole could as well. Maybe Simon could get through to her the way he had with him. She might see there was God's hand in all this, and maybe then she could forgive him.

Simon deposited Tim back into his hut and left. As Tim lay on the threadbare mattress on the floor, he felt alone once more, and he began to lose touch with the feeling of hope Simon had infused in him. He willed himself to hang onto it, but it drifted away.

At some point he must have nodded off because he was woken by a commotion outside his hut. Footsteps raced along the path towards the perimeter fence. There were shouts. Cars started up. His heart was still so heavy with grief that none of it even tempted him off the mattress. He pictured the scenario as it unfolded around him: the return of the cars, the clank of the giant gates, the hushed mutterings of people as they hurried by.

After what seemed like hours, someone walked by, summoning everyone to the prayer hall. His curiosity got the better of him, so he dragged himself up and followed.

He snuck in behind the crowd, and to his amazement he saw Gail standing at the pulpit, flanked by Nicole and Simon. How was this possible? How on earth had she found them?

Then his focus shifted to Nicole. Their eyes met and she turned away. He saw Gail catch it and bristle, and in an instant he could tell she *knew*. Nicole had told her what he'd done. He saw her huddle closer to Nicole and put an arm around her.

Tim's heart sank deeper. Was this what she'd planned all along? To take his place at Nicole's side?

For the rest of the day and into the next, Tim kept his distance. He spent his time wandering through the compound and sitting alone by the pond. He observed the members of the community as they went about their chores: raking the paths, clipping the shrubs and fixing the roofs.

As he sat by the pond and afternoon turned to dusk, Tim was woken from his thoughts by the sound of approaching footsteps. He glanced up to find Gail standing there.

They stared at one another for a moment.

'You've been sitting there all day,' she said flatly.

Tim nodded, at a loss for what she wanted.

'I want you to understand something, Tim. When you go to her to beg for forgiveness you are only intensifying her pain.'

Fury turned in his guts.

'Fuck off, Gail. This is between Nicole and me.'

'It's not,' she barked. 'I am only here because of you. We're *all* only here because of you. Father Jim is dead because of *you!*

Tim felt like he'd been kicked.

'What?'

'He came with me to find you, and now he's dead. You need to think about that, Tim.'

'But how—'

'That lunatic.' Gail locked onto Tim's eyes like a vice. 'Do everyone a favour and stay away.'

Tim buried his head between his knees. He heard Gail's footsteps stride away from him, and when he looked up again she was gone.

Darkness fell over the pond, bleak and still. Tim wanted to submerge himself under the dirty water and let the weight of it squeeze him into the mud until he was ancient and petrified.

But out of the silence, he heard more footsteps approaching. He looked up to find Simon escorting a young woman towards him. Tim was certain he'd seen her in the hut with Simon.

Simon grinned. 'Need some company?' Tim wanted to scurry away, but Simon headed him off. 'This is Joanne.' He guided her to one side of him and then sat on the other, penning him in. 'Tim feels sad,' Simon said to Joanne.

The girl tilted her head to one side and mocked a sad face. Simon picked up one of Tim's hands, and Joanne took the other. Tim didn't have the strength to pull away. If he was honest, it was comforting.

'Are you sad because you don't like us?' Joanne asked.

Tim twisted a pained smile.

'Tim hasn't accepted he's an instrument of God yet,' Simon butted in. 'He resists it.'

Joanne wore a look of fascination. She sat forward, egging Simon on to explain.

'It was because of Tim that Baby Jesus came here in

the first place,' he said.

Joanne's eyes blazed.

'Oh,' she gasped. 'Oh, well you just can't be sad.' She let go of his hand and threw her arm around his shoulder. 'You've changed my life. My God, I owe you so much.' She gently kissed his cheek, then nuzzled her face into his neck.

Simon cupped the back of Tim's head with his hand and gave it a pat.

'Years ago I was in prison,' Simon said. 'I heard God speak to me. And with that, He put me on the path. A year on, He told me to build this community. And I did. Yesterday he spoke to me again.' Simon glanced at Tim. 'He spoke to me through Baby Jesus.'

'Billy … spoke to you,' Tim said doubtfully.

'Yes he did. It was right when Gail arrived, and I'd lost my head. I was doing the Devil's work, and the train had almost left the tracks. That's when Baby Jesus cried. It split my head wide open, and I heard God inside his cry.'

'What did he say, Simon?' Joanne asked, wide-eyed.

'I heard a thousand things in the same instant. He told me to take hold of myself. To let go of the fear. To embrace love. He told me that I must play my part in His story and never lose sight of that. It was incredible. I took myself to the sea, and I dived in, clothes and all. I washed away all the filth, and I returned as a new man. My eyes are clear now. My path is defined. And Tim? So is yours.'

Joanne was crying. She held onto Tim, sobbing into his shoulder.

Simon's words had reignited the feeling of wellbeing he'd instilled the day before. They were comforting in the extreme, and Joanne's tears on his neck felt erotic and heady.

Tim turned to Joanne and wiped the tears from her face. She smiled at him with such purity it made him swoon.

She reached out and touched his face too.

'Thank you,' she said. 'Thank you for what you have given us.' Then she leaned in and kissed him deeply. It was a kiss desperate with gratitude. A kiss that longed to repay the priceless gift he'd brought her.

Tim was transported. He returned the kiss longingly, drinking in her desire for him, giving her back all of his pain and loneliness. He was way beyond the point of being able to stop himself.

Joanne drew him down into the grass and pulled him on top of her. They pressed themselves together, clawing at each other, straining to hold each other tighter.

For a moment, Tim found his kisses couldn't take Joanne in deeply enough. He needed more of her, and her lips were telling him she needed more of him too.

Joanne pushed him off abruptly and glanced breathlessly at Simon.

'Can he come to the hut with us, please?'

Simon beamed. 'Of course he can.'

Tim sobered. His heart pounded with the alarming prospect of it, but a secret part of him was now fixed on going through with it.

'Let go, Tim,' Simon said, measured, reading his fears. 'This doubt of yours is part of another life. You have a new one now. A life where all this can be embraced. You can have whatever you want.'

These were the words Tim had craved all his life. The pathway to all the things he desired and felt entitled to—always stymied, always not quite within his reach—Simon had now opened up before him.

Joanne kissed him again. She reached under his shirt

and ran her hands over his skin.

'Come on,' she said and helped him up.

***

The hut was already bathed in candlelight when they arrived. Mayling was inside reading a book. Joanne shoved Tim onto the bed and tore his T-shirt off. It was all happening so fast that Tim felt like he was on some kind of drug. Then Joanne was taking off her shirt. She was pushing him onto the bed and rolling her naked body on top of him. Next he was inside her, and they were fucking desperately on the silken sheets. Mayling was naked too and lying next to him, ready. She stroked his cheek and kissed his forehead. Tim felt dreamy and ecstatic—like he was riding an acid trip he could touch and taste.

Simon arrived with two more girls. Tim could sense them undressing and then felt their weight displace the mattress. They touched him too, drew him into them. Soon the four of them were all around him, caressing him, stroking him, and Simon was gone.

Joanne rolled away from him, and Mayling took her place. He could taste a different mouth—lips that were fuller—a tongue that probed deeper. Mayling guided him inside her while another of the girls caressed his chest with her kisses.

Everywhere he looked, everything he touched was soft, warm skin, and it was touching him back, caressing him, wanting him. At any moment he could explode with pleasure, but he fiercely hung on, wanting to have all of them before he was finished.

***

Simon stood outside the hut for a moment listening to the quiet ecstasy unfolding inside. He felt peaceful and happy. Tim had taken a giant step into the heart of the community. Now all there was left to do was to cement his place there.

He strode up the path to Nicole's hut and tapped gently at the door.

'Come with me,' he said softly. Nicole hesitated. Gail rose.

'Not you,' he said firmly.

Nicole passed Billy to Gail and followed Simon. He led her down the track to the rear of his hut where he drew aside the curtain for her. He stood back and gestured for Nicole to look inside.

23

Sanjiv Gupta was accustomed to being recognised. With his commanding dark features and greying stubble, he drew a crowd wherever he went. People recognised him from the cover photos of his books and his appearances on TV talk shows. He was an American institution.

But today was different. Today he was flanked by star-power from a different stratosphere. As he wheeled his titanium hand luggage through the airport concourse, it wasn't Sanjiv the crowds were gaping at, it was his best friend, Sean Teale: movie star, fighter for liberal causes, and champion of the African poor.

Sean was one of those rare individuals in whom all elements of perfection converged. Whole magazine articles were devoted to his ice-blue eyes—how they sparkled with mischief, yet somehow remained kind and sensitive. Even in middle age he was crowned the sexiest man alive, year in, year out.

Hysteria ignited around the men like spot fires. Sanjiv

had already signed two books before they'd made it to the bag check. The first, *Find the God Within,* was his most recent and far and away his best seller. But when a fan thrust the second book he'd ever written, *Five Easy Steps to Enlightenment,* in front of him, Sanjiv was thrilled to think that all these years later, it was still someone's trusted travelling companion for a solitary, long-haul flight.

The two stars escaped the mayhem by slipping into a lounge through a door marked "Private". This section was reserved for only the big fish. To enter they needed no documentation and no membership card. Staff had been alerted to their arrival way in advance, guaranteeing their reception would be understated and gracious.

An attractive young woman walked them from the reception area into a lounge that boasted a personal chef, a computer kiosk, a fully equipped bar, and a private masseur, should they need any stress relief before their flight. Both men declined all of this in favour of a relaxing chat over a glass of freshly squeezed orange juice, and Sanjiv used the remote control to change the music from easy-listening pap to a playlist of 60s Motown.

As they reclined into a leather sofa, a red-faced man in his fifties hurried in wearing an airline jacket and a horrified expression.

'Excuse me, gentlemen,' he said breathlessly, 'I'm so sorry to have to inform you that your flight has been delayed.'

Sanjiv and Sean looked at him calmly.

'How long?' Sean asked.

'Well, sir, the aircraft you will be travelling on has had a problem on its leg from Dubai. I'm afraid they had an ill passenger on board and had to turn back.'

'So how long?' Sean repeated.

'Five hours, I'm afraid.'

The man squirmed.

Sanjiv looked at him kindly. Reading the dread in his face, he gave him a smile that instantly put him at ease.

'That is no problem,' he said gently. 'This is a beautiful place, and we are very happy to be here. You will tell us when the plane is ready won't you?'

The man nodded, eager to appear helpful.

'Then everything is perfect.'

***

Days had passed since Nicole, Tim and Billy had vanished. Their story had become such currency that journalists were simply making stuff up. One news syndicate had published the account of an eyewitness who claimed they saw the clouds part and the hand of God reach down and pluck the Blake's car right off the street. Another claimed an international crime syndicate had kidnapped them and was demanding the world's largest ransom.

If the stakes hadn't been of such biblical proportions these stories would have been laughable, but the papers had no choice to publish them because it was all anyone could think about. All around the world, people were glued to their TVs and mobile devices, breathlessly awaiting updates. Social media plumped every piece of gossip. Unsubstantiated rumours were served up as fact, until no one could trust anything they heard anymore. A universal intake of breath had occurred as the world hung on the family's reappearance.

The government too was under siege. Because the family had disappeared on their watch, they were labouring under a scandal so big it could bring them down. The public smelled a conspiracy, and the longer the Blakes remained missing the shriller the howl of civic indignation became.

This wasn't just at home. Governments around the world demanded action. As a result, every resource was being thrown at the search for the family. A special ministry had been formed. Chains of command were hammered out. Heads normally associated with endeavours far more elevated than government were recruited. Police, Army, Secret Service were all deployed.

But even with all the intelligence, the boots on the ground, the forensic searching employed, it was as if the family had simply vanished off the face of the earth.

This was the storm that washed Sanjiv Gupta and Sean Teale up onto Garry and Clare's doorstep. Such was their star-power that, completely unannounced, they parted the grasping media like the Red Sea, sidestepped the security detail and knocked at the front door like they were Sunday visitors.

Clare had spied them coming. Something had stirred the press into a frenzy, and for a gleaming moment she thought it might be Nicole and Billy returning home. But instead the media scrum coughed up the celebrities.

Clare had to slap herself. Both men had played a massive part in her life. Sanjiv's books were her lifeline during her illness and depression, and Sean Teale was the eye-candy that had got her through menopause. She'd watched him since the early days of *Emergency Ward* and seen every one of his movies. How could it be that the police were now ushering these men towards her front door?

'Oh, my God, oh, my God, oh, my God. Garry!' she shrieked. 'Did you see who showed up?'

Garry seemed annoyingly underwhelmed.

'Come on,' she squealed and raced for the door. She wrenched it open to find two star-struck policemen flanking Sanjiv and Sean.

Clare threw herself at Sean first, wrapping her arms around his neck. Then she untangled herself and launched at Sanjiv.

Both men smiled humbly. When she was finished she stepped back, breathless.

'I'm sorry,' she said. 'I had to do that.'

Sanjiv beamed. 'Thank you, I enjoyed it very much.'

Garry stepped forward and offered his hand.

'I'm Garry. And you've met my wife, Clare.'

'The miracle woman,' Sanjiv said, and Clare chuckled shyly. 'I'm Sanjiv and this is Sean. Please forgive us for arriving unannounced. We thought if we requested an appointment there would be many people who would try to put obstacles in our way, and we have something very important to discuss with you.'

'Are you kidding?' Clare barked. 'Any time, Mr Gupta.' She slapped him lovingly on the shoulder.

Garry gestured to the guards that they were no longer needed, and he led their guests into the lounge room. Clare fluffed cushions before she allowed anyone to sit.

Sanjiv and Sean seemed relaxed, like celebrities should be—which only made Clare more anxious. As if he already knew this would be the case, Sanjiv took control.

'I would like to thank you so very much for allowing Sean and me into your home. With so much going on it is very generous of you.'

Clare was sitting forward on the couch smiling ferociously—barely listening.

'You must know that we have come to talk to you about the child.'

Clare nodded.

'Forgive me, and please don't feel you are beholden to answer this question, but ... do you know where the child is?'

Clare and Garry swapped a surprised glance.

'No,' Garry said. 'I don't mind you asking, but I give you my word—we truly don't know.'

'That's fine. I understand that it may be wise for you to keep their whereabouts a secret, particularly from the press. Perhaps even from the authorities as well, but I believe you. I just wanted to clear that up first.'

Sanjiv sat forward.

'Now. Mrs Sharp—'

'Clare.'

'Clare. I want to tell you that I believe you did the right thing telling the world about the child.' Clare beamed victoriously. She even gave Garry a look. 'But if you'll forgive me for saying, I believe you did it for the wrong reason.'

Clare's smile wilted.

'Okay?' she said.

'You have been cured from an appalling illness. It was a miracle. It proved this child has enormous power. You want others to be healed this way too. This is a beautiful sentiment. Very, very beautiful. It comes from a heart that is full of love. But something you must understand about the child is that he brings with him something much, much greater than that.'

Without realising it, Garry and Clare were sitting forward on their seats, spellbound; Sanjiv had the magnetism of a shaman.

'Some people have said that this baby is Jesus Christ reborn. I don't believe that to be the case. People like to see only what is in front of them, but *we* must look deeper. There is no doubt that the child comes from God, a manifestation of Him. Some would say he is an avatar of God. But that doesn't make him Jesus Christ.'

'Then what is he?' Clare asked.

'A being of pure consciousness,' Sanjiv said. 'The most powerful manifestation of consciousness we have ever seen.'

'Then why the star?' Garry said.

'That is indeed a Christian symbol. A very powerful one. But look where he chose to be born. I'm certain if he was born elsewhere, his heralding would have manifested differently. If he was born in say ... Iran, for example, I don't think the same symbols would have been seen. Do you see what I mean?'

'You're saying he chose this place and those symbols intentionally?'

'This is only my assumption. But I can't help but feel that it was calculated that he arrived in a place with such easy access to mass media and then announced himself with such recognisable and powerful symbols.'

Sean cleared his throat. Sanjiv stopped his monologue and turned to him.

'Sometimes I wish Sanjiv would open with how nice the weather's been,' Sean quipped, and Clare and Garry laughed.

Sanjiv beamed, 'Sean is right. I am like a bull in a china shop.'

'The point is,' Sean went on, 'Sanjiv believes that rather than coming to heal on an individual basis, Billy has come to heal the world as a whole. Once people can get beyond the symbolism of what he represents and realise that he is truly God manifested, then everyone on the planet may reach out to him regardless of their faith, and *he* can reach out to *them* too—'

'There is no one he cannot touch,' Sanjiv interjected excitedly, 'because he doesn't belong to any specific race or any one religion; he belongs to everyone.'

'Belongs,' Garry said.

'Poor choice of words,' Sean shot back. 'He is *here* for

215

everyone.'

Sanjiv nodded enthusiastically.

'Sean is always the steady one,' Sanjiv said. 'He saves me when my mouth runneth over.'

Clare and Garry laughed again.

Now that Sanjiv was back on message, Sean seemed to retreat into the background once more.

'This is an opportunity for all mankind to truly engage with God,' Sanjiv said. 'And I don't mean religion, I mean the true essence of God. It is a chance for us to put aside our differences. It's a chance to heal the world.'

Clare wanted to cry. Sanjiv's words perfectly encapsulated her passion to heal, but on a limitless scale.

'What do you need us to do?' Clare asked, already sold.

'We have a plan of how to put into action what we believe his purpose to be, but we would of course need the blessing of his family. And the help of some of the biggest heavy hitters in the religious world.'

Sanjiv paused to make sure he hadn't lost his audience.

'I have made a list of some very fine people. Some of these people are religious figures, some, like Sean, are only on the list to help attract attention and wake people up. I have selected the list very carefully, hoping not to miss anyone and to include only the most vital.

He took a piece of paper from his breast pocket and handed it to Clare.

'Coincidentally,' he said, 'there are twelve names on the list.'

24

Tim returned to his hut, his skin still blooming with the fragrance of sex. But the moment he lay on his bed, he felt an icy kiss of dread creep over his body. Exhilaration deserted him, and all that was left was a turning fear in his guts. Please, God, don't let Nicole find out.

He wanted to hurry back to Simon's hut and secure the secret. To gather the conspirators around him and hear them say the words: We *will never, ever tell.*

In the morning, Tim took the path to the perimeter fence for the jog, praying that if *he* behaved as normal, then everything would still *be* normal.

A crowd had gathered beneath the towering mango tree. The early sunshine filtered through its reaching foliage. Simon had already arrived with the girls, and they all rushed to embrace him. He couldn't help but withdraw. Their affection was a claxon blaring to all what had happened the previous night. But Simon seemed calm. He egged the girls on to nuzzle and fuss over Tim.

Tim followed Simon as he led the joggers, snaking their way past soaring fern glades and clusters of fruit trees so abundant their uneaten harvest littered the track. Tim found the odd moment of contentment, his anxiety dulled by the beauty of the surroundings and the reassuring smiles of his fellow joggers. The air was fresh and sweet, the silence only broken by bird calls and the footfall of his companions. It was pure and seductive. If there was a place to be incarcerated, this was it. Perhaps in the future, when Nicole had forgiven him for posting the video, they would share this morning jog together. She would run alongside him just as Joanne did now. Just as Shayne and Mayling and Kara did. She would share the garden with him, and they would find peace together here.

Simon set them a challenge for the final leg of the run. He picked up the pace and took an unexpected turn through uncharted scrub. It brought determined smiles to the joggers' faces and it demanded extra grit from them all. He pushed himself, leaving nothing in the tank.

When they finally arrived back to the community, Tim felt revived—like he'd shed his unease, dropped it like the tropical fruit on the track. He wanted to pass by Nicole's hut on the way back to his, just to catch a glimpse of her and know she was still there: a prospect, a possibility of something good that was to come. One day, the two of them would enjoy the same sense of freedom he'd returned with.

As her hut came into view, he saw Gail shaking a blanket out front. She caught a glimpse of him coming and stopped what she was doing. Something in her stare caught in Tim's throat. He slowed. Gail looked like she was swallowing against something bitter—stemming some kind of vile eruption.

She threw the blanket into the hut and marched towards him. Tim found himself involuntarily backing away.

She reached him and shoved him so hard in the chest he almost tumbled backwards.

'You are a deeply stupid man,' she screamed.

Tim spluttered as he ducked Gail's slaps.

'What is wrong with you?' she said. 'You've destroyed her. Do you understand that?'

Tim instantly knew the worst had happened. He couldn't imagine how, but it had. Panic set off a siren in his head, which drowned Gail out—drowned out the world and swelled his skull to breaking point. He had to get to Nicole.

Gail was still yelling at him, but he could no longer hear her. The hut was only metres away. He had to get there. Nicole would be inside, and he had to get to her.

As he made for the hut, Gail was in front of him blocking his way. 'Don't you go in there!' she screamed. But she was now just an object, an obstruction. He threw her out of his way, and she crashed into the dirt. Her threats turned to cries of pain, but they were inconsequential.

The hut. Nicole was inside the hut.

It was dark, and the air smelt dank and exhausted. As he stood in the doorway, he cast a dim shadow into the room before him.

Nicole lay on the bed, facing the wall. At first she didn't stir. Even the sound of Gail's cries couldn't bring her back into the world.

'Nic,' Tim croaked.

She turned and looked at him. For a moment her face was unrecognisable. Her cheeks were swollen and raw like a victim of abuse, and her eyes were slits that could barely focus on him.

This couldn't be Nicole. How could tears alone have so distorted her face?

Tim rushed to her, but she fended him off with her fists.

'Nic, I'm sorry. I'm so sorry,' he sobbed.

'Don't touch me!' she screamed.

'No, please, Nic, let me—'

'Shut up,' she spat. 'I never want to see you again. Never!'

Tim sank to his knees.

'Please, Nic,' he pleaded. 'Please…'

The light in the hut dimmed as Gail appeared in the doorway. Tim could sense her hovering, ready to pounce the moment intervention was needed, but he couldn't bring himself to leave. He had to fix this. To put Nicole back together.

Nicole rolled onto her back, drew both legs up to her chest and kicked him. He flew backwards like a rag doll, his head hitting the base of a chair.

The world spun as he tried to right himself.

'Get out!' Nicole screamed. 'Get out!'

Gail had seen enough. She marched over, grabbed him by the arm and dragged him towards the door. He was so weak with despair he offered no resistance.

Gail shoved him out of the hut, and he stumbled away down the path.

Now the compound felt like a prison, and, like any prisoner, his only objective was to escape. In every direction, the perimeter fence seemed to soar to the sky. He began to run. Past the ornamental pond and into the scrub, retracing the steps of his morning jog.

When he was well out of the community's sight, he scaled the fence, dragging himself over the razor wire and slicing his skin. He leapt off the other side, and then he ran. The bracken slashed at his feet, and it felt good

220

that it hurt. He kept running until he was lost, exhausted, and far enough from the compound to scream his guts out without being heard by a single soul.

He lay in the dirt for hours. He had no desire to get up because there was nowhere for him to go. He couldn't return to the compound, and he had no home left to return to. Nowhere to *be* and no one to be *with*.

There was no future stretching out before him anymore. He guessed this was because the next thing he'd do would be to walk out onto the highway and wait for the first truck to run him down. It was the thing he *should* do—the least he could do: imbue this drama with some sad honour. It would show Nicole he was sorry. And when Billy was grown, it would be his message to him from the grave that his father was man enough to concede he'd made a catastrophic mistake. Maybe in years to come they would miss him. Perhaps they'd even forgive him.

As he lay in the dirt, ploughing the fields of his misery, a crunch came from the bush behind him. He turned with a start to find Joanne stepping out of the undergrowth. She made him feel ill. He shut his eyes against the sight of her.

She trod gently through the yellowing grass and stood over him.

'Hello,' she said.

Tim had no energy to respond.

Joanne sat. 'I'm sorry you're so sad.'

'How the fuck did you find me?' he mumbled.

'Simon knew you'd run. When you found out she knew, Simon said you'd run.'

'So what's he going to do now, kill me?'

Joanne chuckled. It caused Tim open his eyes.

She reached out and took his hand. 'We all care about you so much. Simon says you bring blessings. Baby Jesus told him so.'

'What do you want, Joanne?'

'No one deserves to be so sad. I want to make you happy. I want to bring you home to where you are loved.'

Tim couldn't listen anymore. He rolled away and sobbed. Joanne lay next to him, spooning her body around his. She held him patiently and let him cry.

His tears soaked into the ground turning the earth into mud. He could feel it smearing his cheek. But her soft breathing at his back, her heady scent of essential oils, her steady arms around him threw a blanket of wellbeing over him.

'What have I done?' he said at last.

'Simon says you have followed the path of enlightenment. That you're brave because you've sacrificed everything to follow God's plan.'

Tim scoffed and turned to face her.

'And you believe that?'

She nodded.

'God's fucking plan. It's all I seem to hear about.' He screwed up his face against his rage. 'All His fucking plan seems to bring is pain.'

'Tim—'

'I have broken my wife's heart. Twice. That doesn't make me brave; it makes me heartless and stupid. How can I possibly live with that.'

Joanne wiped the muddy tears from his face.

'Every birth brings pain,' she said. 'It's God's will. And now that you're re-born, let me nurse you. Let me take away your pain. We love you. I love you.'

Tim could feel himself spiralling into her kindness, her sweetness dulling the ache in his head.

'We all want you,' she whispered. 'We want you.'

Tim squeezed his eyes tight. He wanted to shut her

222

out, but he could feel her love rolling over him in waves, and it was calming and soothing, and he knew it was the only love left for him in this sullied, confusing world.

26

'Make yourself at home,' Simon said.

Charlie stifled a laugh. As if. With its essential oils and its hanging silks and its stink of women, Simon's hut was everything Charlie knew he was not entitled to. *His* place was a dank lean-to with a dirt floor. And he'd been solid with that—until Simon decided he was happy to let Tim have a taste of it: the man who only a couple of hours ago had run snivelling from the compound like a girl.

Charlie planted himself on a cushion by the bookcase.

'What's going on?' he said with a little more detachment than he should.

'I wanna start putting things in place,' Simon said.

Charlie was always party to Simon's plans. He was the go-to-guy when things needed to get done, but for the last few days he'd been out of the loop. 'Seems to me things are a bit of a dog's breakfast,' he said.

'How so?'

'Well, Nicole's been howling since last night. Half the

compound's heard it. And now the husband's taken off.'

'It's under control,' Simon assured him. 'I sent Joanne after him. He's gonna be fine. The guy's got nowhere to go anyway.'

'What about Nicole?'

'That's what I wanted to talk to you about.' Simon took a moment to gather himself. 'You had a little one once, didn't you?'

'A boy,' Charlie said. 'Ancient history.'

'How old was he when you went inside?'

'Eighteen months or so.'

'So you know a bit about kids.'

'It was a pretty crazy time, Simon.'

'But you were there.'

'Yeah.'

'How old was he before he didn't need his mother anymore?'

'How would I know?'

'How old was he before she started heating up bottles?'

'Little.'

'How fucking little?' Simon barked. 'Baby Jesus is three weeks old. Can he do without his mother, Charlie?'

A chill ran down Charlie's spine. Burying the priest and hiding his car was one thing, but this was another.

'You remember God told me to build this place?' Simon said.

Charlie nodded.

'And you remember he told me I would take our faith out into the world, right?'

Another nod.

'Well, we're ready, Charlie. The time has come. We have the baby now, and with His glory we'll go out into the world, and the world will find God through me. Can you see it, Charlie?'

Charlie *could* see it. It had always been the doctrine of the community.

'Yes,' he said at last, 'but why—'

'We need a willing parent. We can't just arrive out there with the child. Think about it. They'd lock us up. But if we have a parent—who's one of us—then we'll be watertight.'

'He's done a runner.'

'He's with us. Trust me. But the mother ... we only need one of them, Charlie.'

'How do we do it?'

'Up to you. But I need them both gone: Nicole *and* Gail. And it has to look like an accident. If the husband gets a whiff we did it we'll lose him.'

Charlie nodded, his mind already turning to the job.

'Good, Charlie.' Simon gave him a pat on the back.

Charlie went to get up; Simon took his hand. 'Charlie?' he said. 'This is our destiny, old friend. You will be rewarded.'

***

Nicole had lost track of time. It was no longer clear to her if it was morning or afternoon, or whether she'd completely missed something and it was deep in the night. Had she been drifting in and out of consciousness? She only knew that whenever she reached out, Gail was there. If she was thirsty, or if Billy needed a feed, Gail was there.

The bedclothes around her felt damp—the very air itself, damp and putrid. With what? Sweat? Vomit?

She remembered returning from Simon's hut unable to rein in her grief. Like a wounded animal, she heaved cries from the deepest part of her body. Soon, her grief turned to sickness, and once she began vomiting she couldn't stop. She was on the floor, aware of Gail hanging over her, holding a bucket, pulling back her hair, dabbing her face with a cloth.

At some point Billy needed a feed, and she felt Gail coaxing her back onto the bed. She took Billy to her breast mechanically, and Gail threw a blanket around her shoulders. Not even the love Billy radiated could dent the devastation she felt.

She had to get out of this place; she knew that—leave behind the husband who had chosen the fanatics over her. There were no bounds to the abandonment she felt. The loneliness. She and Tim should be fighting this nightmare together; instead he was feasting on the same insanity she was so desperate to escape. Nothing could be more frightening or cruel.

She had no energy left to think about it anymore. Exhaustion overwhelmed her. Without knowing it, her eyes folded shut and she was asleep.

***

Once she was certain Nicole was asleep, Gail crept outside and arched her chest skywards, stretching her aching back. She closed her eyes and breathed deeply. All around her the bush sang. The breeze came rolling out of the trees, perfumed and sweet. If not for all the insanity around her, this place would truly be a hidden corner of paradise. But she knew they had to get out of here. Now.

There seemed to be no guards posted today. Mostly they were obvious: random devotees watching over the prize. Perhaps they were keeping their distance from what was obviously an unfolding tragedy. Maybe they thought Nicole was too distraught to try and escape. Whatever the reason, Gail saw an opportunity. She checked to see if Nicole was still sleeping, and then she quietly crept away down the path.

She followed it through the community to Simon's hut, praying she'd find Adele inside. She knew who to look for; she'd already spotted her in the prayer hall the previous day and recognised her from her Facebook profile.

When she reached the hut, she crept around to the rear and pulled back the curtain. The hut was empty. Her heart sank; there was no time to hunt through the compound to find Adele; guards could return to her hut at any moment. She slid the curtain shut and began heading back.

As she hit the path, she almost ran into someone coming from the other direction. To her astonishment it was Adele.

Gail had to think quickly. Company could appear at any moment, so she needed to engage her fast.

She sidestepped her, sobbing loudly. Adele stopped in her tracks.

'Are you all right?'

Gail's tears were convincing. 'I'm sorry, forgive me, but I had to come and see for myself. This is where it happened isn't it?'

'What do you mean?'

'Were you with them? Tim and those girls?'

Adele sighed heavily. 'No,' she said. 'I wasn't.'

Gail wiped her eyes.

'Sorry,' she said, starting off down the track, 'I shouldn't have come.'

'Wait,' Adele said. Gail stopped and turned back to her. 'I want you to know I would never do something like that.'

'Thank you. Nicole is inconsolable.'

'I would never—'

'Who was Anthony?'

As she'd intended, her question seemed to catch Adele by surprise.

'I'm sorry,' Gail added quickly. 'I shouldn't have. I just ... I saw his shrine and I ... I lost someone too.'

Adele went to say something but stopped herself.

'I feel like such an outsider here,' Gail went on. 'I guess I just need someone to ... if you don't want to talk about Anthony—'

'I don't mind,' Adele broke in softly. 'Everyone seems to have forgotten him but me. I like to speak about him. To remember him.'

'Were you close?'

Adele nodded.

'Was he your boyfriend?'

Again, Adele nodded. It was clearly still raw.

'When did he pass?'

'Two months ago.'

'Did you come to the community together?'

'No. Anthony was a founding member. An elder. Such a beautiful man.'

Gail took Adele's hand.

'How did he die?'

Adele couldn't meet her eye.

'There was a boating accident,' she said bitterly.

'No,' Gail gasped.

Adele managed a nod.

'Simon and Anthony went fishing together.'

Adele's eyes were filling with tears. Gail waited for her to go on, but nothing came.

'Who did you lose?' Adele said at last, steering them off the topic.

'I came here with a priest. We weren't lovers, of course, but we became close ... because of the child.'

Gail decided it was time to throw out the bait.

'Simon *said* he died in the car accident. That's what he told everyone, anyway.'

Adele seemed startled. Gail's insinuation rang in the air, naked and audacious. Time slowed as she waited for Adele's next move, but Adele remained silent. She looked down at the path.

'I need to get to the kitchen,' she said at last.

'Of course you do. It was lovely talking with you, Adele.'

Gail embraced her and hit the path once more, not daring to look back. If she chose to, Adele could end her right then. It would only take for her to repeat her vicious insinuation to Simon, and without a shadow of a doubt Gail would be in a ditch next to Father Jim.

The seed had been planted. Gail returned to her hut knowing that for better or worse things were at least moving.

***

Nicole awoke with a jolt, as though she'd been kicked in her sleep. She must have startled Billy because he was disturbed in the crook of her arm.

Something had changed. Instead of being made of bruised flesh she felt hard as a nut. Membranes had interlaced beneath the solid exoskeleton, and she was impenetrable. She gathered Billy and sat up. Where was Gail? It didn't matter.

The hut was dim, but it no longer contained the shadows of despair. The stink of her grief had somehow been purged through the uneven bark walls, and with the haze of it gone, her surroundings appeared sharp edged as if seen through clear eyes.

How could this be? The last time she was conscious she'd felt polluted, suffocated under the layers the feelings of betrayal brought. She glanced at Billy. Was this his doing? Processing that amount of emotion should take a lifetime.

She held him closer to her. She could smell him. She drew his sweet baby stink in through her nostrils and deep down into her body. It was a physical union that brought a part of him inside her, and she could feel him there, on the inside.

'We're leaving,' she said.

She looked around for something to take with her, but besides a small, dirty swaddling blanket there was nothing in the hut she wanted. She would walk out of this place with the clothes on her back and her baby on her hip.

She made for the doorway, and as she exited the hut, she almost ran into Gail coming the other way. Gail seemed surprised.

'Nicole, you're up.'

Nicole didn't want to engage her. She wanted to move. She gave a nod and headed past her.

'Nicole?' But Nicole didn't stop. 'Wait.'

Nicole could hear Gail trotting after her. Gail ran around in front of her.

'Where are you going?'

'Home.'

'But—'

Nicole took off again. She saw Gail take a quick look around to see if there were any eyes on them. There was fear in Gail's look. Something Nicole had no time for.

Gail was soon after her again.

'Wait. Please, Nicole. You can't do this.'

'I *have* to do this. They can kill me if they want.'

Gail grabbed her by the arm and tried to shush her.

'Let me go.'

'You have to listen to me.' Gail was trying to keep her

voice down, probably in an attempt to not attract attention. But it was too late for that. Nicole leaving the hut on her own was bound to bring the cavalry.

'Let them come,' Nicole said. 'They can't keep me here.'

'Something's happened. Come inside the hut and let me explain.'

'No. I'm finished listening. I'm finished being told what to do. I can only rely on myself now.'

'Trust me—'

'You *broke* your trust with me when you brought the priest. Tim broke his trust with me. The whole fucking world has lost my trust!'

'This is making it worse.'

'What could be worse? Tell me! I have no one. There's no one but Billy and me. And we're walking out of here, understand?'

'Stop!' Gail cried. Her voice rang in the air, and Nicole was taken aback by the force of it. 'You can go when you've heard what I have to say. But you know they'll catch you, and they'll bring you back. And they'll put you in irons … or worse. Now walk with me back to the hut and listen to me.'

Nicole stood silent for a moment. The fear was gone from Gail's eyes. They were locked onto her own and immovable. Nicole could match those eyes now. If she wanted. She was in control. She had to be. Without a word, she turned for the hut.

'What,' she said, as Gail followed her inside.

'Please keep your voice down. I may have found an ally.'

Gail made it sound like there was a plan. Like there was someone ready to help them. But Nicole knew to be doubtful. So far anyone geared up to help them had contributed to landing them in this fucking place.

'I found you because of a girl called Adele,' Gail said. 'I spoke to her just then … when I went out of the hut. I know she has doubts about Simon—I knew that before I came here. So I planted a seed with her.'

'What kind of seed?'

'I hinted that Simon killed Father Jim. If she loses faith with Simon then I think she might be on our side.'

'Might.' Nicole snapped.

'It's worth a try. It's better than a failed attempt to escape.'

'I won't fail.'

'Give me twenty-four hours.'

'For what?'

'If she takes the bait then we'll soon know, and we'll have help on the inside.'

Nicole wanted to walk out and leave everything behind her: her weak husband who'd been so easily seduced, the unending days of irrational bullshit. She even wanted to be gone from Gail and her grasping belief that she was somehow Nicole's champion. But she had to concede Gail was right. There were only Simon's obsequious fanatics out there, and the impenetrable fence beyond. There was no getting past.

'One day. Please.'

Nicole sat on the bed.

'One day,' she agreed.

***

For twenty-four hours, Gail's insinuation ricocheted around inside Adele's head. Once the thought had taken hold she couldn't stop turning it over. Did Gail mean the story about the car accident was a lie? And if it was a lie, then had Simon killed the priest?

She obsessed about it all afternoon as she washed

vegetables and peeled potatoes. She couldn't meet Simon's eye when they returned to the hut for curfew, and she was relieved that there was no evening sex while Simon helped Joanne mend Tim's wounded heart.

Overnight, Adele's doubt bloomed further. Her lingering suspicions of how Anthony died at sea on such a still day began to take root. Could it be—as she'd brooded on in her darkest hours—that Simon had had a hand in Anthony's death? She needed to find out the truth.

Late in the afternoon, Adele entered in the doorway of Gail's hut and quietly called out to her.

Gail joined Adele outside.

'What is it?' Gail asked.

'I need you to come with me.'

Adele saw Gail flinch. This was the typical subtext for the entire compound. God may have been all around them, but no one dared buck the authority of the place or they risked igniting Simon's wrath.

'Don't worry,' she said, 'I only want to talk.'

Adele led her down a track, deep into the bush. The further they went, the more anxious she could feel Gail becoming.

'Won't Simon's guard come after us?' Gail said.

'I'm Simon's guard this afternoon.'

Adele led her to a glade where a fallen tree had flattened the scrub into a secret clearing. Broken foliage carpeted the ground, and young ferns pushed their way through the carnage.

Adele sat next to Gail on the fallen tree. 'Do you know how Father Jim died?'

Gail's heart beat faster. 'Why would you ask me that?'

'I need to know.'

'But why?'

'Because. The way you put it yesterday, it sounded

like you didn't think he died in the accident.'

Gail turned away.

'Gail. Did you see how the priest died?'

'Yes.'

'Well?'

'I don't know if I can tell you.'

'Why?'

'Because if I tell you, I could get into a lot of trouble, and I can't do anything that might endanger us.'

'You don't trust me.'

'I didn't say that. I need to be careful, that's all.'

'You can,' Adele said urgently. 'You can trust me.'

'Simon sent you to guard me. Why should I believe you're on my side?'

'Because I think we're both victims.' Adele took Gail's hands. 'Did Simon kill Father Jim?'

Adele could feel herself shaking with rage. And she could see that Gail wanted very much to trust her. 'Please. If you tell me, I promise I will try to help you.'

Gail took a long breath.

'When Father Jim went through the windscreen of the car, he was alive. Then I saw Simon crush his boot into his throat until he was dead. Simon doesn't know I saw him.'

Adele pulled away. There was no longer any doubt in her mind. Now she could see what Simon was capable of, she knew he'd got rid of Anthony. 'I believe you,' she said.

Gail sat forward and gripped Adele's hand. 'We have to get out of here,' she said. 'If we stay, something bad will happen.'

'We'd never make it. He has eyes everywhere.'

'Then what can we do?'

'I'll go for help. It's the only way. I know a way out of the compound. If I went during the day and came back before my kitchen shift he'd never know I was gone.'

'When will you go?'

Adele took a breath and steadied herself.

'First thing in the morning.'

26

Morning rang with birdcalls, which echoed through the valley. Adele lay watching the sun filter the warm light into the hut and wake the sleeping occupants. She tried to calm herself about the day that stretched before her. Today would be no casual outing to Garnerville; today would bring Simon's downfall.

Kara was the first to stir. Then Simon. Soon the big bed was filled with stretching bodies, drowsily kissing each other and pulling on clothes.

'The Lord has given us another beautiful day,' Simon chirped. 'Who's coming for a run?'

As the girls dragged themselves off the bed, Adele pulled the sheets over her head and let the others trot away into the morning. After breakfast, she completed her cleaning roster, and by 9.00 am it was safe to disappear.

She left the mess hut and headed past the pond, making for her secret escape route under the fence. She dragged at the wire, but as she went to slide under it the fence stayed strong. The hole had been filled in. Fear turned in her stomach. Someone was on her tail.

She dashed back into the bush and flattened herself into the grass. For minutes she lay there silent, listening for any crunch of approaching footsteps, but nothing came. Finally, there was no choice but to keep moving. She needed to be back in the compound for her afternoon kitchen shift or everything would go straight to hell.

The scrub around her was littered with fallen branches and bark. In her Light Up days, Adele had learnt stilts and trapeze, so she knew how to assemble a structure that would get her over the fence.

She fossicked some branches and leaned them against the fence, and she gathered some bark to drape over the razor wire at the top. Then she threw two poles onto the other side ready for her return trip.

Now for the hard part. She launched herself at the branches, scaling them like a tall, rung-less ladder. She had to press outwards with her feet to get traction, but her sandals kept slipping. At about six feet off the ground, she lost her footing and came crashing down. Winded, she tore off her sandals, threw them over the fence and made a second attempt.

This was easier. She quickly reached the top and folded the bark across the razor wire. She threw a leg over, slid her toes into the wire on the other side of the fence and began her descent.

When she hit the ground, she crashed into the undergrowth, sweat pouring off her, and she didn't stop until the highway came into view. Beyond it, green pastures ran down to the endless beaches, which brought board riders from all over the world. The pounding surf reminded her that this was the water that had taken Anthony. She imagined his swollen body washing loosely along the reef. His sweet, innocent eyes still wide with the shock of his guru's treachery.

Garnerville had no police station, so she'd need to head south to Cook, twice the distance away. The highway was empty, and for fifteen long minutes she danced impatiently, willing God to send her a ride.

Finally, the sound of a motor came over the rise. She was filled with terror that it might be Simon, out on the hunt for her. She dived for cover on the side of the road only to see a rusting tractor appear over the verge, spitting globs of mud from its tyres as it bobbed past.

She sat up and waved at the farmer, promising herself that she'd hold her nerve the next time a car came past.

***

Simon's secret pleasure was a bush shower. It was the only thing he didn't like to share with his brothers and sisters. After the morning jog and a hearty breakfast, he'd fill a bucket, walk into the bush and stand under the cool stream letting it cleanse and revive him. He'd shake himself off and let the warming air dry his naked skin.

It was his only real opportunity to snatch some solitude. For a brief moment, he could feel the touch of God's hand all around him, without being distracted by the constant grasping of the community. He could order his thoughts and make his plan for the day.

Today his mind turned to Adele. Dealing with all the recent drama the visitors had brought had taken him away from her; their crazy dash to Garnerville seemed like a lifetime ago.

As he climbed back into his clothes, he realised that he missed her, and that today would be the day for them to reconnect.

He imagined them walking together through the fern glades to the east of the property, talking about her time in Light Up and holding each other under the tall canopies of green. He would run his fingers through her silken hair, and they'd laugh about the times they'd fought. Maybe they'd have sex. Maybe she'd push him to the ground the way she had on that crazy night when they'd broken curfew and fled the compound.

Simon emerged from the bush feeling weightless. He took the path to the mess hut, nodding kindly to his followers as he passed them, only to find Adele had already finished her shift.

'Do you know where she's got to?' he asked Mayling, who was already chopping pumpkins for lunch.

'No, Simon,' she said with a shrug. 'Who knows where Adele gets to?'

Simon wandered the paths checking all the places she might normally go: the ornamental pond, his hut, the vegetable garden—but there was no sign of her. Slowly, his mood began to sour. He could feel his pace quickening along the paths, and his greetings to those he passed were no longer so breezy.

Adele was nowhere to be found. She could have gone walking in the bush, but if that was the case it would take the whole day to find her, and knowing Adele, as he did, his money was on her having done a runner.

He took the path past the pond and up the track to where he knew she'd dug her hole under the fence. He arrived to find his repair job still intact, but seeing the bark draped across the razor wire at the top of the fence told Simon all he needed to know about how Adele had made her escape.

Brimming with rage, Simon stormed back to the community and hunted down Duck.

'I want you to get the SUV and drive to Garnerville,'

he snapped.

Duck was milling wood. He took off his safety glasses and swiped at the sawdust on his shorts.

'Sure, Simon. What do you need?'

'Adele's gone missing again. I need you to go and find her. She's probably in the pub.'

'Drinking?'

'No, not drinking,' he barked. 'She'll be on the internet. Just fucking find her, Duck, and bring her back.'

Simon made for Charlie's hut, but now his eyes were set on the path in front of him, and anyone passing got no greeting at all.

Charlie was lying on his mattress, smoking, when Simon burst in.

'I need you to go up to the fence where we filled in that hole. Adele's done a runner. I want you to stay there and wait for her.'

Charlie calmly stubbed out his cigarette.

'She'll be back, Simon. Do we really need to sweat this?'

Simon turned on Charlie, eyes blazing. 'You want me to let her walk all over us? What if she's off telling someone about the child!' Simon headed for the door. 'And bring her to me the moment she's back.'

'Simon?' Simon paused at the door. 'I've had a think about that thing we discussed.'

'And?'

'Well, it's simple really. If we burn their hut while they're sleeping it'll look like an accident.'

Simon made a face. 'But you'll kill the baby too.'

'No. We get the baby out *before* we set the fire.'

'Everyone will come to save them.'

'Not if I do it at night.'

Simon rolled this around in his head.

'When?'

Charlie shrugged. 'Whenever.'

'Okay,' Simon said. 'Do it tonight.'

***

It had already been half an hour, and Adele had got nowhere. Since the tractor, the road had been deserted, and the longer she stood there the more she feared her absence would be discovered. If she could just put some distance between herself and the compound.

Mercifully, the sound of a motor materialised from beyond the rise. Adele braced herself. If it was a white SUV rounding the bend, all would be lost. She might get a moment to dash into the scrub, but would it be too late?

Before she could give into her fears, a bright red sedan came into view. Adele pumped the air, and rather than stick out a thumb, she ran right out onto the road and waved the car down.

The moment it stopped, Adele ripped open the door and jumped inside.

'Oh, thank you, thank you, thank you!' she cried.

The driver had the road-weary look of a travelling salesman.

'Whoa … everything all right , young lady?'

'I need to get to Cook.'

'I can see that. You're a long way from anywhere.'

'You're telling me.'

The car started off, and Adele felt herself relax.

'Just need to get out and see some people I guess,' she said.

'Hallelujah to that. Sometimes when I get out of this car I just sit on a corner and watch the passers-by. It's a lonely old place, a car. Where ya from?'

'I can't say exactly.'

The man spun to look at her. 'You don't know?'

'Well, it's not exactly a *place*, if you know what I mean.'

'No, I don't,' he chuckled.

'I live in a commune. About half an hour south of Garnerville. It's a religious community.'

The man's eyes widened.

'You don't say! Well, I imagine you guys'd have the 'no vacancy' sign up right now.'

Adele didn't follow.

'Well, you know … with all the excitement about that child that's been going around. Churches must be doing a roaring trade.'

Adele was still confused. The man took a moment to take her in.

'You haven't heard, have you? Whoa, sorry to tell you this, sweetpea, but you really have been under a rock.' He paused and set his face with a smug grin. 'While you've been off hugging trees, there's been a Second Coming. Jesus Christ has been re-born.' The man cackled. 'You must be the only person on the planet not to know about it!'

'Wow,' she said weakly. 'Where *is* this child?'

'No one knows.'

The man guffawed so hard Adele thought he was going to drive off the road.

'Here's the thing,' he said. 'The Catholics dug him up, the world went nuts, then suddenly—bam—he disappears! Someone snatched him. I can't believe you don't know about it.'

The man collapsed with laughter again, but Adele couldn't even pretend to find it funny.

'It all sounds like a load of bullshit to me,' he said. 'Sorry, you're probably a full-on believer. But really—a

243

Second Coming—gimme a break.'

Adele wished she was bouncing Billy on her knee right now, just to see the look on his stupid face. What would people do when Billy did finally appear? When he was real and not just a story anymore? What would they do when faced with undeniable, flesh-and-blood proof that God truly existed?

When they reached Cook, the man took delight in pointing out the billposters outside news agencies, sneering at their feeble stories about the God-child. Adele did her best to tolerate him until he dropped her to the front door of the police station.

As she hurried up the steps, the enormity of what she was about to do hit her. This was history. When Billy was carried out of the compound, the world would surely change forever, and she would be there to see it happen.

She rang the bell on the reception desk, and a young man in a freshly pressed uniform emerged from behind a mirrored glass door.

'I've come to report a crime,' she said.

The policeman gave her a look that suggested he'd never heard of such a thing.

'Okay?' he said, picking up a pen. 'What kind of crime?'

'The child that everyone is looking for, the Second Coming? I know where he is.'

27

The pocket-sized holding cell contained one plastic chair, a squat laminated table and a CCTV camera that monitored her relentlessly. For forty long minutes, Adele had been locked in this capsule. Kitchen duty loomed, and the thought of not making it back was unthinkable. What was their problem? If she had information, why the hell were they treating her like a suspect?

Fed up, she climbed onto the table and waved at the camera.

'Hey!' she cried. 'What's going on? Can someone please tell me what's going on?'

As if her cries had actually made a difference, the door burst open, and a large man barreled in. Unlike the constable at the reception desk—who had followed him in—this man wasn't in uniform, and although he was greying he still had the dash of a young man and a chest you could bounce bricks off. His head was buried in a clipboard, which he didn't bother looking up from.

'Sit,' he barked, and parked himself on the table. Adele did as she was told. 'I've had to drive up from Lismore, so please don't make this a waste of my time.'

His manner made Adele feel instantly guilty of something.

'Now,' he said, looking at her for the first time, 'let's start at the beginning. I'm detective John Wright. You are Adele Blanche. Constable Sawyer here has told me you allege to know the whereabouts of the Blake family.'

'That's what I've been trying—'

'Everyone else that's come forward with sightings of them has turned out to be a nut-job. Why should I believe you?'

'What?' Adele said, indignant. 'I didn't think I'd have to bring proof.'

'Sawyer tells me you come from a religious community south of Garnerville.'

'Yes.'

'How long has the family been there?'

'Since Wednesday morning.'

'Is the whole family there?'

'Yes. And Gail, their midwife.'

Wright sat forward, his interest seemingly piqued.

'Tell me about her. Did she arrive with them?'

'No. She arrived the following day with a priest.'

Wright glanced at Sawyer, and then he leant closer to Adele.

'What's this priest's name?'

'Father Jim. But he's dead now. Simon killed him.'

Wright's expression darkened.

'Okay. Tell me about this Simon.'

Wright began scribbling on his clipboard.

'He's the spiritual leader of the community. He was the one who kidnapped the family.'

'Did you see him kill the priest?'

'No, but Gail did.'

'Why did he kill him?'

'I think he thought he'd come to take the baby.'

'I think he may have been right. There's been a separate investigation running.'

'I can tell you for sure they came looking for the child, but I don't know how they found us.'

There was a fire in Wright's eyes now. He reached across and put a hand on Adele's arm.

'Ms Blanche. I believe you. What I need from you now is as much detail as you can give me about the community. Can you do that?'

'Yes, but I need to be back at the compound before my kitchen duty. If they find out I've gone—'

'I'm afraid I can't let that happen.'

Adele's throat tightened. 'But there'll be big trouble if—'

'You've just told me this man, Simon, is a murderer. I can't put you back into harm's way.'

'You have to! If they find me missing, something terrible could happen to the family. It could make things much worse for them. Simon is dangerous. He doesn't like it when things don't go his way.'

'Is the community armed?'

'Yes. They have guns. They use them on the raids.'

'Explain "raids".'

'When the community runs out of food, Simon and the men go out and steal what we need.'

Wright gave Sawyer a look.

'Okay. I'm going to need you to talk me through some things, and I'll try to make it quick. When do you need to be back?'

'Four.'

Wright glanced at his watch.

'Then let's do this.'

Wright put a pile of notepaper in front of Adele, and she began drawing maps. The first would get them to the community. She drew a circle around the perimeter to warn against vehicles getting too close. If the guards heard them approaching they'd go straight for their guns.

Then she drew up a more detailed map of the compound itself and marked out Simon's hut. If they captured him first the rest of the community would most likely roll over for them.

She then circled Nicole's hut, then Tim's. She marked out the huts where Charlie, Duck, Aamir and Rob would be, and finally the places where the guns were stowed.

She identified the best entry points through the fence and made certain Wright understood that a raid just before dawn would be by far the best option.

Wright had his own questions; Adele was sharp and handled nearly all of them.

Finally, Wright seemed satisfied.

'Listen to me,' he said seriously. 'No one can know about this. No one on the inside, no one on the outside.' He turned to Sawyer, making sure his point wasn't lost on him too. 'Imagine if the press got hold of it? Now, the Constable will drive you back to the community.' Wright stood. 'Adele. Please stay safe until we arrive.'

***

Sawyer kept the lights flashing all the way up the highway. Adele made him drop her by a patch of thick scrub, and she made a breathless dash from the highway all the way to the perimeter fence. By the time she arrived, the afternoon was well upon her.

She quickly stacked her hidden poles against the fence

and climbed. At the top, she threw a leg over the bark that covered the razor wire and began her descent. Her heart pounded the entire way. Please, God, let there be no eyes waiting at the bottom.

When she hit the ground, she shoved the poles away from the fence ready to make a dash for the community, but as she turned she found Charlie, arms folded across his chest, blocking her path. Adele leapt with fright.

'Where the fuck have you been?' he barked.

Adele was shaking. What orders had Simon given him? Would she even make it back to the community?

'I was in Garnerville—' she blurted.

'Save it for Simon.'

He grabbed her by the arm and shoved her towards the track. Adele stumbled forward. At least they were headed for the community. A detour off the track could mean a quick, ugly death.

They walked in silence, Adele using the journey to concoct her story. She knew it had to be a good one.

When they reached the community, Charlie steered her towards the prayer hall. Afternoon prayers were breaking up, and a few stragglers were wandering home. Adele caught a glimpse of Simon, who slipped through the drapes at the back of the hall when he saw her. Charlie marched Adele over to meet him.

Adele felt sick. She couldn't predict what Simon would do. In the past when she'd arrived back from Garnerville, she hadn't cared if Simon was mad at her. He'd have done her a favour if he'd kicked her out of the community back then. But that was before she knew for certain what he was capable of. Before she'd stolen out of the community to betray him.

'Follow me,' he said to Charlie, and led them deeper into the scrub.

Adele's heart was racing. How could it be that she

might die, right on the cusp of her escape? How could she stop Simon from killing her? Was it too late to leverage the crush he had on her?

They walked for ten minutes until they ran out of track and began stepping over fallen branches and knee-high bracken. When he was satisfied they were alone, Simon turned on Adele.

'Where the fuck have you been?'

'Garnerville.'

'Bullshit.'

'I have, I promise.'

'Duck drove up there.'

'I went to check messages, and then I went walking in the bush.'

'Bullshit.'

'It's true.'

'Why did you go?'

'I told you.'

'Did you speak to anyone? Did you tell *any*one about the baby?'

'Of course not.'

'Don't lie to me!' Simon roared.

'I promise, I didn't.'

'I don't believe you.'

'It's true.'

'Why would you leave?'

'I had to get out for a while,' Adele pleaded.

'Why. Do you know how risky that is?'

Simon took Adele by the arms and shook her; his fingers squeezed deep into her flesh.

'What am I going to do with you, Adele? You can't stay in the compound now, but I can't let you leave either.'

'I promise I'll never do it again.'

Adele's pleading had no effect on him.

250

'Why do you do this to me?' he yelled.

Adele sank to her knees, tears streaming.

'Sorry, Simon. I'm sorry…'

Adele disintegrated. Simon glanced at Charlie who was ready to carry out whatever command he was given.

Simon sank to his knees, put his lips up to her ear and spoke very softly.

'You have run out of chances, Adele. Do you understand? Nod if you understand.'

Adele nodded.

'You are no different from anyone else here. When I say you can no longer leave the compound, I mean it. Things have changed.' Adele convulsed with sobs. 'You are confined to Charlie's hut indefinitely. You will not leave there unless I say. I will send Margaret Greer over to help you reintegrate into the community. She will work intensively with you until you get over this disdain you seem to have for us.'

Adele shuddered at the thought. Margaret Greer was the worst of Simon's fanatics. Obsequious enough to have climbed high, but so vacant she could barely draw breath.

Simon let go of her and marched away, and when she looked up he was already disappearing into the scrub.

Adele almost laughed for joy. She was spared, and the only thing that had saved her was Simon's lack of imagination. He couldn't picture the magnitude of what she'd just done.

Clemency felt intoxicating. Her heart beat fast with the satisfaction of knowing she'd won. Now all this would end. She would see Simon's face as he watched his empire crumble.

For the entire journey back to Charlie's hut, Adele reassembled herself. All she needed to do was behave, take her medicine like a good girl, and wait. Wright would arrive with the cavalry, and she would walk out of the compound gates forever.

When she entered Charlie's hut, Margaret Greer was waiting for her with her oily devotions at the ready. Adele spent what was left of the afternoon in prayer, and repeating mantras only fit for a Hallmark friendship card.

When Margaret Greer was finished with her, Adele was offered a meal. She realised it was the first food she'd had since breakfast.

Dead on curfew, Duck arrived.

'Simon wants to see you,' he said.

Adele's heart quickened. Was this trouble? Had something reignited his temper?

'Why?' she said, calming her voice as best she could.

'Go!'

Adele rushed along the path to Simon's hut. Inside, she found that Simon wasn't there. Tim had taken his place, and the girls were busy undressing him.

'What's going on?' Adele said.

'Simon wants Tim to stay with us tonight,' Joanne chirped, and the others giggled.

'Are you serious?'

'It's a celebration,' Shayne said. 'Tim has embraced the community.'

'He's one of us,' Joanne said.

'Simon wants you to lie with him too,' Mayling said.

'What if I don't want to?'

'Please, Adele,' Joanne crooned.

'Simon said you mightn't want to,' Mayling said.

'He was right,' Adele shot back.

Shayne sat up taking a serious tone. 'He said if you didn't want to be with Tim you had to go to him. He's in Tim's hut.'

The whole arrangement sickened her, but she knew

she couldn't make waves now. One last night and then she would be free. She left the women to their sordid task and headed to Tim's hut.

She arrived to find Simon lying on Tim's bed, reading by candlelight. He glanced up at her with a smug grin.

'I guessed you'd end up here.'

Adele wasn't amused.

'Well, I'm not having sex with Tim, that's for sure.'

Simon shrugged.

'Then come here.'

28

If Wright didn't feel part of something big before, he certainly did now. Forty men in battle fatigues and bulletproof vests were at his back, bashing their way through the scrub behind him. His kit was heavy. Sweat soaked his back and stung his eyes as he raced to outstrip these younger men, eager to test his mettle.

From the moment Adele had left the station, Wright felt like he'd been shot out of a gun. Having the first real bead on the baby made him everyone's main man. Within the hour he'd found himself in a helicopter speeding towards Command, clutching Adele's maps and preparing to be grilled by people he'd only read about in newspapers.

In a meeting with the Commissioner, cabinet ministers, and a clutch of advisors, Wright got the treatment he'd given Adele. Knowing the top brass had short attention spans, he gave them the short version, and the moment they realised his story was worth getting out of bed for, Adele's hand-drawn maps were replaced by satellite images with exact dimensions superimposed upon them. A task force was rallied. Command personnel appointed. Logistics organised. By midnight, a force of forty armed men were on choppers heading north, ready to be dropped into scrub five Ks from the compound.

Wright had been appointed leader of one of the three groups going in. He still couldn't believe it—a country cop like him mixing it with the steely-eyed boys from the city. He guessed his local knowledge put him in the mix. That and possibly a reward for landing them such a big fish.

Wright was running on adrenaline and not much more. His team had been on the go for about half an hour. The others had split off soon after the drop to assemble at their respective entry points. All teams were to be in position by 4.30 am, ready to cut through the compound fence. Their coordinates showed them where to cut, then pointed to the exact positions in the compound where they needed to be.

The towering perimeter fence appeared ahead in the moonlight. It seemed to go for miles. Whoever this Simon was, he was an organised son-of-a-bitch.

The night had been sympathetic so far. A blanket of cloud dimmed the moon, giving them a little cover. The rain held off. Their only foe was the stillness. There was no breeze—not a breath—so every footfall seemed shrill in the naked bush, and their whispers amplified.

Wright's team reached the fence and dumped their bags. While the rest of them drained their water bottles, Wright dragged a pair of wire cutters from his kit and found his place to cut. No sensors or electrical charge, so all was clear to go.

He worked the cutters fast while the men gathered,

ready to go on his call. At precisely 4.30 am, Wright peeled back the wire, and one by one his men threaded through the fence into the darkness beyond.

***

Nicole woke to feel Billy slipping from her arms. In her drowsy head it was feed time, and she needed to put him to her breast. Maybe he'd rolled away.

Was that smoke she could smell? She started to cough, which stirred her properly from her sleep.

She reached for Billy. He was gone.

The baby was gone.

The shock of it made her suck in a sharp breath, but it felt like she'd breathed in gravel. She coughed it straight back out again. Where was Billy?

Her eyes were open now, blinking painfully through smoke. At the other end of the hut, the door swung shut. Someone had her baby.

She opened her mouth to scream out for Billy, but as she drew in a breath more smoke caught in her chest and stifled her cries.

The hut was now filling with smoke. She glanced around to see where it was coming from. It was impossible to tell. What could be on fire?

Gail began to stir, coughing her way out of her sleep.

'Billy!' Nicole croaked. She dragged herself off the bed and crawled towards the door.

Gail was quick to follow.

Nicole tugged at the door, but it wouldn't open.

'No,' she coughed, banging on it. 'Help us. Help us.'

She put her shoulder to the door and tried shoving it outwards, but it was jammed. Gail arrived to help, and the two of them slammed their shoulders into it. There was no budging it. Something was wedging it shut.

This couldn't be. Was somebody trying to kill them?

With every attempt to open the door their lungs sucked harder at the choking smoke. Nicole could feel the heat at her back and her head beginning to spin. How much longer could she beat at this door before the smoke defeated her?

Through the smoke she could just make out that the back wall of the hut was now completely ablaze. Flames licked their way deeper into the hut, reaching out for them. It wouldn't be long before this tinderbox was engulfed. They had to get out, now.

They gave another desperate shove against the door, but the smoke was overwhelming. Every breath had become a solid object. There was no longer any oxygen to keep her upright. She slid to her knees, all her strength draining from her.

Nicole knew Gail was somewhere close by. She could hear her coughing weakly. She reached out to her and felt a hand grip hers, and they lay together on the floor, fighting for every breath.

***

The track was well worn, but Wright and his men trod carefully. The crunch of their boots was amplified in the stillness. If they weren't vigilant, it would be the first thing to give them away. They reached an incline that led down to the pond. Beyond was a clearing where the huts were just visible in the moonlight. Wright signalled for them to cut their pace, and they crept past the pond in single file. Wright's heart pounded faster. This was where the operation got serious.

They were at the outskirts of the community. Simon's hut was deeper in, so they moved stealthily along the path, each tread of their boots threatening to stir a sleeper in their hut, mere inches away.

They arrived at Simon's hut. Wright silently gathered his men and waited for the signal: once Simon's arms had been secured, team one's commander would beam a message—a flashing red light—to his coms.

Suddenly, shouts rang out across the compound. Then a gunshot. Wright spun around to face the noise. The glow of a fire was visible above the line of the bush. Something was going down, and it was likely to wake the entire compound. It was now or never. Wright gave the signal, and his team plunged into Simon's hut.

***

Across the compound, team one was standing in Charlie's empty hut, the armoury behind it already secured. It had come to them so easily that they all knew something had to be wrong. Where was Charlie? Securing him and the other hard men was paramount, and so far they had none of them.

Two cops stayed with the guns, plucking out their ammunition and throwing the magazines into a pile, while the others congregated outside, frantically reworking their plan.

Not far down the track, cries broke the silence. Shouts and a scuffle. A gunshot. Things were unravelling quickly. They needed to get moving and secure the other names on their list. Charlie would have to wait. Whatever was going on down the track would have to be left to the responsible team to deal with.

The team broke into a sprint making for Duck, Rob and Aamir's quarters. But the gunshot already had them out of bed, and they were charging towards the team, guns raised. The cops hit the dirt.

'Drop your weapons!' one of the officers cried.

Duck was leading the charge. He ignored the instruction and got a shot off. An officer answered with his own. Duck went down.

Rob appeared behind Duck, two guns raised.

The cops rolled off the track and took cover. This was where their training made the fight unfair. A couple of shots and Rob was already dead.

Behind him, Aamir had more sense. He left the track and scampered for the darkened scrub. One of the cops gave chase, while the others went to secure the shooters.

Duck was badly hit. In moments he was bound at his hands and feet, his struggles more a show of pride than any real attempt to fight back.

Rob was no longer a problem.

In the scrub, Aamir had made good distance. The pursuing officer hadn't lost sight of him, but Aamir's knowledge of the bush gave him the advantage. The pair crashed through the night, breaking everything in their path. The officer stuck close, waiting for Aamir to run out of puff, or belief, or both.

Aamir hit a steep drop down into a creek bed and began running along its dry sand. In an instant the cop was behind him.

'Stop, or I *will* shoot!' he cried.

Aamir didn't even slow. The cop squeezed off two quick shots above Aamir's head to let him know he meant business, and Aamir shied like startled game.

'Get on the ground or the next one won't miss.'

Aamir was having second thoughts. His pace slowed. He was no longer dodging imaginary bullets. Knowing the drill, he fell to his knees and put his hands behind his head.

The officer was on him in moments.

'Wise choice,' he said, giving him a quick whack for his troubles.

***

Simon was awoken by shouting. In an instant he was on his feet, his senses bristling. He gave Adele a shove.

'Listen,' he hissed.

'What's going on?'

Simon put his finger to his lips.

'Someone's raiding the fucking compound.'

He dragged on some pants and rushed for the door. There was movement down the path—police bounding towards him. He ducked back inside, his mind racing for an explanation for all this—and for an exit strategy.

'Where the fuck did these guys come from?' he whispered, struggling into a shirt.

And then it came to him. He turned to Adele.

'You,' he spat. 'You fucking did this.'

Adele backed away into the corner of the hut, a look of guilt spoiling her perfect features. He wanted to charge at her, to destroy her, but two cops appeared breathless in the doorway. He spun around to face them.

'Come on,' one whispered, holding out a hand. 'We're going to get you out of here.'

What they were talking about? Shouldn't they be cuffing him? He stood motionless, trying to drill down into the unfathomable logic of it.

One of the officers moved towards him, but he backed away. For a moment he thought he might take his chances and rush them. But then he had a better idea. Simon threw himself at the side of the hut—just as Tim had done on the day of his arrival. He crashed through the wall and bolted into the darkness.

***

All Tim knew was that someone was dragging him out of bed. The girls were screaming, struggling against a gang of men. Someone was attacking them, but who?

As his eyes adjusted he noticed battle fatigues. A rescue! But before he could open his mouth to say anything he was on the ground, and his face was being pushed into the dirt. Who ever had their knee in his back let their two-way dangle against his head, and he could hear the whole world of the operation playing out.

"*Two in custody, two dead,*" it crackled.

"*Roger that,*" another voice barked.

It suddenly dawned on Tim that the reason he was being treated like this was that they thought he was Simon. It was almost laughable. He opened his mouth to explain, but the knee in his back shoved him deeper into the dirt.

The cacophony died down, and the officer dragged him up and shoved him after the girls, who were being marched smartly out of the hut, hands bound. Tim went placidly. Sooner or later things would calm down, and he would sort out this stupid mess.

***

Nicole felt herself being dragged. In her delirium, she resisted, knowing that, inside this nightmare, it could only be someone coming to harm her. At least Billy had got out. Wherever he was, he was safe from the flames.

Suddenly, the ground beneath her felt cool. She tried to open her eyes, but her head was swimming, and the world felt like it was miles and miles above her.

A shot of sweet air plunged into her throat—a breath that didn't hurt like all the previous ones. How had she inhaled without knowing it? Without even trying, the breath left her again. She felt her chest collapse, and then another breath took its place filling her lungs, sending its cool potency straight to her brain.

She found she could open her eyes, and a cough came hacking out of the deepest part of her. A man was over her, saying her name, willing a response. He pressed his lips to hers and breathed into her. He pulled back again. 'Are you Nicole? ARE YOU NICOLE?'

'Yes … yes…' she spluttered.

She took another breath—this time on her own—and she felt the first clear thought enter her head: Billy.

'Where's my baby?'

'We have your son, Nicole, and he's fine.'

Beyond the group of men hunched over her, she could see Charlie lying in the dirt, hands bound. Cradled in an officer's arms close by was Billy. The brawny man wept gentle tears as he pondered a vision he could never have imagined.

'When you're ready to move, we're going to get you out of here.'

***

Simon had hit the ground running. He assumed at least one of the cops would give chase, so he weaved his way through the thicket beside the path to make his escape.

Up ahead he saw a group of police coming towards him, leading their captives out of the compound. He ducked for cover in a dense patch of bush, laying quietly and listening for their approaching footsteps. As they came into view, he could see it was Tim and the girls being marched towards the compound gates.

In one glorious moment, the truth dawned on him, and he caught a tiny glimpse of God's great plan. The cops thought Tim was *him*. They thought they'd captured the leader. It was beautiful. God was never beaten, but this time His victory was immense. Simon now understood that he was bulletproof. With God at his back like this, anything was possible. He smiled as a sign to God that he was listening, and that he trusted His plan. Emboldened, he waited until the group approached, and then as they passed he sat up and revealed himself. He was easily visible in the moonlight, but no one in the group noticed him. No one but Tim. While the rest of them kept their eyes on the path ahead, something made Tim turn towards the scrub and look directly at him. Their eyes met. Neither of them spoke or made any gesture. Tim could have blown the whistle, but he said nothing.

The moment they were gone, Simon leapt from the scrub and onto the path. He ran past the pond and plunged into the bush.

***

Adele hadn't been spared the zip ties. When Simon had bolted, the officers assumed she was a flight risk too and had taken her down. Their brief hadn't mentioned a woman in Tim's hut, so they'd erred on the side of caution.

Adele was happy to let Wright straighten it all out later. The last thing she wanted was for the community to know it was her who had brought all of this down on them.

They led her down the path towards the compound gates. Police roamed freely from hut to hut, dragging out occupants and binding their hands. There was little resistance. Most seemed dazed by their rude wakeup call.

One or two howled with the injustice of it all, demanded to see Simon, but overwhelmingly there seemed to be an acceptance that their time here had come to an end.

Outside the gates, transporters arrived, waiting to take their human cargo. Floodlights turned the field beyond into daylight, and the rumble of military transports filled the air with diesel fumes.

When they arrived at the gates, Adele joined a queue waiting to have her head counted and her name entered on a list. It was breathtaking. A simple joy flooded her. So often she'd doubted this place and doubted Simon— her dream of finding Jesus incrementally damaged day by day thanks to Simon's self-serving salesmanship. But now it was over, and it was time to leave this place knowing that her instincts had been right all along.

She scanned the scene for those who had already been ejected: Charlie and Aamir under heavy guard, Duck and Rob, dead under a blanket. Tim and the girls were seated in a circle in the field, their hands bound behind them, a few officers keeping them company.

But where was Simon?

Had they found him after he'd crashed out of the hut? She knew none of this would be finished until they led Simon out of the gates.

***

The compound seemed to pass by in slow motion. Someone had insisted Nicole remain on the stretcher until they'd reached the med unit, but it was completely unnecessary. She could have flown there. Watching the compound being dismantled around her had given her wings. And knowing she could finally go home dulled the terrible ache in her lungs.

She held Billy to her, enjoyed the lazy equine sway of the stretcher. Through the barricade of guards that surrounded her, she could see Gail lying on her own

264

stretcher. The nightmare was over. They were finally safe.

Tim didn't even cross her mind until she saw him seated in a ring of girls beneath the floodlights outside the compound. She turned away before he could catch her looking. What would happen between them now that they had to face each other in the real world? A chill went down her spine.

Her journey came to an end at a large, white van, where she was gently dismounted and handed over to the medics. They wasted no time steering her inside.

She didn't mind getting the once over, and she was relieved to have Billy in front of some medical care. But what she really wanted was to put this place way behind her.

Gail sat opposite, draped in a blanket. A medic asked Gail questions and listened to her breathing. Gail's face was filled with victory, like she'd pulled off this rescue singlehandedly. Nicole caught her eye and smiled.

***

Simon took the trail through the bush behind the prayer hut. He knew the place like he knew his own name. Five trees along and to the right of a fallen log, loose rocks concealed a rifle he'd stowed for emergencies exactly like this.

He tore at the rocks until a canvas bag revealed itself. He dragged it out and checked the gun was loaded. Now he was ready. Scouts were bound to be out looking for him, so he'd need to be fast. He looped back through the scrub behind the community and crawled on his belly for the final leg to the kitchen hut.

There he found a box of matches and set to work. The bark on the outside of the kitchen hut was tinder dry, so he struck a match to it and let it catch. Flame licked up the wall in liquid streams.

Knowing the job there was done, he raced through the undergrowth to another hut and put a match to that. He stood back and watched the fire take. Behind him, the kitchen hut was well ablaze. In the distance, voices were raising the alarm. Was this a contingency they'd planned for?

Now the second hut was on fire, he took a burning piece of bark and tossed it into the dry bush, watched it catch in the bracken. It crackled loudly, flames reaching greedily in all directions. In minutes, the entire valley would be ablaze. This was the perfect decoy.

He made a dash through the undergrowth to the far side of the compound and skidded to a stop by the fence—his secret part of the fence where an escape was hidden. He dragged the camouflage away and rolled under, clutching his gun.

Hugging close to the fence line, he followed it around until it brought him to the front of the compound, where he saw the full scale of what had come after him: the trucks, the personnel, *the might*. All this to take him down.

The fire he'd set had disturbed their plan. Men were scattering, orders were being shouted, as fire dabbed its fingers into the dawn sky behind them.

His followers were spilling out of the gates quickly now, the field outside the fence a sanctuary from the flames. They were being herded like sheep towards military buses.

He crawled on his elbows until he was close enough to make out faces. He'd eventually find his target, if he was patient. One clean shot was all he needed, and then his work there would be done.

He scanned the crowd through the telescopic sight on

his rifle. His eye settled on the baby and Nicole, standing by a medical van. Nicole was wrapped in a blanket, talking to a policeman.

Simon moved his sight to take a closer look at the cop, and as he did the officer raised his arm to greet someone approaching from the compound. Simon panned the gun sight to see who he was waving at. It was Adele, walking towards them, smiling.

What kind of a smile *was* it? A smile of relief? A smile of victory? Rage turned inside him, deep as the oceans. Adele was never his.

Simon's finger tightened on the trigger. He squeezed. The gun cracked, and Adele went down.

A scream cried out into the night. Simon didn't wait to check his precision. She was hit, that was all he needed. Time to go. He crawled back into the shadows and melted into the bush like a ghost.

***

Wright saw Adele go down. He knew exactly what had happened. He hit the dirt, eyes darting for the shooter. The way she'd fallen meant the shot had to have come from outside the compound, but there was no sign of who'd pulled the trigger.

Behind him, the unit was in disarray. Men ran in all directions, barking orders, guns raised, but Wright only wanted to get to Adele. She couldn't die, not after all she'd done.

He raised himself up on his elbows and heaved himself along the grass towards her. 'Adele,' he whispered urgently. 'Adele.'

As he reached her he saw why she hadn't answered. She'd have been dead before she hit the ground, the bullet finding her left eye. He helplessly swept her hair from her face.

Not many things in his long career had torn out his heart, but this did. Wright reached under Adele's body and picked her up.

***

Nicole felt numb. She couldn't shake the image of Adele falling right in front of her. Someone had shot her—maybe killed her—right there under the floodlights. So close to Billy. So close to her.

Someone bundled her, Gail and Billy into an SUV, which took off at speed for the far side of the unit, and took cover behind one of the transport vehicles.

The door swung open. She looked up to see an officer silhouetted against the fire-lit dawn.

He must have caught the terror in her eyes. 'I'm sorry, Mrs Blake,' he said quickly. 'Everything's under control. We'll be transporting you to Cook now. Just quickly, this man claims to be your husband. Is this true?'

The officer gestured to Tim, who was standing beside him, handcuffed.

Nicole was too stunned respond. The mere sight of him made her stomach turn. She went to close the door, but the officer caught it.

'He was found in the hut belonging to the leader of the community,' the officer said, appearing slightly confused. 'Is this your husband or not, Mrs Blake?'

Tim was framed in the doorway, with the glow of the compound blazing behind him. This was a man she could no longer love, his true character laid tragically bare.

Nicole nodded.

'Then I guess he can travel with you.'

'No, he can't,' she said flatly, and she tugged the door out of the officer's grasp.

'Can we go please?' Nicole called to the driver, and the SUV jolted into motion.

As they drove away into the rising dawn, she turned to see the compound ablaze behind them. She could hear Maurizio's words: Where there was God there was also fire, if you chose to see it. Was this the case now? Had God had a hand in the destruction of this place? She was too tired to think about it anymore. All she knew was that fire was ending it, and driving away felt like she was finally escaping from the jaws of hell.

29

The media pack washed over the car like an angry sea, pounding the cabin with their fists and barking questions through the tinted windows.

Inside, Nicole and Gail shrank from the roar. Hands pawed at the windows, faces pressed against the glass, cameras thrust through the solid crowd, in the hope that one blind shot might catch a glimpse of the child.

Nicole turned to see a car pull up behind them. Through the window, she could see Tim riding in the front seat. The onslaught of the press didn't seem to faze him; he was just staring passively at them, wearing an odd smile.

Nicole's door was torn open. She shied away, but a man in a tailored suit reached out for her.

'Please come with me,' he barked, and he leaned into the car and grabbed her by the elbow. 'Follow me closely and don't get separated!'

Nicole's heart pounded. She tucked Billy in close and

stepped out of the car.

The frenzy went up a gear. All around them, police pushed back against the mighty pack and brayed at them for calm. Photographers scrapped for any glimpse of the child as he passed them.

Nicole and Gail shadowed the man as he wove them through the crowd and up the steps to the police station, where they were sucked inside.

The group exhaled as one. Nicole was so shaken that she hadn't noticed Tim and his girls had arrived with them too.

The man who had secured them inside was already shaking the chaos off, and Nicole saw him turn to get his first glimpse of Billy. He wasn't ready for the impact. He hesitated for a moment, then gathered himself and then took off again, leading them deeper into the complex.

He led them into what looked like a lunch room. Plastic chairs circled a long table, and the room smelled vaguely of toasted sandwiches and soup. Yellowing safety-in-the-work-place posters hung crookedly on the walls.

'Well *that* was a bit of fun,' he said dryly. 'My name is Chief Commissioner David Bird. I can't apologise enough for putting you through that. I promise you it'll never happen again. Not on my watch.' He gestured to the chairs around them. 'Sit, please.'

Nicole and Gail took seats next to each other, while Tim and the girls settled at the other end of the table.

'I understand someone at our end leaked the operation to the press,' he said. 'It's unforgivable. The culprit will have their nuts crushed. Pardon the French.'

'There's so many of them,' Nicole said in awe.

'That's nothing. You should see what's camped outside your house.'

'Our house?'

Bird paused.

'Okay. You need to understand that the world has changed for you since you've been away. Billions of people now know who you are and what you look like. Nicole, you've been on the cover of every woman's magazine in the world. You guys are the biggest story on the planet.'

Bird let this idea settle.

Gail seemed distracted. At the end of the table, Tim—surrounded by his little party of fanatics—watched on with the same self-satisfied conceit Simon indulged in.

'I'm sorry to interrupt,' Gail said, 'but why are *they* here?'

'Who?' Bird said.

'The girls. Why are they here?'

'They're not part of your group?'

'No. They most definitely are not.'

Bird glanced over to Tim, seeking his response, but Tim remained aloof. He shrugged, which Bird took as acquiescence.

'Err … ladies? If you don't mind,' he said, gesturing for them to leave.

The girls looked to Tim for his approval.

'Don't look at him!' Gail yelled.

Bird glanced from Gail to Tim.

'Please,' he said more insistently.

Tim nodded to the girls, and they obediently rose and left the room. Gail watched them leave, then, once they were gone, she marched over to Tim.

'How dare you do that to her,' she spat, and she slapped him across the face so hard he almost fell backwards off his chair. Tim saved himself and was on his feet ready to swing at Gail. Bird was across the room

272

in a second, stepping between them.

'Okay, okay,' he said and led Gail back to her seat.

Tim was still on his feet. He grabbed the chair in front of him and threw it, sending it crashing across the room.

'Hey!' Bird cried. 'Let's take it down a notch here.'

'Why is *she* here?' Tim yelled, jabbing a finger at Gail.

'Because if it wasn't for her we'd still be in that hell hole!' Nicole shouted back. 'We owe her!'

'I owe her nothing,' he said. 'If she stays, my girls stay.'

'Okay, okay, okay,' Bird cut in. 'I clearly have a little catching up to do here. Tim, why don't we get you checked out by the med staff. Nicole, Gail, you can stay here while I fill you in on what happens next.'

'I'm staying,' Tim said.

'Is that really such a good idea?' Bird said. 'We need to focus on a few things without any feelings getting in the way.'

'I'm fine.'

Tim didn't move. Bird glanced back to Nicole, who was breathing through her fury.

'Okay,' she said. 'If he can resist throwing the furniture around.'

Tim found another chair, sat on it and crossed his arms.

Bird sat on the table and waited for calm.

'Okay. Clearly, you've all had a very distressing time. My job here is to try and make the transition from what you've been through to your new lives as smooth as possible. You need protection.' He gestured to the door. 'Everyone out there wants a piece of you guys. You can't underestimate how big this is. I'm only here to greet you because the Prime Minister couldn't get here in time. Otherwise he'd be standing on the steps out there grinning for photos with you right now. Every religious organisation in the world has been trying to get their hands on you. World leaders, you name it. Do you understand what I'm saying?'

'How do they know about us?' Nicole said bitterly. 'Did they trace the video as well?'

Bird was confused. 'I'm not sure what you mean.'

'How did they find us?'

'Your mother.'

Tim snorted. Nicole did her best to ignore him.

'My mother?'

'I'm afraid so. The day you were kidnapped she rang a radio station and told them all about you. While you were in the compound, the entire world has been out looking for you.'

Nicole couldn't put it together. 'Why on earth would she do that?'

'I can't say for sure,' Bird said. 'I can only imagine the stress she was under at the time. I'm sorry. You can talk to her about it soon. We're organising a call for you.'

The thought of speaking to her parents practically split her open with joy; there was so much to say.

'So,' Bird went on, 'let's talk about your living arrangements. Your house is under siege from the press, so we've organised alternative accommodation for you at a secret location. It's a safe house operated by the government. You don't *have* to take it, but I strongly encourage you to. At least for the time being—'

'I'm happy to take it,' Nicole butted in, 'but you'll need to find somewhere else for him.'

Bird glanced over to Tim, who turned away.

'Tim?'

Bird paused; it didn't look like Tim would ever answer.

'I'm happy to stay in our house,' Tim said flippantly.

'Are you certain? You might find—'

'You heard what I said.'

Bird nodded and turned to Gail.

'Ms Alvarez?'

Gail never had a problem asking for what she wanted, but imposing on Nicole now seemed too much. Nicole saw her hesitation.

'Gail. You're welcome to stay with us. For as long as you want.'

Gail sighed with relief. 'Then I'm happy to do that.'

'Good. Okay. Now before we can get you out of here, we'll need to ask you some questions. After that, I'm afraid we're going to have to present you to the media.' Nicole went to protest. 'There'll be a riot if we don't,' Bird added quickly. 'I know it's the last thing you feel like doing, but if you do it now it'll get them off your backs for a while.'

Nicole didn't feel ready. She was still shaken from the frenzy on the way in.

'I promise it'll be better managed than before,' he said. 'Now. Nicole, Gail? I'd like you to take Billy to see the med staff and get checked out—'

'We were checked at the compound,' Nicole said.

'I know, but it can't hurt for them to take another look at you. Tim? Can you stay and answer some questions with me please?'

Tim shrugged.

Bird went to the door and waved an officer in.

'This is Constable Carpenter,' he said to Nicole. 'She'll take you down to the sick bay.'

Nicole and Gail followed, as Carpenter led them away.

***

Bird turned to Tim. 'Do you need anything? A coffee? I'm sure there's a doughnut around somewhere.'

'Both,' Tim said. 'Thanks. I'm starving.'

Bird waved down another uniform.

'That's it? A coffee and a doughnut?'

Tim nodded.

Another man entered the office. Tim recognised him from the raid. He remembered how effectively he'd shoved his head into the dirt.

'Tim, this is Detective John Wright. He led one of our teams this morning.'

Wright dragged up a chair and sat. Tim gave him a thin smile and shook his hand.

'Hello, Tim. How are you feeling?'

'Tip top.'

'Right. Stupid question. Sorry. Look, I know you've been through a lot, so I'll try to keep it brief. We understand that the man who kidnapped you was called Simon. We also understand that this is a pseudonym. Do you know anything about that?'

Tim shook his head.

'He never indicated to you what his real name was?'

Tim shrugged "no".

'Okay. Who was present when you were kidnapped?'

'Simon, Duck, Charlie, Rob and Aamir.'

'Good. Aside from the deceased we have the rest of them in custody—except for Simon. Now tell me … Adele spoke of Simon committing a number of violent acts. Are you aware of this?'

'What kind of acts?'

'Robbery … murder—'

'I know they stole provisions for the compound, but I don't know anything about any murders.'

'He never mentioned how Father Jim died?'

'In a car accident.'

'He told you that?'

'Yes. He said he wanted to talk to him, but Gail took off. Drove the car into a creek bed or something.'

Wright glanced at Bird.

'Were there any rumours around the place that that wasn't true?' Wright said.

'No. Look, Simon was not to be fucked with, but I don't think he killed anyone.'

'Why were you in his hut when we arrived?'

Tim detected a tone in Wright's question.

'Why?'

'I'm interested. You were his captive, yet you seemed to be using his bed and sharing his girlfriends.'

'Is that a crime?'

'No, but the reason he hasn't been caught was because of this confusion. We want to be sure there was no collusion going on.'

'What? You think I helped him escape?'

'Did you?'

Tim thought back to the moment on the track when he was being led away. Simon was within reaching distance of the police, yet he'd said nothing. He couldn't explain why. For an instant he was in a nether world where Simon's conviction that he was part of God's plan had cast its spell over him. It seemed true: Simon was right there in the scrub next to the path, yet he was invisible to the police. If it wasn't God's will, how did he do that?

'Of course I didn't,' Tim said at last. 'It was a coincidence. None of us had any idea you were coming. I was in Simon's hut because he wanted me to adjust to the community.'

Wright and Bird shared a look.

'Okay. Finally, what was Adele Blanche's relationship with Simon like?'

'How do you mean?'

'Were they lovers?'

'Yes. But she wasn't like the others. She played hard to get.'

'Do you think he would kill her?'

'What? Kill her? No. Why?'

'Adele was shot dead this morning.'

Tim gasped despite himself. 'No.'

'We suspect it was Simon who pulled the trigger.'

'No, that's not possible.'

'He was the only member of the community unaccounted for at the time.'

'Then it had to be one of *your* lot.'

'That's also impossible. The gun has been retrieved and it's not one of ours. Forensics is looking at it now.'

Tim stood. He couldn't fathom Simon doing such a thing. He paced the floor.

'Look, this is upsetting,' Bird said. 'I'm sorry to have to bring it up. Why don't you go and get checked out, then we can get you out of here.'

Tim was in a daze. Wright led him from the lunch room and down the corridor, but his mind was with Adele. Why would Simon shoot her? He loved her so much. There had to be some mistake.

The corridor echoed with the footsteps of busy officers mopping up after the raid. There was the kind of buzz that only followed a successful operation, and Tim felt like the star attraction. They all knew who he was as they hurried by, and he could feel their eyes lingering on him.

As they passed another interview room, he noticed his girls languishing under the guard of a uniformed officer. Tim stopped.

'Can I see them?' he said.

Wright took a look at his watch. 'Don't be long.'

Tim pushed through the door. The moment she caught sight of him, Joanne ran to him.

'My darling,' she cried, kissing him desperately. 'What have they done to you?'

'I'm fine,' he said. 'Truly. They're looking after me. What about you?'

'They won't tell us what's going to happen to us. I just want to go back to the compound.'

Tim knew without the sanctuary of the compound Joanne was lost. It broke his heart to see her so rudderless.

'That's not going to happen,' he said tenderly. 'The compound's finished.'

'But where's Simon?'

'He's taken off. They didn't catch him.'

Joanne stared at him helplessly. Tears welled.

'What can I do?' she said softly. 'I don't know where to go.'

Tim held her.

'It's okay,' he said. 'You can come and stay with me.' He turned to the other girls, whose faces betrayed the same fear as Joanne's. 'If you have nowhere else to go, you can all come and stay with me.'

The girls rushed him, and Tim found himself buried in a grateful embrace. He squeezed his face through a gap only large enough to catch a breath and noticed Nicole returning from the sick bay.

She turned to see him locked in the girls' embrace. Tim saw her squeeze her eyes shut—as if to blink away what she was witnessing. As if seeing them together brought back the most painful sight she'd ever seen.

The elation he'd felt moments before vanished.

'I have to go,' he said. 'But I promise I'll get you out of here. You haven't done anything wrong, so you should be free to go.' The girls drew him tighter. 'Don't be afraid,' he said, 'we'll work something out.'

He extracted himself and made for the sick bay with Wright.

***

Tim's check-up was brief, and the attending nurse was more than a little star-struck. When she took out her iPhone to take a selfie with him, Wright stepped in to put a stop to it. But it fed Tim's craving for celebrity. As he left the sickbay, the nurse's lingering farewell hug sent a shiver of fulfillment through him and made him walk just that little bit taller.

When Tim arrived back at the lunch room, Nicole was talking on the phone and bouncing Billy on her lap. He could tell it was her parents on the line, because her face was awash with tears.

Gail was being interviewed by an officer, and seemed to be relishing her chance to point the finger at Simon.

'We'll find him soon enough, Ms Alverez,' Tim heard the officer say. 'There's a lot of country up here, but not many places to hide.'

Nicole handed the phone back to Bird and joined Gail. 'They're getting on a plane now,' she said. 'We'll see them tonight.'

Gail threw her arms around Nicole and held her close.

Bird, who was hovering, crept a step closer. 'Okay. How do we feel about facing our first press conference?'

'Daunted,' Nicole said.

'They're really only going to want to photograph Billy, but it would be extremely wise for you to take a few questions. Are you okay to do that, Nicole?'

Nicole hesitated.

'Look,' Bird said, 'you may as well give them a few

headlines. If you don't give them one, they're going to make it up anyway.'

Nicole smiled. 'Okay.'

'I have some clothes for you to change into, and a makeup artist to make you look pretty.'

'Seriously?' she gasped.

'Are you kidding? These photos are going to be beamed around the globe. You may want to look your best.'

Nicole nodded.

'Okay then,' Bird said, 'let's get pretty.'

***

Nicole and Gail spent an hour in makeup. Billy was given a fresh jump suit, and Tim wore a deep blue jacket. By the time they were finished, they looked like they were ready to step onto a yacht.

As they assembled at the front door, the racket from outside sounded like Mardi Gras, and they could see TV lights on stands already blasting the front of the station.

'Just so you know; they've been ordered to behave,' Bird said. 'There will be *no* repeat of what happened this morning, understand?' Nicole nodded nervously. 'Now I'll be running this thing. If you want to stop at any time throw it back to me. Okay?'

With a nod from Nicole, Bird pushed through the doors. Nicole saw police members lining a steel barrier, which ran all the way down the stairs to where a podium had been erected.

A deafening roar went up. Nicole's heart pounded as they were bathed in a thousand camera flashes. She held Billy tighter to her.

Bird stepped up to the podium. Nicole and Tim assembled awkwardly behind him, and Gail stood back out of the way.

'Good morning, everyone,' Bird said. His voice echoed out of loud speakers up and down the avenue. 'As you know, we've recently arrived back from a successful operation to free the Blake family from a community just north of here, where they've been held captive since last Wednesday. I'm delighted to confirm that the family members are all in good health, thanks to the courageous endeavours of local police and a specially assembled task force. Now, I'm sure you're already sick of me and would like to hear from Nicole Blake, the mother of this very special child. She has generously made herself available to answer a few questions.'

He turned to Nicole and nodded.

All she could see were faces and camera flashes, and the world around her sparkled and crackled. She made an unsteady step up onto the podium, while Billy lay peacefully in her arms, unfazed by the uproar.

As she approached the microphones, she made sure Billy was upright and visible to the crowd, which seemed to stretch back for a hundred metres. Beyond the scrum of media, people held up placards that read: "*the Lord is come*", and "*Jesus is reborn*".

Billy's halo glowed, dreamlike, in the soft morning light. People gasped. Some of the photographers were so stunned they lowered their cameras and stood motionless. Others fell to their knees.

'Hello,' she said, testing the reach of the microphones. A hush fell over the crowd. 'My name is Nicole. I'd like to thank the very brave officers who rescued us. I can't tell you how relieved we are to be back, believe me.'

A roar went up again. As one, the media pack began to yell questions. "*Nicole, are you a virgin?*" "*Were you commanded by God to call him Billy?*" "*Have you met God?*"

"Did God come to your house?" "Are you going to give the child to the Church?"

And then one question rose above all the others. *"Nicole, what was it like living in a fanatical religious commune?"*

'Unpleasant,' she said shyly.

The crowd roared with laughter. More questions came. Again, Nicole heard one rise above all the rest. *'What will you discuss when you meet with Sanjiv Gupta and Sean Teale?'*

Nicole was thrown. She knew their names. One was the self-help guru Clare read when she was sick. And *everyone* knew Sean Teale. What was the connection?

'I ... we don't know anything about that.' Nicole felt herself floundering. Suddenly, it all became too scary. 'I'm sorry. We really need to get some rest. And this little one needs a feed.'

While the crowd thundered more questions at her, Nicole turned to Bird and mouthed, "Can we finish?" Bird was on the podium in a flash calling it off, and with that he shepherded them back up the stairs and into the station.

***

For a moment, Tim didn't move. Wasn't it his turn to speak? How was it that Nicole was suddenly the protagonist? He followed the others into the station, where Bird rubbed salt in the wound by wrapping Nicole in a hug and saying, 'You are a natural.'

'No,' she said. 'That thing with Sanjiv Gupta threw me! What was he talking about?'

'No idea. But you handled it perfectly. Only answer the questions you want to answer. Now, I promised to get you out of here and I will. Your transport is ready to take you to your accommodation.'

Bird led them through the police station and out to the car park, where a helicopter sat idling loudly. Bird had to yell to be heard over the din.

'Nicole, Gail, this is your ride. It'll take you to your new home.'

Nicole looked exhausted. She thanked Bird and headed for the chopper with Gail.

Bird turned to Tim. 'If you can wait for a few minutes, I'll sort you out once the others have gone.'

Tim nodded vacantly and watched as Nicole ducked under the blades and climbed aboard. He hung onto the thought that she might look back at him—just once. He waited, but she disappeared inside the belly of the craft, all without a single glance behind her.

With her went his child. The one thing that made him special in the world. How was it that his role as a father was so easily ignored, and the assumption that Billy could be separated from him so effortlessly made?

The idling surged to a deafening whine, and the chopper lifted off. It fidgeted above the police station for a moment, rotated, and then punched away towards the horizon.

30

The suburbs of Cook gave way to outlying pastures, and then to the massive plantation forests beyond. Through the bug-eye of the helicopter, Nicole could see for miles, but what lay ahead of her was a mystery.

Billy rested comfortably in her arms, his eyelids heavy against the already long day. Gail was beside her in the cabin, staring out at the landscape. She owed this woman so much. Without her, they'd still be back in the compound—or worse. She took Gail's hand and woke her from her thoughts.

'Okay?' she said, and Gail nodded.

The chopper banked right, and beyond the rocky ridge of a soaring mountain range a small hamlet appeared nestled between two thundering mountain streams. They squared up over a large football field, and Nicole could see at least half a dozen cars parked below. The helicopter swung its tail around until it found the right place to descend, and as it touched down a man in a uniform rushed to the door and swung it open. Nicole saw his military efficiency momentarily undone by the sight of Billy. Quicker than most, he recovered and yelled over the whine of the aircraft, 'Mrs Blake, Ms Alvarez, I'm Lieutenant John Gable. I'm here to escort you to your accommodation. If you'll come with me please.'

Gail stepped out first, followed by Nicole, who sheltered Billy from the turbulence. Gable led them across the turf to one of the parked cars, and they were showered with leaves as the chopper roared back into the embrace of the mountain range.

Gable ushered them into the back seat.

He gave a hand signal, and in unison the cars that surrounded them simultaneously roared to life.

Gable climbed into the driver's seat and headed the car off the oval and onto the road. As if some silent instruction had been given, the other cars took off in different directions.

'Where are they going?' Gail asked.

'They're decoy vehicles, ma'am. We have to be certain that where we're taking you remains one hundred per cent secure.'

'Where are you taking us?'

'That's confidential.'

'My parents are arriving,' she said. 'Will they know where we are?'

'Already sorted, Mrs Blake. Just sit back and relax. We'll be there in no time.'

After thirty minutes on the road, the car turned off the highway into a housing estate that was still under construction. Neatly paved bitumen rolled through street after street of half-dug allotments, filled with teetering stacks of bricks and earth dumped in gigantic piles. The skeletons of unfinished houses were scattered about, abandoned. In the distance, a miniature skyline of the city rose over the uneven flat of the landscape.

As they drove deeper into the estate, the construction became more complete. Semi-finished houses dotted the streets, each a slight variation of the next. They arrived at an oasis of fully completed houses, replete with tended gardens of instant turf and tethered saplings. The oasis stretched for about three streets around them before it fell away again into the desolation beyond.

Gable pulled into the driveway of one of the completed houses. Neither Nicole nor Gail moved. The house towered above the street with its faux everything—a cake decorator's idea of architecture.

'Welcome home,' Gable said with a wink. The women were still too stunned to speak. 'We haven't managed to bring many of your things yet, but over the next few days they'll start to arrive.'

'Won't the neighbours recognise us?' Gail said.

'There are no neighbours, ma'am . The government owns the entire site.'

'All of it?'

Gable grinned. 'Yep. It's probably the most secure site we have, leaving aside those facilities that would make you feel like prisoners again. We call it "The Film Set". It's designed to look like an estate under construction, but of course with the discovery of methane in the soil, it will never be finished.' Gable read the look on Nicole and Gail's faces. 'Don't worry, that's a cover story. It's perfectly safe. Shall we?'

Gable led them inside through the faux Romanesque porch. The cavernous entrance foyer narrowed to a hallway, which ran deep into the house, terminating in a giant family room at the rear.

Sweeping skyward from both sides of the entrance foyer was a mock plantation estate staircase, which led to God knows how many bedrooms. Ornamental tables dressed the hallway and had already been set with knickknacks lifted from Nicole's home: photos of her and Tim, her parents, her wedding day. As Gable led them down the hallway to the family room, Nicole turned the photos of Tim face down.

In the family room, the furniture and fittings all felt temporary. The white leather couches still smelt of the store, like the plastic had only been stripped off moments before they arrived. Standing amongst all this spruce and neatness, Nicole didn't quite know what to do next. Her instinct was to rearrange everything.

'They've put you in a bedroom upstairs,' Gable said to Nicole. He turned to Gail. 'And you're first to the right downstairs, Ms Alvarez. I'm sorry, we haven't been able to bring any of your belongings yet. They'll be here tomorrow. There's food in the cupboards and sheets on the beds.'

Gable shuffled. Now he'd delivered them he was clearly keen to take off.

'You have two security personnel here looking after you twenty-four seven. These men are the very best. Commissioner Bird has ordered a communication blackout for you, so you can feel free to get some rest.'

Nicole breathed a sigh of relief. All she wanted was to hit the sack and sleep.

'Now unless you have any questions?'

Nicole shook her head, and with that Gable was gone.

Nicole took Billy up the grand staircase to her bedroom. Like the rest of the house it was bloated. A king-sized faux-Napoleon four-poster bed sat in the middle of the room. On the chest of draws that faced it sat familiar objects snatched randomly from her real home, looking as out of place as she felt. She wandered over and slid open the top drawer. Inside, she found some of her clothes, gathered without the slightest thought for what went with what.

The second drawer down was filled with Tim's clothes. The sight of them repulsed her so much she scooped them up and tossed them into the hallway. Then she lay on the bed with Billy, and within moments was asleep.

***

Nicole couldn't tell how long she'd been asleep when the sound of voices woke her. She sat up, completely disoriented.

She gathered up Billy and carried him down the staircase to the ground floor. There she found her parents in the lounge room, talking to Gail. Her fatigue evaporated, but just as she was about to race over to them she noticed two men standing with them. They didn't look like police or army. They radiated success, holding themselves the way only influential people do.

That's when it hit her. They were Sanjiv Gupta and Sean Teale. She had to take a moment to fully comprehend it was really them. Why on earth were they here? And how did the journalist back in Cook know to ask her about them?

She was still gaping at them when the group sensed her presence. They turned as one. Clare squealed and ran to her, burying her in her arms. The two held each other and wept, then Clare kissed Billy and fussed over him.

Garry approached, patiently waiting his turn. Nicole turned to him. 'Dad,' she said, nuzzling into him, and Garry threw his arms around her.

Sanjiv and Sean politely stood back as the reunion

unfolded. Sanjiv, in particular, didn't take his eyes off Billy.

Nicole finally unfolded herself from her parents and turned to Sanjiv and Sean.

'Hello, Nicole,' Sanjiv said. 'My name is Sanjiv, and this is Sean.'

'I know who you are,' she said with a grin. 'You're pretty famous.'

'Well *he* certainly is,' Sanjiv said nodding to Sean. Nicole laughed. 'I know you've been through a terrible ordeal. I truly hope we're not imposing on you by being here.'

'I'm sure there's a good reason,' Nicole said.

'I'm very keen to explain. But first, do you mind if I hold Billy for a moment?'

Nicole was taken aback. When first encountering Billy, most people were too overwhelmed to hold him; Nicole gladly offered him to Sanjiv, who took him and looked down at him with kind eyes.

'Hello, Billy. Aren't you beautiful?'

Nicole felt her heart fill with joy. She expected Sanjiv to give his attention back to her once more, but his eyes stayed fixed on Billy, and he continued to address him tenderly.

'Most of my life has been spent exploring the esoteric,' he said. 'Questioning, searching for truth—but nothing could have prepared me for you. I feel God all around you, little one. Only good can come of you. You will teach us, and lead us, and show us how to love. We'd almost forgotten how before you came.'

As Sanjiv held the baby, all the noise seemed to be sucked from the room; Nicole watched on, spellbound. It was a moment of pure presence—as if nothing else existed. It was like encountering the intersection of two profound paths in one perfect moment in time.

290

Sanjiv looked up and returned Billy to Nicole's arms.

'You have business with your family,' he said. 'You want to talk about what has happened to you and what has happened to them. When you are ready, I would like to talk to you too. About some very important things. I have a proposal for you and your son—a task that I believe is what Billy has come to this earth to do.'

After the ordeal she'd just escaped, Sanjiv's words should have repulsed Nicole. But there was nothing grasping about him. His way was generous and genuine, and for the first time Nicole didn't fear that someone wanted to steal her child away from her. She would have given anything to hear what Sanjiv's proposal was— except she needed time with her parents. They had so much to say to each other, and all of it needed to be covered before she could even think about talking to Sanjiv and Sean.

***

While Nicole debriefed with her parents, the two famous men sat in the back garden and waited patiently. As evening fell they made a meal, and they coaxed the family to the dining table and served them delicious curries and naan bread. Wine flowed.

Clare drilled Sean about Hollywood, turning him into a wellspring of celebrity gossip. Finally, Sanjiv turned the conversation to Billy. He reached across the table and took Nicole's hand.

'You've had one hell of a day, my dear. Would you like to go to sleep now, or would you like to hear my crazy proposal?'

31

Tim watched until the chopper cleared the hills to the far side of Cook. Even after he'd lost sight of it, he listened until the hum of the engines faded. Nicole was gone. She was starting a new life without him, and she'd taken their son with her.

'I'm sorry,' Bird said, placing a hand on his shoulder and breaking him rudely from his thoughts. 'You okay?'

'Not really. I need to ask you something.'

'Shoot.'

'This is all so thrown together.'

'What do you mean?'

'Well, where have you taken them?'

'To a property set aside for high-target witness protection.'

'But where?'

'That's classified. I'm sorry.'

Tim shook his head cynically.

'What if I want to see Billy? How am I going to do

that?'

'We'll arrange it. We needed to get you settled first. We had no idea there were issues between you and your wife.'

Tim felt the stab of being a forgotten part of the picture; he craved for something to be in it for him too.

'What about Joanne?' he snapped, 'And the other girls? I'd like them to come home with me.'

'I'm afraid that's not possible. The rest of the community needs to be processed.'

'Processed?'

'Questioned. There's been a murder. Possibly three. We need to determine who, if any, is implicated in a crime.'

Tim laughed bitterly. 'You're kidding me. You seriously think the girls had anything to do with that?'

'That's what we need to clear up.'

'Can't you question them and release them to me now?'

'They've already left for the city watch house. After they're processed, if they wish, I'll arrange for them to be escorted to you.' Tim was seething. 'It's procedure.'

Tim wanted to take it further, but the roar of an approaching chopper drowned him out. It touched down, and Bird gestured for him to get in.

As they lifted off, Tim could see the scale of what had just taken place. The crowd that had assembled to see Billy was breaking up, but it flooded the streets below— like the scatterings from a music festival. A line of media vans stretched out along the main street and made him feel like a rock star making a secret escape into the open sky.

They flew most of the way back to Melbourne, and then met with a motorcade that delivered them to the cul-de-sac, where Tim caught a glimpse of what Bird had warned him about. The street was choked. Scores of media personnel languished in tents or on blow-up mattresses, sunning themselves in the afternoon heat, doing their best to break up the boredom of waiting.

The sound of the approaching cars stirred the hornet's nest. As one, they sprang into action, swarming them, cameras and microphones at the ready.

Tim sat to attention, taking it all in.

Bird slowed to a crawl as the media pressed in on them.

'Police,' he said flashing his badge. 'Let us through, guys.'

The crowd parted reluctantly as they shouted questions and snapped pictures through the windows.

After easing their way through the crowd, they pulled to a stop at the driveway. Two guards were already standing their ground out the front of the house. Bird gave them a nod, and they came forward to escort Tim inside.

'The press has been cautioned not to enter your property, so when we get out of the car go straight inside, and we shouldn't have a problem. Okay?' Tim nodded. 'Good. Let's go.'

Bird leapt out; Tim followed. The world lit up around them as the lens of global media turned his way— everything and everyone angled in his direction. Journalists bleated desperately over each other, some in foreign accents.

Tim ducked under the flimsy perimeter tape, which marked out the no-go zone. Bird started up the driveway towards the house, assuming Tim would follow, but rather than go with him, Tim turned to the crowd and waved. It sent them into a frenzy.

"Tim, where's the baby?" "Tim, where were you being held captive?" "Give us a smile, Tim." "Where's Nicole?"

It was like a dream. Hundreds of them, grasping at him, calling his name, wanting him. Anything he chose to tell them would be flashed around the globe instantaneously. It stirred something inside him: a sleeping beast, and he felt an ecstatic ache as it woke.

"Tell us a bit about yourself, Tim."

He craved to answer the question. So many times he'd dreamed of this moment, fantasised about what he'd actually say in this situation, and there was so much to tell them.

He searched the crowd for the questioner. 'Okay,' he said with a grin. A hush descended. 'I can tell you about myself.'

Bewildered, Bird tried to catch his eye, but Tim sailed on.

'I'm Tim Blake. Billy's dad. If you hang around here you'll be seeing quite a bit of me.' The crowd laughed. 'What can I tell you about myself? Well, for a start, I'm a musician.'

"Sing us a song."

More laughs from the crowd.

'What, right now?' he quipped. 'No, I need my band for that. Or my guitar. But I'll tell you what; I *will* come and play you something soon. In the meantime, if you want to hear some of my stuff, it's easy to find online.'

"What's it called?"

'Butterfly Kiss. It's a band I fronted. There's a whole EP on iTunes called *Get Some.*'

Bird leant into Tim.

'We need to keep moving.'

But Tim was on a roll. 'In fact, why don't I go inside right now and put up some of my new stuff. Have a listen and let me know what you think.'

Questions rained down on him, but Tim was finished. He waved again and turned for the house. Bird followed.

When they made it inside, Bird shut the front door and turned to Tim.

'What was that?' he said reaching for a calm tone.

'What?'

'If you engage them like that, it makes our job that much harder. You watch, there'll be another hundred here by morning.'

'I don't give a fuck how many come. Let 'em all come.'

Bird seemed to bristle.

'I'm not going to hide away like some recluse.'

'Then you need to go somewhere more secure.'

'I like it here.'

'What if someone wants to take a swipe at you?'

'Don't we have guards?'

'It may not be that easy.'

Tim shrugged. 'Look, I'm going to be fine.' And with that he turned and headed for the study. Bird followed. Tim had fired up his computer, already acting on his promise to get his music online.

'I'll have some uniforms do a shop for you and bring you some lunch,' Bird said.

'Great, I'm starving. Can they bring pizza?'

'Sure.' Bird pulled a business card out of his jacket. 'Here's my number. Give me a call if you've got any questions or if you need anything.'

'I'd like the number of where Nicole is.'

'I'm sorry. I can't risk giving it out. Not even to you.'

'I'd like to know when I can see Billy.'

'Give me a few days.'

Tim nodded, but his focus had already left Bird. He opened his song folder and selected tracks to upload. Bird hovered for a moment.

'I'll tell the boys outside about the pizza.'

'Uh-huh,' Tim grunted absently.

By the time Bird had left, Tim had already pulled out a dozen songs and was uploading them to iTunes. He'd done it a hundred times for the bands he'd recorded at the studio. He created a self-titled album and then Photoshopped an image of himself for the cover. In ninety minutes flat the album was up.

He opened his YouTube channel. After the demise of Butterfly Kiss, he'd posted a bunch of solo songs there in an effort to showcase his own work. To his astonishment, within an hour of talking to the press, he'd already gained half a million subscribers.

He leapt to his feet and punched the air. His future was set. The music he'd fought so hard for—which had failed so miserably before—was now going straight to the top. Finally, he'd be a household name. He could tour. He could handpick his band. He could record any music he damn well liked, and the record companies would eat it up.

His head throbbed with exhaustion, but he was fuelled with the adrenaline of promise. Today had started with a gun being pointed at his head and had finished with his musical dreams coming true. The void had been filled. Maybe Simon was right after all. God *did* have a plan for him.

He marched down the driveway to the waiting press. Lights erupted around him.

'I've got an update for you. I've just uploaded my new self-titled album, *Tim Blake*. It's available on iTunes right now. Stay tuned for my tour dates.'

32

James Conroy, Arch Deacon of the Anglican Church. Tareq Hasis, Supreme Imam of the Sunnis. Hassan Braqu, Supreme Imam of the Shiites. Karl Gurder, Cardinal of the Catholic Church. Philip Castel, High Priest of the Mormon Church. His Holiness, the Dalai Lama of the Buddhist Church. His Holiness, Raj Bendal, spiritual leader of the Hindu Church. John Xasvenios, Cardinal of the Greek Orthodox Church. Joel Bergman, Chief Rabbi of Tel Aviv. Kagiso Mkandla, chairperson of the African Council of Religious Leaders. Sanjiv Gupta, spiritual healer and psychologist. Sean Teale, actor and ambassador for world peace.

Twelve names.

Sanjiv talked Nicole through every one of them and why they deserved a place on the list. Each represented their faith on the international stage, and their faiths combined reached around ninety-five per cent of the world's people. They were holy and respected church leaders, and—as far as Sanjiv was concerned—true servants of God. Gathering them together wouldn't be easy. He wasn't even certain it would be possible. But as Sanjiv pointed out, could there be a bigger or more compelling drawcard than Billy?

Sanjiv sat opposite Nicole at the dining table with the list spread out before them. The wine, the headiness of the evening, the wonder of fame made his words swim. She was inside a dream where celebrities dined at her table, and laughed, and flipped out the kind of anecdotes that only appeared in women's magazines. It was flattering and rare. She felt special—like a celebrity herself.

'War is the major cause of poverty, human displacement, and environmental destruction,' Sanjiv said. 'It perpetuates a cycle of hatred. The majority of wars are driven by religious differences. My philosophy is this: that essentially all human beings are the same; we all want the same things. Peace is one of those things. Faith is another. Nicole, we have a unique opportunity here to end the conflict between religions. If we can unite the twelve people on this list around Billy, and with their blessing and guidance take him out to the world and show the people that God unites us—not divides us—then I believe it will cool the temperature of hatred and suspicion between people, and bring the world together in peace and in faith. This, I believe, is the reason Billy has come to us.'

After enduring Simon's puerile ramblings in the compound, Sanjiv's words felt selfless and pure, and Nicole connected with them whole-heartedly.

'Sanjiv is the perfect facilitator for this endeavor,' Sean said. 'He's spent his entire life promoting interfaith communion, and he's as admired and accepted by the Hindus as he is by the Muslims or Christians.'

Sanjiv smiled and waved Sean's words away.

'He's too humble to admit it, but it's true,' Sean said. 'If peace is what you're after, Sanjiv's your guy.'

Sean flashed one of his winning smiles.

'I am a rich man,' Sanjiv said. 'I wish to use this wealth, all of it if I must, to bring the people on that list here, to your house. To meet Billy. I want them to know the truth about him, to experience him firsthand so they can understand the vision as I see it. When they meet Billy, they will feel his power and understand his potential. And when they do, we will all unite to heal the world. Our message will be simple. God is real. He is here, and he belongs to all of us without favour.'

Nicole needed no more convincing. She glanced at her parents, who'd already had days to digest this and had asked all the hard questions they could think of: Where will the army of support staff come from? How to do it without inflaming religious rivalries? Where to start to set the tone for the tour? Security? Cost? What if it fails?

Sanjiv had stated that he'd contemplated these issues and observed the answers in meditation. He'd promised he was prepared, but added it was as important to be instinctive and blindly optimistic as it was to plan, because if they let the size of the task enter the frame it could easily frighten and swamp them.

'Logic and intuition must be the two sides of the one coin that we take with us on this journey,' he said.

Nicole was silent. The prospect was scary but exciting.

'I have given you my vision, Nicole, and now I must ask you for your answer. You are the child's mother and therefore will ultimately decide his future. Do you want Billy to be part of this vision? Or would you like for Sean and I to leave you and your family in peace? The choice is one hundred percent yours.'

He sat back waiting for her answer. Perhaps he imagined she would need some time to think, but his respectful tone had made her heart soar and the decision came easily. 'I don't even need to think about it. I'd be honored.'

Sanjiv burst out of his seat and embraced her.

Clare threw her arms around both men and celebrated too.

'I believe this will be a new awakening for us all,' Sanjiv said.

***

Sanjiv went to work. He converted one of the sprawling, upstairs bedrooms into an office, and he hit the phones. The first calls were to the names on his list. The nervous days leading up to gaining Nicole's approval had been spent constructing a database that would, in a few easy steps, get his chosen few straight on the line. But now the time had finally arrived for him to make those calls, he felt a strange unease as he lifted the phone. What if they were suspicious or defensive? How would he convince them to trust him?

His misgivings proved justified. The first call was to Karl Gurder, the Cardinal of the Catholic Church. It seemed the Church hadn't quite recovered from losing Billy in the first place, and the revelation that Sanjiv was now calling the shots was a bitter pill to swallow.

'How is it,' Karl Gurder said, making little effort to sound civil, 'that *you* see fit to grant yourself the authority over what happens to the child?'

'Please believe me that is not the case,' Sanjiv replied politely. 'This is what his mother wants as well. What I bring to the table is merely a paradigm for all faiths to discuss and agree upon. I have no desire to dictate the outcome. Every church in the world should feel included in this plan. That is the point.'

'But we found the child. It is for us to bring him to the world.'

'And you will. But with all the other faiths standing beside you. This is an opportunity to unite rather than divide. Isn't that what God would want? Is that not what you want?'

There was silence on the line.

'What do you want from us?' Gurder said at last.

'Join us. Come here and engage in the discussion of how we will bring Billy to the world.'

The Cardinal had been left with no choice. As Sanjiv had already declared, Billy was the biggest drawcard in history.

Sanjiv found the Sunnis reluctant to share a room with the Shiites, but the prospect of being excluded was too much for them too. No one could afford to be left out; the moment was too big, and once they got beyond the politics, everyone soon discovered the beauty in the idea.

Before he knew it, Sanjiv was able to shake a date out of everyone and put into motion the immense task of planning the meeting. The magnitude of the assembly meant security would have to be top priority—the meeting held in utmost secrecy. Governments would need to be involved. But bringing Government on board meant risking the event becoming political. Sanjiv soon encountered some tough lobbying from political heavyweights desperate to join the list. He responded by smiling calmly and reminding them that this was not an exercise in self-promotion. The meeting would need to be supported by Government, but not controlled by it.

To his astonishment, Government and the Church put their hands in their pockets. Sanjiv found himself with both a budget, and a team of assistants drawn from the Federal Police to help him pull the meeting together. Commissioner Bird was brought into the frame, once more assisting Sanjiv with the logistics of the meeting. They drew up plans together, rallying the security forces to take charge of getting the esteemed guests into the country under the radar.

The event was penciled in to run for two days. A plan would be discussed and agreed upon by everyone present. The twelve would decide the sites where they would present Billy to the masses, in which order they would present him, and the items they would include in the presentation. Sanjiv was determined that as much of the world's population would be covered as possible.

Nicole was shielded from the heavy lifting that was happening around her, and if she was honest it was a relief. She'd settled into the peaceful routine of being a nursing mother. Each morning at dawn she'd take Billy downstairs to feed him on the deep sofa in the lounge. Only Sanjiv was awake at that hour, rattling around in his office upstairs.

Sanjiv and Sean had taken to working sixteen hours a day, every day. An army of assistants had arrived at the house, and the more that arrived the more they seemed to need, and the more hours Sanjiv and Sean seemed to work. But as intense as the workload was Sanjiv remained cheerful, and he somehow always seemed to have time for Nicole and her parents. He'd stop for regular meditation breaks, would walk in the sunshine, and insisted on the odd cuddle with Billy.

People came and went, rushed off their feet, but never without a smile. Everyone knew they were privileged to be involved, so the work was a pleasure. The output was staggering, and at the end of the day people were happy to stay and unwind with those they'd spent the whole day working alongside.

The appetite of the press had not subsided. They felt entitled to know everything about Billy, including his whereabouts. Nicole was required to appear at regular press conferences—sometimes daily—a payoff for the house and the security detail. She regularly found herself shoulder to shoulder with prime ministers and world leaders. Everyone who considered themselves important wanted a photo opportunity with the child, so it became a virtual diplomatic necessity for the government to provide them with one.

Nicole quickly got the hang of fronting the press, and with a few tips from Sean and Sanjiv, media calls became a cinch. As she became more relaxed, her breezy personality emerged, and the press fell in love with her as much as they had with Billy.

As the weeks passed, Nicole felt like she was putting the horror of the compound behind her, and there was a real sense of purpose swirling around her as the build up to the meeting drew nearer. But this sweet sense of ease came to a crashing halt when Bird rang to discuss Tim's request to see Billy.

'He has a case, Nicole,' he said. 'I held off as long as I could to let you get settled.'

Nicole was silent for a long time before she responded.

'Could we wait until after the meeting? It's only a few days away. I know it's only fair he see Billy, but it's crazy here at the moment.'

'I can put it to him.'

Nicole found it hard to even picture Tim's face. It was like he was becoming a shadow from a former life.

'What's he doing?'

She felt sick asking, but she couldn't help herself.

Bird paused.

'He's fine. He's recording some music, I believe.'

Nicole shuddered. Even Bird couldn't disguise the disdain lurking beneath his words. She hung up and waited for a response. Bird was back on the line within the hour.

'He wasn't happy, but he's agreed to wait.'

'Thanks, David.'

'I'll organise a visit once the meeting's over.'

***

Finally, the day came when the guests were due to arrive. Sanjiv and his assistants emerged from upstairs battered and exhausted. As a celebration, lunch was served in the back garden, and the entire entourage gathered, joking and laughing. Sanjiv stood on a chair and addressed them all.

'Ladies and gentlemen. I have worked you all like dogs.' Everyone laughed. 'Those who want to kill me, please form a line.'

Everyone knew nobody had worked harder than Sanjiv. It was a miracle he was on his feet.

At dusk, the ten began to filter in. Their arrival was staggered to avoid attracting attention, and their trip from the airport had been guarded with the utmost secrecy. Security forces had unlocked another ten houses in the street, so the group could stay in close proximity to one another, and their security could be managed more effectively.

Sanjiv greeted each of them personally and helped to get them settled, ready to meet Billy the following day.

***

In the morning, Nicole was up just after dawn. She

watched as the house was transformed into a pleasure dome. Platters of fruit and baskets of flowers perfumed the air. The family room was emptied and then refilled with opulent couches covered with feathered cushions. Silks were hung from the walls and the ceiling. Sculptures were brought in to watch over them. A mere twenty-four hours before, the house had had no character at all, now it had the atmosphere of a sultan's caravan.

At 10.00 am, one by one, the guests emerged from their mansions all along the avenue. They strolled the freshly swept footpaths, ready to join the gathering.

Sanjiv could sense a shiver in the air. Something big was about to happen. All of the ten betrayed their nervousness and excitement at meeting Billy; their greetings were distracted with anticipation. They knew that any moment now He would arrive in the room and God would be before them in the flesh. It was to be the pinnacle in their lifetime of faith.

The group gathered in the opulent lounge. Calming music played. At 10.30 am precisely, Sanjiv turned down the music and called them to order, standing shoulder to shoulder with Sean.

'Before we begin, I'd like to thank you all for having the courage to be here. This is truly a great day for all of humanity. I would also like to clarify something in everyone's presence. This is very important. You are each representatives of different faiths. Being here means you also respect each other's faiths. The media has frequently referred to Billy as the Second Coming of Christ. I would like for us to let go of that idea. It's an idea that may be inflammatory to some of us. When you meet him I'm sure you will see that that description is a misrepresentation, and he is simply an incarnation of God.'

A murmur filled the room. Sanjiv took it as an echo of support.

'Now, if you will excuse me, I'll ask Nicole to bring the child to you.'

Sanjiv left them to their nerves and disappeared up the grand staircase.

Nicole couldn't help but be excited, and she fed off the exhilaration in Sanjiv's eyes. The first stage of his dream was unfolding before them.

'Let's go,' she said.

They found everyone waiting at the bottom of the stairs, silent—their lungs seemed to barely move, but their hearts had to be thrashing. These esteemed holy men, accustomed to projecting finishing-school authority, appeared dizzy with anticipation. Sanjiv paused before them.

'This is Nicole. And I'd like to present before you her son, Billy.'

Nicole pulled back Billy's blanket and presented him to them. There was a collective gasp as they caught a glimpse of him—of his electric halo. Each face was frozen in the same degree of wonder.

'Please,' she said, 'I'd like for each of you to have a turn holding him.' She approached the Imam. 'Here, Mr Hassan. Why don't you take him?'

The Imam took Billy from her and held him. It was impossible to anticipate the sensation holding Billy brought—the connection to God, the feeling of calm and wellbeing, and, without question, the Imam was feeling that now. His eyes filled with love as he looked down at the baby.

The Imam passed Billy to Arch Deacon Conroy. Each member had their turn holding him. It was an initiation. A conversion. The atmosphere was sacred and the room silent. Billy was the hub in a wheel of spiritual energy that turned powerfully in the room. It was a coming together of a few, but with a reach of millions.

When all had taken their moment with Billy, Sanjiv called them to order and the meeting began. Everyone present now understood what was possible. They had seen Billy with their own eyes—had felt his power—and were convinced of his legitimacy. The rest was now a matter of process.

Nicole sat with the twelve around the huge wooden table. Sanjiv spoke first and outlined how he visualised the plan: Nicole, Billy, Gail and the twelve would travel as one to an agreed list of religious hot spots around the globe. They would present Billy at a number of large rallies. It was crucial that as many people as possible had a chance to see him in the flesh. Travelling together as one was vital. It would be a sign of unity.

He made suggestions for the prospective venues: Mecca, Rome, The Ganges, Bodh Gaya, The Temple Mount. Each location should hold great religious significance and be capable of accommodating large crowds. It was a must to include as many religions and denominations in the tour as possible. The size of the events would also attract the attention of even the most rusted on atheists, and offer them the possibility of connecting with Billy.

Sanjiv was careful to give each member the chance to share their ideas and have their suggestions heard, but his vision was so complete, his plan so fully realised, that they could find only harmony. Their input identified a more comprehensive list of venues, but soon the conceptual discussion was over, and the twelve turned their thoughts to logistics.

Organising the gatherings for hundreds of thousands of people would be, by far, the most difficult part.

Governments as well as the Churches would need to be involved. There was security to consider, politics, crowd control, finances.

They agreed that upon their return to their home states, each member would begin work on gathering assistance from their own countries.

They drew up a media release to be published simultaneously around the world.

The discovery of Billy may have been a big story, but this one was going to be beyond anything anyone could imagine. It was audacity on an unimaginable scale. Now, it only remained to be seen if it would be a catastrophe of blind faith, or a spark that would ignite a great light in the world.

33

The media had been quick to realise that Billy was never going to return to the cul-de-sac, so only days after Tim had arrived home their number had thinned. Some remained to cover what they could of Tim's movements, but titbits about his fledgling music career didn't cut it with their editors. The real story was with Billy.

When Bird released Joanne and the other girls a day or so after their detention and they arrived to Tim's waiting arms, the threadbare media that remained saw a story they could actually use.

As the girls stepped out of the police car, Tim emerged from the house to greet them. He lifted the perimeter tape, and they circled him, smothering him in kisses. The cameras ate it alive. *"Not very God-like"*, one headline screamed. *"Orgy in the house of the Lord"*. *"God is love and Daddy's 'got some' to spare"*.

Tim was happy to let them feast on it. He even smooched the girls as he led them up the driveway. Fuck it, he thought. There's no bad publicity, right? Nicole had had no trouble finding the lens, why shouldn't he share in the spotlight.

He welcomed the girls into his home, and they spent the afternoon making love and telling stories of their unfair incarceration. Tim played them his music, and they swooned over it like groupies.

Having the girls with him was like a breath of fresh air. Life had become strangely sour with the online haters eager to knife his music. Even though his sales had skyrocketed, the internet chatter had been cruel. He was labelled bland. Derivative. Uninteresting. He waved it away, promising himself he'd still take his music on the road, his sweetest revenge, international success.

Once he'd got his back-catalogue of music online, he put a call through to Mark Richards, the A&R guy of the label that had released *Get Some*. There was something sweet about dangling himself in front him now that he was a "somebody". Not only would Mark have no choice but to beg him to re-sign, but with all his music now online, the company would have to fork out to get any new material recorded. That meant stumping up for the best musos and a recording studio.

The receptionist put Tim straight through.

'Mark,' he said, like they were long lost buddies, 'Tim Blake.'

'Tim. Wow.'

'Yeah, I know, right?'

'What's happening?'

'You tell me.'

'Some crazy shit's been going down your end.'

'Don't I know it.'

'Well, what's up? You gotta be running around like a mad dog.'

'It's why I'm calling.'

Tim fed him some of the numbers he was doing online and put it to him that it might be time to get back into the studio. There was a familiar silence on the other end of the line.

'You wanna come back with us?' Mark said.

'It had crossed my mind.'

'Right. Right.'

Another pause.

'Well, sure, Tim. Look send some stuff through, and I'll have a listen.'

Tim couldn't believe his ears.

'You know my music, Mark. It's a simple yes or no.'

'Is it like the stuff you put up the other day?'

Rage started to burn deep in Tim's guts. This was the same charade he'd endured years before.

'You know my next call will be to Sony,' Tim said.

'Kudos. You might be more suited to them anyhow, Tim.'

Sony was no different. Or EMI. Something about him was on the nose.

Tim Googled himself. It sickened him to find that almost every article he found overlooked the fact that he had brought the new messiah into the world. Instead, he was painted as some kind of sleazy philanderer, and there was almost zero mention of his music. No wonder he couldn't make any inroads. The cards were stacked against him.

The stories of his polyamorousness had an unexpected spin-off though. Young women began to arrive at the cul-de-sac in their droves, seeking to stay with Tim. What could he do? Turn them away? He made a policy to grant them no more than two nights with him before they had to leave. And he was extra cautious to use protection, as he suspected a good deal of them may have had their sights set on having a mystical baby of their own.

His girlfriends didn't seem to mind the company. They were convinced that these ring-ins were only seeing the same things in him that they did—he was blessed by God and it was their duty to adore him. As Simon had declared, they touched divinity when they touched him.

Tim threw himself further into his music, but it had spoiled. He was convinced he was belting out killer riffs and catchy hooks, but whenever he took a break and returned to them they sounded empty and cheap. Nothing fitted together. He'd ditch everything and start over, but the new material always felt as bad.

He couldn't stop his mind turning to Nicole and Billy. Nicole's press conferences were massive affairs, and she was becoming increasingly self-assured. Where he'd become a footnote, she attended functions with world leaders and major dignitaries. It seemed so unfair. Where had it gone so spectacularly wrong for him?

As his arranged visit with Billy approached, Tim became increasingly demoralised. He didn't feel strong enough to face Nicole. He was haunted by failure and accusations of sleaze, while she was dancing in the light of success.

Days before the visit, he was watching the evening news when Nicole, Sanjiv, and Sean stood shoulder to shoulder to announce the first stage of their world tour. The announcement was massive news. The religious muscle they'd enlisted, the places they planned to hit, the reach they would achieve with Billy as their Prophet—it was beyond belief.

Tim shrivelled. After weeks of slaving over his music with nothing to show for it he felt more abandoned and worthless than in all his years of rejection. Sales of his music had stalled. He was already yesterday's man.

He abandoned his studio and spent the next two days buried beneath his girls. When the day of his visit with Billy arrived, he felt like he was coming up for air.

He waited until his ride appeared and went out to face the dreggy remains of the media haunting his driveway. *"Tell us where you're off to, Tim."* *"Out on a Tinder date?"* *"Off to the chiropractor, Tim?"*

Tim paused beside the giant SUV.

'You know what? Fuck you, guys,' he said. 'I'm going to see my son.'

Tim climbed into the car nursing the soft toy he'd bought as a present for Billy.

To complete his humiliation, Tim was blindfolded for the trip. They changed cars three times. His phone was confiscated and the SIM card removed. When he arrived at the new estate, the house had been vacated. The celebrities and their support staff had left, his in-laws were unwilling to meet him, and Nicole was absent.

A security guard escorted Tim up the lonely staircase to see Billy, who was asleep in his cot. He didn't want to wake him, so he sat, holding his hand and cried for an hour. When Billy finally woke, he looked at his father with kind, forgiving eyes. Tim wanted to cry for another hour; the love Billy so effortlessly radiated filled the empty pit inside him. He wished, in the deepest part of himself, that he were a better person. Being with Billy was like standing on a path with the ability to look back at your past mistakes littered behind you. Like broken pieces of furniture they lay there, unrepairable, unreachable, serving only as a reminder of the failure you had been. Tim wanted only to turn around and face the other direction—towards the future—and find a way to be a better man, but he'd begun to know himself too well. He lacked the strength to break the addiction he had for all the things that were destroying him.

Soon, he was bundled back into the SUV and run home like a political hostage. When the car delivered him back to the cul-de-sac, Tim alighted to the catcalls of the press. *"No luck, Tim?" "Losing your touch, buddy?"*

He stood gazing up at the house for a moment, searching for the will to go inside. The joy of seeing Billy had drained away, and he was once again back to where he'd started.

When he finally dragged himself through the front door, he found the house strangely quiet. For a horrible moment he feared the girls had left him too. He tiptoed down the hall towards the lounge and found it bathed in candlelight. The girls were sitting in a circle holding hands, silent in prayer. And in the middle of the circle sat Simon.

34

Six hundred thousand people were crammed into the courtyard of the Great Mosque in Mecca, and another million and a half were in the surrounding vicinity—more people than the annual Hajj. Worshipers flocked from all over the world, and cameras were ready to beam live into homes across the globe.

From the beginning, this gathering had been run like a military operation. The security force was formidable, donated by the United Nations, host countries, and the religious bodies themselves. Motorcades whisked the twelve and their entourage from airports to hotels, where they waited for the first of the rallies to occur. Every street, every plane, and every hotel room was swept meticulously before them. With so much at stake, everything had to run like clockwork.

The build-up hadn't gone without controversy. An element believed that the rally was offensive to Allah and the Prophet Muhammad—particularly the idea of holding it in his home town. The twelve were acutely mindful of this. The Islamists in the group used their position to hold off the doubters until they could see Billy's legitimacy for themselves. It was a fragile truce, but it held.

The twelve had agreed early that Mecca should be the site for the first gathering, as it would be a statement to the world that the child was not—as some had proclaimed—the Second Coming of Christ, but simply a child of God. Mecca was the heart of Islam, and making Billy's debut there would confirm the stake the Muslim world had in the tour.

The Vatican had pushed to have it in Rome, but Sanjiv insisted that Rome would get its turn a fortnight after the Saudis.

The courtyard began filling before dawn. The city itself had been packed for days, and the anticipation was intense. Nicole and the twelve were escorted through tunnels beneath the mosque by elders of the church— bearded men in white gowns who'd walked these cobblestones for decades. It was the only way to get around the massive crowd that had built in every direction.

They threaded through ancient passageways, worn down by centuries of imams making their way to prayers. The tunnels were dark and smelt of damp. Nicole could hear the footsteps and chatter of the worshipers on the streets above her, and their own feet echoed deep into the passageways ahead. She imagined these tunnels running for miles beneath the streets, all the way into the surrounding countryside.

They reached a stone staircase where they found sunlight again. It was a relief to finally leave the tunnel, but the closer they got to the open air, the louder the noise of the enormous crowd became. Soon they would take to the stage.

Gail stayed close by Nicole and Billy. Nicole felt stronger knowing she was there with her. Sanjiv didn't leave their side either.

'Oh, my God, I am *so* nervous,' Nicole whispered to Sanjiv.

He laughed. 'You think you're the only one?'

Beneath the grin, Sanjiv looked terrified. The culmination of his dream was finally upon him. Every day he encouraged his followers to *'visualise what you want and give yourself permission to move into it'*. Now it was the master's turn to practice what he had preached.

The group was greeted by a stage manager, who escorted them to a specially erected stage overlooking the mosque and the Kaaba. She seated them backstage, ready to be announced to the crowd.

Nicole held Billy in her arms. He was wide awake. She'd never seen him so alert. It was as if he knew something big was about to take place.

On stage, Hassan, the Imam of the Shiites spoke in Arabic to the crowd. He was flanked by the Saudi King, the Prince, and the imam of Mecca. Although she couldn't understand what he was saying, Nicole knew he was talking about tradition and a new way forward, preparing the crowd for what was to come. Billy's unprecedented divinity had flung open the doors of the Muslim world, and for the first time, they would welcome other faiths onto the Haram of the Great Mosque—the heart of Islam.

But for all the preparation and all the good will, no one could predict what was going to happen. How would the crowd respond? Would Billy have the same impact on them as he did on smaller gatherings? And would they see—as Sanjiv hoped—that he belonged to everyone equally?

318

Hassan finished his address and called the rest of the twelve onto the stage. Nicole was surrounded by them. They stood together, a posse of leaders bouncing on their toes with nerves. Before anyone moved, Nicole called for their attention.

'Thank you, all,' she said. 'I guess it's up to Billy now.'

Everyone laughed.

'Let's go,' Sanjiv said.

Nicole gave Gail a nod, and she stood back as Nicole led the others onto the stage.

As she stepped forward she saw a sea of people stretching out before her. A hush fell. Not a single sound floated back to them on the baking breeze. Nicole felt giddy, praying their silence was inspired by fascination and not a growing wave of hostility. She observed how colourful they were. Not just the headdresses and the silks, but the faces. Skin tones from every country peered up at her, eyes wide with wonder. In the distance she could hear birdcalls and the odd toot from a car miles away—one of the few in the city who had shunned the divine child.

As Hassan gestured for Nicole to come to the front of the stage, fear stabbed at her. Her legs were jelly, and the walk to the front seemed endless. Murmurs rolled back at her through the crowd, and the anticipation was palpable.

Nicole focused her mind, concentrated on not passing out.

Now was the moment. Now was her time to finally present Billy to the masses. She took a breath and gently pulled the blanket back from Billy's face. Then she lifted him up and held him out for all to see.

A roar filled the courtyard. Her body was crying out for her to flee, but she stood steady, holding Billy high.

His halo blazed in the midday sunshine, and his eyes

were alert, taking in the crowd, almost as if he knew they were watching. The moment they saw him, thousands fell to their knees, and hands stretched to the sky or towards the baby. Others howled exultations. Some stood mutely, too overwhelmed to utter a sound.

That was when it happened.

Without warning, Billy's halo expanded. Gradually at first, it grew to three times its size and became brighter than ever before.

It was frightening—the way it grew and then continued to grow. Soon Nicole found herself engulfed inside the massive circle of white light. It grew further—to the size of the stage itself.

Panic set in. The audience cowered, frightened by the unknowable unfolding before them.

Then—like a bomb—it exploded outwards through the crowd at unimaginable speed. A single, unbroken band of light ploughing through everything before it, reaching out in all directions at once. It raced across the heads of the gathering, toppling each person gently to the ground.

When it reached the walls of the courtyard, it continued out into the city, along the streets, through crowds of worshippers that had gathered on the city's sidewalks. From there it pulsed out into the countryside all the way to the surrounding deserts, then, as if it had reached its zenith, it stopped and began to roll back the way it had come—contracting in on itself—like a giant wave being sucked back into the ocean. It sizzled towards Billy once more, finally snapping back to its usual size above his head.

Every soul in the city felt it. It was as if the miraculous rolling white light had penetrated their bodies. As it touched them, it filled them with light. It vanquished all hatred, and it cleansed them of fear.

Hundreds of thousands of people wept in the streets, crying out with voices of joy. Mecca was a city converted to Billy's legitimacy. Nicole stood looking out over the scene in shock, wondering if for the rest of time, this day would be spoken about as the day miracles had returned to the world.

***

Like the rest of the world, Tim, Simon, and the girls were gathered around the television. What they saw was terrifying. When the light raced through the crowd it appeared to pulverize them. It knocked people down like ninepins, and the speed of it kicked up clouds of dust as it passed. It was so bright that the cameras flared and turned the TV screen to white. It was as though a bomb had exploded.

Tim leapt out of his seat in horror. He raced for the television, as if being closer to it would undo what he'd just seen. But it quickly became clear that this was no terrorist act. As the dust settled and the vision returned, pictures began to reveal the ecstasy rippling through the Grand Mosque. It was another of Billy's miracles.

Tears of despair turned to tears of joy. The six of them sat watching in wonder, slowly coming to understand what had happened.

Only Simon looked sour. He flicked the television off.

'Let us pray,' he muttered.

His tone was hard to read. He didn't seem to be filled with the same wonder as the rest of them.

The group formed a circle and held hands as they'd taken to doing many times a day since Simon had arrived. He'd effortlessly slipped back into ruling the roost, and Tim was content to relinquish the reins as it made him feel less rudderless, more secure.

Simon's mood was prickly, and the prayers were short. He cast off the girl's hands and stood from the circle. All watched uneasily as he paced the room. Mayling became frightened and started to cry, which made Simon turn on her.

'It's no use weeping!' he bawled.

Shocked, Mayling stopped.

Simon rolled his shoulders like he was spoiling for a fight.

'I have made contact with twenty-three members of the old community. All of them want to come home. Our compound may be in ashes, but I've found a new place. Together we'll start again. Who will join me?'

He levelled a look at the girls. No one moved.

'What we witnessed today was an affront to God!' he barked. 'I was supposed to take the child to the world. It was ordained. And if not for the betrayal—' Simon broke off, words failing him. 'Who will come with me?' he repeated.

'I'll come with you, Simon,' Shayne said.

'Me too,' Kara said.

'And me,' Mayling and Joanne repeated.

Simon gave a satisfied nod.

'Good. I love you all very much.'

He turned to Tim.

'What about you?'

Tim was too shocked to respond. Return to the compound? How could he make that choice without decent consideration?

Simon bristled. 'Three months. That's all I need to start again. In that time you can watch your ex-wife exploit your child. After that, you'll beg to come and join me.'

Tim was still unready to give an answer.

'They'll be bringing the child home in three months,' Simon continued. 'By then the community will be set up. We'll rescue him and bring him to the place it was always ordained he should be. With us. He will be the centrepiece of a living, breathing place of worship. And you will join us, Tim, because you are a part of God's plan too. You are the cornerstone of our future life together: you and your son, Baby Jesus. We will have everything we need. And for that to work, Tim, I need for you to tell me where I can find him.'

35

Simon had his bearings now. As the estate became denser and every second allotment contained the bleached bones of a half-finished house, he knew he was close. Soon he'd reach the manicured rows of the completed mansions Tim had described. He could just make out their Hammer Horror silhouettes in the moonlight.

He was able to remove Tim from the rescue with the promise of reuniting him with his child once the new community was set up. His main sell was that Tim had just as much right to the child as Nicole. Worshipers would come to visit Billy on Tim's terms rather than those laid down by a cheesy, American self-help guru. With the girls backing him up, Tim finally relented and spilled all he knew.

Tim's description gave only a scant picture of the place, without detail or direction, but it was enough to give Simon the scent. It set him on a search that had lasted almost three months, hitch-hiking, walking, exploring—his days of being a nomad paid off.

Back in the day, he'd traversed Melbourne over and over, sometimes sleeping in empty estates like this one. He knew them all, but that was years ago now, and things change. This estate didn't immediately spring to mind, because he'd assumed it would have been completed by now. But here it was: desolate and unwelcoming. The perfect camouflage for Baby Jesus.

Because it was deep in the night, Simon knew the eyes of the security detail wouldn't be as sharp. He was counting on it. Although he couldn't see them, they were bound to be there—strolling the chilling air, stopping to check social media on their phones, listening idly for intruders they trusted would never come.

Simon floated through the skeletal carcass of a half-finished house and found his first obstacle: a guardhouse the size of a granny flat, radiating orange into the cool moonlight. It looked freshly constructed. There was no sign of movement inside. Perhaps the occupant was out on a sweep.

He side stepped it and made a circle around the estate, only to find another guardhouse blocking his path. This was a pattern. A ring of defense around the child.

Simon needed to become invisible as he was in his dreams: large crowds would walk by him without anyone noticing. Alone and insignificant, a rage burnt inside him that commanded them to turn their heads, but everyone passed by—no one saw him. Now was the moment to test his apparent invisibility.

Circling the area would only send him to another guardhouse. He needed to push through, so he flattened into the dirt and propelled himself forward on his elbows. Each slow drag inched him closer to the guardhouse. His heart pounded as much from fear as from effort.

He reached the guardhouse and dropped flat to catch his breath. There was still no movement from inside, but logic said it would be manned.

After a moment of rest, he raised himself onto his elbows to press on, but he caught a glint of red—inches from his face. Running like gleaming wires between the two guard houses was a laser sensor. Simon pulled back. It was only the dust he'd kicked up, filtering through the beam, that had alerted him to its presence. God was truly with him.

This fencing would surely run the entire perimeter. There would be no way through it.

Simon eased himself back the way he came. In an abandoned house he found a short piece of timber wide enough to use as a digging blade. He tucked it into his pants and returned to the laser. He could hear voices in the house now. A laugh. A boiling kettle. Military men at ease. Every move from here on must be made in silence.

The soil was loose beneath the beam. Simon slid the timber into the dirt, collected a tiny load, and dragged it out. With patience, he dug until he could use his hands to claw out a hole, deep enough to slide through.

Clearing the beam gave him confidence. Beyond this invisible barricade, few would expect him. He needed to make it past without getting a bullet in his back, then he'd be in open space.

Silently inching his way forward, he found himself on Jackson Terrace. Finished houses surrounded him, just as Tim had described. It meant he was almost there. His pulse quickened, and he reached for his knife to reassure himself he had protection.

At the end of Jackson Terrace he turned left into Meadow Mews and edged into the darkness. Ahead of him was the house that contained Baby Jesus.

Out the front, he spotted a security guard. This guy was still getting used to the family being home. He was yawning when he shouldn't be. Dancing on his toes to keep his lids open.

Simon sneaked unseen around the side of the house and waited. As the guard made his next absent-minded pass of the garden, Simon stepped out of the shadows and buried his knife deep into the man's heart.

The guard's look of astonishment became glassy as Simon helped him onto the blue-green turf. He raced around to the back of the house. Tim had only mentioned the two guards. If he was wrong, Simon's night was already over.

But Tim wasn't wrong. As he entered the back garden, Simon saw that the only other guard present was resting his oversized butt on an exercise trampoline, as he rolled a cigarette.

There were no shadows to help Simon this time. If he was going to finish the guy off, he'd need to cross half the yard to get to him.

With God at his back, Simon took his chances. He raced across the space before the guard even noticed him, and slid the knife between the guard's ribs. The man fell forward onto the trampoline, dispatched before he knew what had hit him.

Simon turned to the house. It was quiet and dark, the shade cloth taking care of any moonlight that might wish to squeeze through the uneven cloud cover. He gently turned the doorknob. It was locked. He twisted harder to make sure, but it didn't budge, so he trotted back to the guard to search his pockets. Nothing. He patted down his vest and heard a jingling. Perfect. He reached inside and pulled out a chain, heavy with keys.

Simon slipped inside the house and headed for the

grand staircase at the end of the hall. All was silent apart from a muffled snorer behind one of the doors. The bedrooms were full—guests and family most likely. Assistants. Nobodies. The people bent on exploiting the child and hijacking His real purpose.

For three months this group had been spreading their McDonald's faith to the world. Using the baby. Offending his father, the Lord God. At every gathering, one after the other, Billy had conjured his rolling white light. The gift denied to Simon. But not now. Now he was doing God's work again—even if he'd told some lies to get here. Like telling Tim and the girls he was setting up a new compound. How could there be a new compound? He was a man on the run. His photograph was up on every police notice board in the country. It was another of God's miracles that he hadn't been caught.

At the top of the stairs he reached a bedroom. He stood at the open door and listened for the gentle breathing inside. Nicole was asleep in the grand bed, Baby Jesus in his cot. Simon approached and carefully gathered him up, smelling his sweet baby smell and bathing in the light of his halo. The baby didn't stir. Simon held him for a moment, feeling the familiar swoon he projected.

Simon reached into the back pocket of his jeans for a folded piece of paper and let it drop into the cot. As it lay there, it opened to reveal a message. 'I am Simon,' it read. 'Baby Jesus is back where he belongs.'

Simon knew he needed to move fast. One squeak from the child would stir the sleeping house. He ran down the stairs and was out the front door in moments.

A car was parked in the driveway. He checked the crowded ring of keys he'd stolen from the guard and picked out the only one branded with a vehicle logo. He dropped the baby into the passenger seat and fired the engine. Then he gently backed out of the driveway and onto the tarmac.

One by one, the lights inside the house popped on. Panic would be spreading like a firestorm from room to room.

The guardhouses reacted slowly at first. The sound of an engine caught their attention, and soon personnel left their buildings with mouths pressed to walkie-talkies.

Simon flashed through the laser perimeter and into the ruins beyond. There was nothing in the rearview mirror yet. He wondered how long it would take for his taillights disappearing out of the estate to be deemed hostile.

He drove with the windows open. It was the way he liked it—the wind in his hair, and the cool air chilling the sweat on his clinging shirt. Next to him, Baby Jesus was still asleep, peaceful and silent.

By now they'd be after him. Helicopters would have been scrambled. He turned off the highway into a satellite town. He dropped his speed and took to the backstreets, meandering his way patiently onward.

Within two hours he was in the centre of the city. He parked the car away from the city's main cathedral, ready to make the final leg of his journey on foot. He gathered up the sleeping child and headed off.

The gardens surrounding the cathedral provided him with all the cover he needed, and he made it to the steps without being seen.

He paused in the shadows and glanced down at the child one last time. From this moment forward, for all time, their paths would be inseparable. No one would ever utter the child's name without remembering Simon and his brand of faith.

'Farewell,' he muttered, tears in his eyes. 'Lord? Thy

will be done.'

And he put his hands to the baby's throat and tightened his grip.

**

Billy sees the earth from above: the tops of trees, a flattening of the landscape. It's only been a matter of months since his birth, but the unusual feeling of being in spirit again takes some getting used to—the freedom of it, the weightlessness, the fragile touch of being connected to everything.

Below him, he watches Simon streak out of the shadows and up the stairs of the cathedral. He's laying a child's body across the cold bluestones at the top of the stairs. Nothing connects Billy to that body anymore even though, minutes before, it was him. To anyone passing by it will look like a forgotten doll. Or a regular little baby, fast asleep. No halo anymore. Just a child, abandoned in the tender hours of the morning on the raking steps of the cathedral.

Simon doesn't linger. He hurries down the steps and into the maze of city streets, heading for the river. Billy can feel Simon's exhilaration. This man has put his entire trust in the Lord, but as he closes on the towering bridge his mind begins to torment him with flickers of doubt. He wants to be drawn into the embrace of God for what he has done. He craves greatness amongst men. But in the moments before he plunges from the tallest part of the bridge, he cries out for understanding.

Billy senses another disturbance. It kisses him like a ripple of air. Ninety-seven minutes after Simon rushed away from the cathedral, out from the morning foot traffic, a young woman emerges to discover the body of a child. She identifies him instantly. Her desperate cries draw a crowd, and they make a doomed effort to revive him.

Billy wants to comfort them, but he feels himself being drawn away. At first he had felt as though he was floating on high, but now it's as if he is joining with all things. He is becoming part of everything around him. His consciousness spreads. Time drifts.

As Simon's body floats out to sea with the ebbing tide, the crisis shuts down the city below. Word travels. People stop what they're doing and weep helplessly.

Billy can only feel empathy.

He becomes aware of the news reaching his mother. Nicole. Gail and the family, gather around her, and she howls to the sky in despair and disbelief. Billy wants to touch her, but he's too far away now.

In the cul-de-sac, Tim's despair only confirms the disgrace he's become, and he banishes his girls into the barren morning to prepare for the inevitable. Billy can see forward—to days later— when his father's body will be found swinging like stinking fruit in the carport.

Billy feels love for him.

The world opens before him now. He can feel all of it. There is a numbness across the globe that only comes with pointless tragedy. He sees whole nations wake to the news, or go to bed with the news—everyone sharing in a mother's pain—all the world united by the same desperate sadness that losing a child can bring.

And as he becomes part of the suffering earth itself, he is aware that a new plant has begun to grow. This is a plant of peace. How could any soul raise a fist to another who lives with suffering such as this? They are all too much alike now. They have seen the darkness and have seen the light, together.

Billy can leave now. As he blends back into the earth, it is a new world and a new time—a time for all to take a new path together as one.

Acknowledgements

My background as a performer meant that the process of writing this book felt extremely lonely at times. I craved an audience for what I was doing. I'd have struggled to get past the first few chapters without Marcus Schintler. Not long after I'd started writing *Rapture* he told me he needed something to read, so as a joke I sent him my first chapter. His response was, 'More, please.' So as I finished each chapter I'd email it to him. This gave me a time pressure, an audience, and an immediate response. Uncritical to the quality (most of the time), he offered his eyes. I can't thank him enough. Once the first draft (the story) was done, I had to learn how to really write the thing. Again, eyeballs were valuable, and John O'May, Greg Stone, Stephen Stanford, Rhea Stanford, and Marija Stanford all provided a sounding board. For a more professional opinion, I worked with Charlie Carmen—who added her impossibly clear insights on character and narrative into the mix—and then Sarah Lewis, who worked with me as a more conventional editor, reminding me that this was a novel and not a screenplay. More re-writing followed. The lonely self-doubt set in and so again I sought out readers I respected for some clues to where I was at. Steve King and Jo Dodds provided some great suggestions and their encouragement. That got me ready for submission. Louise Ryan, as usual, was a fountain of knowledge and provided the inside info. Steve Worland gave me some vital nudges in the right direction, and Eddie Perfect cast his brilliant mind over the manuscript. Once signed to Tale Publishing, I began working with Kathryn Moore. Nothing could have been more deluxe. To have her by my side offering her intelligence, her experience, insight, encouragement, and her steady guidance was a genuine treat. I can't thank Robert New enough for believing in me and being that exceptional guy who gets the things he believes in, done. Thanks to Shayne Frances for giving the book its first public outing. And finally, as with all my creative endeavours—well, all my endeavours really—I couldn't have done it without the support of my incredible wife, Annie, who makes the unusualness of my creative world feel natural and accepted. As with everything, I dedicate this book to her.

About the author.

Jeremy Stanford has had a long and varied career as a performer, which was kicked off with his portrayal of Buddy in *The Buddy Holly Story*. He went on to play many lead roles in other plays, TV shows, and musicals most notably recreating Hugo Weaving's role of Tick in *Priscilla Queen of the Desert – the Musical* which inspired his first book, *Year of the Queen* about his rocky journey through the creation of the show. Jeremy then retrained as a film maker at The VCA School of Film and Television and set up his own media company for which he developed content for TV and Film. In 2013, he directed and co-wrote his first feature film, *The Sunset Six*. Since then he's split his time as a writer, actor, and director. *Rapture* is his first novel.

www.ingramcontent.com/pod-product-compliance
Lightning Source LLC
Chambersburg PA
CBHW030659120726
47905CB00001B/289

* 9 7 8 0 9 9 4 4 3 9 9 9 4 *